THE PRICE OF SUCCESS
A Steve Quinn Novel

By CJ Vermeulen

To: Richard Barton
- Enjoy - !!

[signature] 3/6/2020

Copyright © 2019 CJ Vermeulen

This book is a work of fiction. Any references to historical events, real people, or real places, are used fictitiously. Other names, characters, places, and events are products of the author's imagination, and any resemblance to actual events or places or persons, living or dead, is entirely coincidental.

This book is dedicated to Albert Benson who unfortunately, is no longer with us. Connie and Albert were great RVing friends even if I couldn't persuade them to come to Mexico!

Also I must include Laszlo Bastyovanszky in this dedication. Laz is one of the greatest raconteurs it has been my pleasure to know. And besides, Laz has to take all the credit for arranging that Kathy and I met, and married. Thanks for everything Laz!

Other Titles by CJ Vermeulen
In The Steve Quinn Saga

The Broken Road
The Road North
The Final Chapter
(Coming March, 2020)
The Beginning
(Coming December, 2020

Special Note:
The very old Scottish word "fey" is used in all the Steve Quinn novels, and sometimes is referred to as Steve's "spidey sense". It is a word seldom used these days but is in fact a very real ability. It means to be able to sense future events. Some people have the ability to foretell other's deaths, others can foretell the outcome of travel plans, or investment opportunities. In Steve's case he can usually sense when events that will do him harm or give him unusual rewards may happen in the near future. His sense also seems to be able to steer him in the correct direction to take advantage of, or to escape whatever is coming.

Chapter One - Surprise

Eleven o'clock on a Friday morning in the spring of 1990 in Regina, Saskatchewan, and Steve Quinn was sitting at his desk disposing of the last of the week's paperwork. Betty Cookston, all six feet tall in heels, quietly approached Steve's desk and stood waiting to be noticed.

"Damn it! Don't do that!" he exclaimed, startled. "You scared the shit out of me! One minute you're there and now you're here," he said, waving at the front office.

Betty smiled her secret small smile. It was an old game between them, a trick that she played on him about once a month, just enough to keep him aware.

"You have an appointment at one, right after lunch. And yes, I know you're trying to leave on holiday."

Steve had learned to listen to Betty. She seldom said much and, along with Sharon Hardesty, had been an employee of the bankrupt courier company he'd bought some six years ago. In spite of her silence she managed to maintain a significant influence on the business and his life. He looked at her and, slouching back in his chair, sighed, "Okay, what's up?"

"Lia, Toni, and Michael Barchetti from Barchetti LLP, the lawyers, want to meet you. They want to discuss a problem."

"And?"

"That's it. You should talk to them. They insisted on coming here to talk."

"But," Steve said, waving his arm around, "I don't meet people here; you know this isn't a proper office."

"That's why you should meet them here. They also didn't want you at their office. I gathered that their problem is serious and there's some rush to solve it. And no, they wouldn't tell me what it is."

As she turned to return to her own office, she added that Sharon would also attend.

Steve hung his head and quietly swore. After months of too much pressure and too much work, he'd finally booked some time off, beginning this afternoon. But Betty had good instincts. And his fey sense of anticipation had been tingling for the last several weeks. He'd originally thought it had to do with his holiday, or his problems with Claire, his wife, but now, maybe not. He didn't think there was trouble coming, but perhaps change? Big change? He wasn't sure. But this meeting felt like the right thing to do.

Sharon Hardesty, all six feet, one inch and 160 pounds of stunning, aggressive good looks, suddenly came wheeling in.

"What's up? It better be damned good or I'm going to be right pissed off," she said, standing in front of his desk, hands on hips, clearly irritated.

"Don't know. What do you know about Barchetti LLP?"

"Their office is two blocks down Albert Street. We do some courier work for them on land title issues, but that's all."

"Better check them out. They have a problem and think they need our help."

"With what? Our transportation division, the consulting people, or something else?"

"I dunno. But I can't see how we can help a bunch of lawyers, unless they're really into something weird."

"Okay, but if they're just a bunch of lawyer assholes, I'm ending the meeting and sending you home."

And Steve knew she meant it.

"And don't call Ted Andrusiv (Quinn's corporate lawyer). Let's leave him out until we see what this is all about."

Sharon went storming out and Steve knew she was really pissed off. She guarded him like a momma bear with cubs and had fought long and hard for his time off. She was the general manager of the transportation division of his holding company, Quinn Enterprises, and also his unofficial consigliere. She'd been the manager of the courier company, City Express, which he'd bought just after he'd been fired by the Saskatchewan Provincial Government. She was also a lawyer but, in spite of being called to the bar, had never practised her profession. Steve still didn't know her story and wasn't sure that he'd ever know.

Quinn Enterprises' offices were on the second floor of an old beat up building above a restaurant and pizza parlor. The stairs up were wide and steep, and the offices were a mishmash spread out all over the building's second floor. As his business had grown, they'd become crowded and had used up every bit of available space. Steve was reluctant to move because the radio antennas for the courier and trucking companies were on the roof, and this was an excellent radio reception and broadcasting location. As the operations had grown, his reward had been to have his office pushed into a former small storage room in a back corner.

The Price of Success

Steve had been a young and fast rising senior manager in the provincial government, but when they'd lost the election, all the senior managers, as usual, had been fired. That had been six years ago. Not wanting to leave the province, Steve had taken his severance pay and bought a bankrupt courier company. His wife, Claire, had disagreed with the purchase and wanted him instead to buy a bigger, better house and look for a regular paying job. She simply didn't understand that such jobs, at Steve's income level, outside of government in Regina, just did not exist. With the help of Sharon and Betty's hard work, his innovative ideas, aggressive drive and his bank's money, in less than 18 months he'd turned the company around. It was now the largest privately owned courier company in western Canada. And, the company, thanks to having a completely redesigned operations department and a well-trained staff, produced a river of cash. But Claire had never forgiven him for taking the gamble.

The account manager at Steve's bank had closely watched his rescue efforts and when it became clear that he was going to be successful, had suggested he knew of another transportation business that might be worth looking into. With the help of Ted Andrusiv, Steve negotiated a deal with the bank that if he turned the new business around, he would acquire a controlling interest in it, and the bank would finance the rescue effort. Steve rescued the ailing heavy trucking company, Rayner Freight Lines, forced out the original owners and created a transportation division within Quinn. Sharon hadn't wanted the division manager's job, feeling she didn't have the necessary skills. However, when Steve pointed out that the salary involved, plus bonuses, would allow her to escape from the clutches of her useless drunken husband, she'd taken the job. Within months both companies, feeding off each other's customers, were pumping out even more cash. By rebuilding other struggling transportation companies and then taking control of some of them, Quinn had been able to acquire a large warehouse, cross dock, and more customers for the heavy trucking and courier companies.

And those deals had set the pattern for subsequent rescue deals with banks, then credit unions, and finally private individuals. It had also shown Steve the need for a consulting company that specialized in reorganizing small businesses. He created that company, Merit Consulting, as another division of Quinn Enterprises, and it had been busy and growing ever since. Merit had also created an additional growth direction for Quinn by applying its expertise to companies in other fields. As he repaired the companies, some he sold, and some he combined into larger units, but all contributed to Quinn's growing influence and supply of cash. Quinn now owned 12 other top-of-the-line businesses in a number of different fields.

Shortly after lunch the Barchettis showed up. Betty showed them into the converted storage room that Steve was using for an office and offered coffee. Steve was the only one who wanted some, so while Betty organized it, Sharon and Steve apologized, laughing at the tiny, crowded room they were in. And it was funny. The

Barchettis, very well dressed in the European manner and trying to be very formal, had been placed in an awkward situation. They were not ready for these surroundings. Which had been Betty's plan. She didn't like lawyers, assholes or not.

But Lia Barchetti was tougher than her little 4' 9" doll-like frame suggested. Ignoring the discomfort of her brothers, she asked Steve to outline his company's consulting practice. Steve explained that their usual practice was to be invited to analyse a business, which included the business's internal structure, organization and personnel, its functional organization, that is, how well it did what it was trying to do, its financial structure and, lastly the market it was trying to function within. They would then present a rescue plan to the owners and proceed with the rescue, or not. He explained that most business owners knew when they were in trouble but few really understood how they'd gotten there or how to get out. Which made some of them reluctant to listen to and adopt change. And finally Steve said they generally limited clients to those with annual sales of less than $4 million. And the majority had annual sales of less than $2 million. Bigger than that they had found the troubled organizations to just be too slow to accept change. But now many of them were considerably larger than those beginning positions. Lia asked what types of businesses they handled and Steve replied that so far it didn't seem to matter; in addition to their transportation division, they'd worked with everything from tire shops to grocery stores. While most were mom and pop shops or single proprietors, they'd worked with several professionals, including a newly set-up law firm. He went on to explain that they had six full time analysts and a larger number of contract staff for computer work, accounting, financing and legal issues. Lia looked at her brothers, but they had no questions, so she asked, "And you? What are your qualifications?"

Sharon bristled but Steve answered, "I have a Masters in Economics from York University in Toronto with a minor in Computer Science plus years of experience in both private and government business operations."

Lia asked, "How do you get paid? We understand that you usually take an equity position in the business."

"Well, that depends. If we're invited in by the principal financial backer like a bank, then we usually are just paid our fees by the banker. Whether we get involved in an equity position or not depends on the individual deal. We may even just buy a distressed business outright and possibly fold it into another one we own. Actually, each deal is unique; however, we try to keep only companies with the potential to climb to the top of their field."

"I didn't know that. You actually own businesses other than in the transportation and consulting fields?"

"At the moment we own 12 other fully functioning profitable top of the line businesses. And have another four under reconstruction. And no, I won't detail them for you. Let's just say they run the gamut."

The Price of Success

Into the silence, Sharon, impatient and forward as usual, interjected, "What do you need?"

Lia glanced at her brothers and said, "What do you know about our firm?"

Sharon continued, "Your father, Frank, originally became a lawyer with the idea of providing legal advice to the Italian immigrant community. In those days, legal advice really wasn't available to any of the ethnic immigrant groups, except those from the United Kingdom. Over the years he got involved with everything under the sun, including city politics. In many ways, he is a modern Godfather. Now he wants to retire, and there's some thought that he's ill. He wants you three to carry on his work."

Lia looked at her and said, "How do you know all that?"

"We do our homework. Now Steve is trying to leave on holiday so, again, what can we do for you?"

Toni Barchetti stood and finally irritated by Sharon's in-your-face attitude, looked around in disgust, said, "Come on let's go, we don't need this crap."

Sharon jumped to her feet and, towering over Toni's slight 5' 4" frame, said, "Fine! Steve, clean your desk up and get the hell out of here. You are now officially on holiday."

Lia, caught unaware by Sharon's aggressive interference, said, "Wait! Wait! Please! Toni, shut up and sit down. Sharon, I apologize for Toni; we really, really need your help."

Sharon, still on her feet, crossed her arms, paused and said, visibly bristling, "I'll give you another two minutes."

Meanwhile, Steve had leaned back in his chair and, amused, watched Sharon in full song. He'd never seen her back down from anyone, especially a man.

Lia began. "You're right. Frank, our father, is sick. In fact, he's dying. Our firm, Barchetti LLP, owns all or part of 31 different companies. Frank personally owns all or part of another 12. They're in all kinds of different industries, and some are not even in Regina, although all are in Saskatchewan." She looked at the floor, gave a little shudder, and said, "We never were involved with the companies. They're Dad's baby, his connection with his Italian community roots. But," she said, looking up, "It's time to move on. Dad somehow heard of what you did for Marsala Industries and decided you should take over all the companies. He also realizes that most of the companies need work, and some actually should to be closed."

Sharon said, "Wait a minute! Your father just decided that we should take over 43 companies? We don't get a say in it? We don't do that; we pick and we choose! Steve, this is just getting really, really stupid."

Lia, turning pink in embarrassment, finally realizing that Sharon was considerably more to Steve than just a division manager, said, "Sharon, please. I apologize again. That was a poor choice of words. My father is used to telling everyone what to do, and that's what he said to us. We're here to just talk about it."

Steve finally spoke up, "Just a second, Sharon. Let's at least hear what they have in mind."

Betty, overhearing Sharon's loud angry voice, opened the door and asked if anyone wanted more coffee. Steve, recognizing that Betty was trying to slow Sharon down, asked for a fresh cup. Lia too decided that a coffee break would help calm everyone down.

Coffee in hand, Steve said, "Okay, let's get back on track. Miss Barchetti, what do you have on these companies? Tax returns? Corporate statements? Anything? And what do the companies think? Do they know about this? What kind of deal are we talking about for the package? I'm assuming you want to do some kind of a package deal? And finally, what role is your father going to play in all this?"

While Lia made notes, Steve continued, looking at Sharon, "We can do nothing today. I have some concerns about the number of companies and a suitable financial arrangement. How about you send over all the paperwork you have and we'll take a look. Send over a two-way confidentiality agreement too. As I've been told, I'm going on holidays in a few minutes and I'll not look at anything until at least Tuesday."

Sharon, having slowed down slightly, interjected, "We also don't really have a surplus of staff or office space to tackle a project of this magnitude."

As Steve stood up, Lia remained seated and said, "Well, we may have a solution for that too. The building we're in is also for sale. It's owned by one of the companies Frank owns and they want out. Its five stories with stores on the main floor, a drive in parking lot on the second floor, the third and fourth floors are rented out, and the fifth is empty. We thought the second floor would be perfect for your courier operations, and the fifth developed for your business offices." Looking at Sharon, she said, "We too do our homework."

Sharon, annoyed, jumped in, "Why don't you just take it over?"

"We talked about it but none of us knows anything about property management. And we understand you do. As far as we know, the existing tenants don't want to move, and they know the rent is well below market. Even so, even with two empty floors, it still has a positive cash flow."

"And how much is it?"

"It's assessed at $700,000 – $750,000. But they'd take about $450,000. They've been trying to sell the place for several years and are getting desperate. The problem is the second floor; it's a drive in parking area, but no one wants it or can think of a use for the space."

Steve looked at Sharon and said, "Sharon, do you think you could go and look at it? I know you're busy, but just a quick look and a walk through would give us an idea. Then if you like what you see, call our building guy, I can't remember his name, and get him going on a formal survey. And on that note, ladies and gentlemen, I'm going home. I have a Jeep that needs putting back together."

Chapter Two - New Directions

Steve stopped on the way home and picked up a kilo of raw large shrimp, a tuna steak, a large piece of arctic char, and a half kilo bag of black rice. With his wife Claire away in Calgary with the three boys and his daughter away in Saskatoon at a volleyball training camp, Steve could indulge in his taste for seafood. He also picked up a bottle of Jack Daniels Black Bourbon and some ginger ale. As a special treat, he also picked up a bottle of Taylor Fladgate Port wine. Claire hated the smell of this one too, but Steve loved its soft aroma and flavour.

Once home, Steve changed his clothes and, it now being nearly four o'clock, decided that it was too late to start work on the Jeep. He poured himself a rare afternoon bourbon and ginger and went to sit in his office to check into his current state of mind, the Claire situation and the Barchetti deal.

Steve knew he was what was called "a late blooming personality," and hadn't really begun to mature until he was in his late twenties having by then completed university. Up to that point he'd been satisfied for years with a life of exploring his well-hidden extraordinary genius and trying to understand the kindergarten world he found himself locked into. Now at 38, he'd matured into a dominant, driving personality. He stood a solid 6'2" and weighed in at 205 pounds. He was a natural blond, had a short brown beard, and wore his hair in a long ponytail. He liked exercise and was a competitive mountain bike "age-class" downhill and cross-country racer. He was quick, a usually gregarious person in social situations, and very protective of his family and friends. But what he didn't know about himself was that the lifelong pressures of trying to both hide his brilliance and survive in a kindergarten world were slowly pushing him to be fundamentally unstable and potentially a very dangerous man. Even so, he was a natural leader; men easily followed him and he was very attractive to women. As he sat sipping his drink he thought that it prolly (probably, a Steve speech idiosyncrasy) was a good idea that he was taking time off.

The Price of Success

First, he was really going to have to do something about Claire. He'd known for nearly a year now that she was fooling around, and with his lawyer and supposed friend, Ted Andrusiv, yet! And lately, possibly others. Steve thought that she was either on drugs or becoming unhinged, or something. Or she had decided that it was simply time to move on. Steve knew she did hate the fact that she couldn't control him and run the marriage. His increasing success in business, fame and growing wealth also pissed her right off, even though her own life style benefited from his success. Claire's father had been a rather unsuccessful newspaper editor and the family didn't know success or wealth. Both were treated with suspicion by her politically left leaning family because, like many, they simply didn't understand the power and meaning of wealth. Her sister and brother had both married submissive partners, and neither sibling liked Steve. He shrugged. He realized that, until he knew exactly what was going on with her, doing nothing was just an excuse for delaying the inevitable.

Second, what kind of crazy deal had the Barchettis brought him? Forty-three different companies! Shit-on-a-stick, in the past six years they hadn't handled that many consulting clients in total! He was making a good living from Quinn Enterprises; maybe he better leave it at that. That building sounded like a possibility though. If they wanted $450K then they'd prolly take $375K, cash. That he could afford. The latest rescued business sale had netted over $500K, and he now had over $800K sitting in the bank. According to Cheryl Letti, his Merit Consulting manager, two more businesses were ready to be sold. Better wait until next week though, to think about buying it; he didn't have enough information. This weekend it was reassemble-the-jeep time, and nothing else!

As Steve got up to refresh his drink and start supper, the phone rang. Recognizing Ted's home number on the call display, he debated about answering it. Could Ted have found out already about the Barchettis? He quickly dismissed the thought and picked up the call.

"Hello Ted, what's up?"

"It's Grace."

"Well, hello there! If you're looking for Claire, she isn't here; she's in Calgary with the boys."

There was a long silence on the line until Grace came back and said, "Can I come and see you? I need to talk to someone."

Ah shit, Steve thought. Now what? I hope she doesn't know Ted is screwing around with Claire, among others.

"Well, I'm here alone and I was about to put supper on."

"That's okay, I'm alone too. Ted went to Calgary to see a client, and Billy is at his grandparents for the weekend. What are you making?" Knowing Steve was a superb cook, she teased, "Ordering in pizza?"

Laughing, Steve said, "Nope. Shrimp with peas and black rice. Ice cream for dessert. With a light Merlot I made last year, and finishing up with a good Port. And yes, there will be enough for two."

After a pause, he continued, "I'll leave the right-hand garage door open. Drive in, close the door and come on in."

This time there was no hesitation, "I'll be there in half an hour."

Goddamn it, Steve thought, this is all I need. Grace and Ted were, or had been his and Claire's good friends, and he knew Grace well. She was a few years older than Steve but kept herself in shape and looked younger than him. She too liked to cycle, and she, Claire and Steve had often ridden together. She was a visual artist and had a successful career on the edge of really taking off. Grace too was someone Claire was beginning to be jealous of, both for her good looks and successes. Ted at 48 had really let himself go physically, and he also did not like Grace's success. While she tried to support Ted, Steve knew that the marriage was on rough ground.

Steve went to open the garage door and returned to the kitchen to begin deveining the shrimp. As he prepared the shrimp and put the rice on, his thoughts slowed down and he enjoyed the simple act of getting supper ready for two.

Grace showed up right on time, dressed in old soft jeans and a V neck cashmere sweater. After giving Steve a hug she began setting the table. As old friends do, they quickly fell into a comfortable mode, talking about her latest work and the possibility of a Toronto show. After supper they stayed at the table and, with small crystal glasses of Port in hand, the topic shifted.

"What's the problem Grace?"

"Did you know that Ted was going to Calgary this weekend?"

Ah shit, Steve thought, here we go. "No, I didn't know that."

"Claire is there too, isn't she?"

Steve slowly put down his wine glass and, taking Grace's hands, said, "And so is my private detective with a camera."

Grace started. "You know!"

"I've known for a long time that Ted screws around, and for the past year or so, has been seeing Claire."

Grace started crying as she said, "But why? He's got a good home life, his business is making good money, and Billy thinks the world of him."

"Because Ted wants more. He's pushing 50, his law practice has stopped growing, and the fling he took this past summer into that retail business failed. You're doing better than he is and will soon be famous. I'm doing better than he is and even my office staff is better looking than his!"

"But I do everything for him. There hasn't been anything I haven't done for him," she said blushing slightly. "What am I supposed to do now?" After a moment she said, "And what are you going to do about Claire?"

The Price of Success

"Nothing at the moment. I've got all the proof I need, I just haven't figured out how to do it in such a way that the kids aren't upset more than necessary. But I rather suspect that the kids are already poisoned. We haven't had a happy family meal together for a long time. Even Skip (Steve's youngest son) doesn't care when I come home anymore. Claire and I haven't shared a bed or had sex for several years." With a rueful look and a grin, he said, "I just go to work and look at Sharon and Betty."

"You know that Claire hates both of them? I too wonder how you can work around that temptation all day and not end up a drooling idiot. Every time Ted comes back from your office, he raves about them. And that other woman, the one that runs the consulting division?"

"Cheryl. Well, actually Cheryl is gay and has a partner. It's tough, but someone has to work with them. They're all very good at their jobs, their good looks are a bonus, and you do get used to it."

Grace stood and went to wash the tears from her face. Steve cursed under his breath and wondered how he was going to get rid of her. When she returned, she wobbled slightly and asked for more wine. Steve said, "I think you've had enough. How about a coffee? I've got some Blue Mountain already ground up."

Grace slowly wobbled up to Steve, put her arms around his neck and said, "Steve, haven't you figured it out yet? I'm staying the night."

Ah fuck, Steve thought. Then, well why not? She was a good looking sexy woman. He asked her if this was really what she wanted to do. Grace replied that right from the beginning he had interested her. She added that she'd been faithful to Ted, but if Steve had asked, she would have gone with him in a minute. She added, now that she'd had enough to drink, she was really going to do this. She started grinding her hips into his and told him that she wanted him to hurt her, control her and fuck her right now. Steve moved them both into his bedroom where he slowly took off her clothes and pushed her down onto the bed. Holding her arms above her head and biting her nipple, he slid into her, making her moan as they both very quickly came.

After he came back from the bathroom, Grace slid down and took him in her mouth. As he became hard again, she slid her hand between the cheeks of his ass and, gagging, worked at keeping all of him in her mouth. Later as they lay quietly, she told him she had never done that before and needed to be drunk to do it the first time. But she liked being in control, just as she liked to be controlled, and could she do it again? It was very late when Grace left, and Steve did not get up as early as he had intended.

Over the weekend, Steve worked at reassembling his Jeep. It was an old CJ-2A built in 1942 that Steve had found behind a barn near Wynyard, south of Big Quill Lake. It had originally been used as a farm tractor during the war when new tractors were not available, and it still had the implement attaching points on the bumpers. Steve, in a moment of weakness, had purchased it and hauled it home. His excuse was he didn't have a rough country tow vehicle to pull behind his RV and thought this would be perfect. Claire had been infuriated. Having a derelict Jeep in the driveway, covered in straw, dirt and chicken shit had not been her idea of class. The fact that all the neighbourhood men and kids thought it was cool made her even madder. Over the past two years he'd disassembled the Jeep and sent most of the parts out for rebuilding and powder coating. He'd purchased custom modified Toyota axles, a rebuilt Buick V6 complete with a turbo, and a new transmission and transfer case. The body had gone out for repainting in a brilliant yellow with matching seats and upholstery. He hoped that he'd collected all the other parts needed, along with all the required stainless steel nuts, bolts and screws. And this weekend he was finally beginning the reassembly.

Steve found this physical work to be very satisfying. For some reason, like cooking, it allowed his brain to slip out of its normal frantic multi path operating mode and slow down to a near normal speed. Strangely he'd discovered that the danger and dramatic action of downhill mountain bike racing and the serenity of lonely long-distance bike touring usually accomplished the same thing.

By late Sunday afternoon he had the powertrain including the axles, suspension, steering, wheels and tires installed. He'd just finished mounting the body and was making the basic wiring harness when Claire pulled into the driveway. Putting down his tools, Steve walked out to help unload the van. And found a large gouge running from front to back along the van's right-hand side.

"Whoa! What happened here?"

Claire replied with a snarl, "Nothing! Just grab the bags."

He shrugged. It was her car.

"Hey guys, how're ya doing?"

A chorus of "Fines," was the response as the boys headed inside. "Hey guys," he said, "Grab a bag."

After moving the bags inside, the boys scattered to watch television and Claire went for a shower. Steve, left standing in the kitchen by himself, realized that no one was interested in his weekend. Or his Jeep. He realized that, really, all was irretrievably lost. There simply was no need to procrastinate. Tomorrow he would take his file of pictures, hotel receipts and the prenup to Cynthia Sharpe, his divorce lawyer, and activate "The Plan."

He went back out to look at the van. The damage was extensive, and it looked like the right-hand doors were jammed shut. It actually looked like someone had taken a giant can opener to the body. Steve surmised that Claire had somehow hit the exposed end of a steel guard rail. As he looked closely at it, he thought she might even have caused enough damage to write off the van. He shrugged; if that's the way Claire wanted to play it, fine, she can get the damn thing repaired herself. After all, he owned a well-known body shop. He returned to the garage to finish installing the primary wiring harness in the Jeep.

The Price of Success

Before he went to bed, he packed up all the tools and parts and washed down the garage floor. Claire or the boys had never reappeared to talk about his, or their, weekend.

In the morning as he poured his coffee, Claire appeared fully dressed. She said she was going into the school today, it was her turn to supervise spare classes, lunch rooms and recess. Steve, who didn't know she was doing this work, shrugged and said that, as planned, he would be at home all day. She didn't mention the damaged van, and Steve let it go. Later he would realize that she'd deliberately planned this move, knowing he'd be home all day. As soon as he was alone, he first called Cynthia and asked her to proceed. She told him that he had three days max before the shit hit the fan. His second call was to Sharon. He told her the prearranged moving plan was to be activated immediately. In minutes a large moving van appeared complete with a trusted packing and loading crew.

He started them packing and loading all the tools, parts, and pieces from the garage. When a small flat deck trailer arrived, he had the Jeep itself loaded and hauled away. A second smaller truck then appeared, and they packed up his music, sound system and photographic collections. His book collection and Eskimo artwork soon followed. A third crew started with his clothes and finished with cleaning out his office, the rest of his art work, and his antique desk and filing cabinets. When they got to his prized secretary, he watched them with some concern. The secretary had been made by one of his distant grandfathers in 1832 in England and had been bequeathed to him by his Mother's father. By noon it was complete. Nothing he wanted remained in the house, except some of the wine in the wine cellar. All the tools, the Jeep and its parts were now in his main warehouse, in a locked bay. This would become his new shop. The clothes were all packed in labelled boxes at Sharon's apartment, and the rest of his stuff was in boxes in another secure bay in the warehouse.

In the afternoon, he went to see Cynthia. As she led him into her office, she said, referring to his very casual and worn working clothes, "Do you always do business dressed like that?"

While she was kidding him, he didn't like it. Stopping, he said, "Is it a problem?"

Realizing at once that his calm demeanor hid a very angry man, she apologized and asked his forgiveness. She'd also caught a glimpse of unrestrained violence in his eyes and told herself she'd badly misread this client. She asked her secretary to join them, using a phrase that warned her secretary that this client could be a problem. She served him coffee and made small talk while he doctored up his brew. She sensed that he was calming down, and he surprised her by apologizing for his abruptness. Steve grinned as she asked her secretary to leave.

"Now you're out of the house? And moved everything out you want? And the bank accounts?"

Steve had nodded at the first two questions and then said, "I handle all the money so, yes, I long ago organized the bank accounts so that the house money and Claire's money is in one bank. She has no access to any of my personal accounts nor to my business accounts. Like all the investments, they're in yet another bank and are in my name, so they're safe."

"And you really want to give her the house and what remains of its contents?"
Steve nodded.

"And the house is paid for? And is still in your name?"
Another nod.

"And you want to give her $50,000 per year for 10 years?"
Steve nodded again.

"Okay, but as I told you earlier, this is most unusual."

"And don't forget," Steve said, "All this is contingent on her agreeing not to contest the divorce or settlement. And one more thing, I want Ted Andrusiv to present the deal to her and get her to sign it immediately."

Cynthia snapped her head up and she just stared at him. "What don't I know?"

"Let's just say that he goofed rather badly and now he's going to pay." He paused, "I also expect you to receive a call from his wife Grace any day now."

"You're not going to tell me, are you? God, how could Claire look at him? Ted's such a pig!"

"It's easy if you're trying to shoot down someone and are slightly crazy. I think you know Ted's been screwing around for years, and he thinks all those women actually want him."

"You mean that she chose him because he's your friend and lawyer?"
He nodded again.

"And if he refuses to do it, or can't persuade Claire?"

"Then you will proceed in the courts, and I'll make sure that Ted's life is ruined. If he can do it, then he still has a chance of successfully dealing with Grace and saving his career and marriage. Although personally, I don't think he has a snowball's chance."

"You know, Steve, I've heard that you can play rough, but this is a classic. Forcing the guy who screwed your wife to save his neck by persuading her to accept an unfavourable divorce settlement! I love it!"

"When will the papers be ready? I want to take them over to him ASAP."

"Tomorrow at 10:00 or so."

After leaving Cynthia's office, Steve called Grace and asked her to meet him for coffee. He then called Sharon and had her give, in cash, a bonus to the movers for a job well done. Just one of the reasons the staff would do anything for him.

The Price of Success

Chapter Three - A Score Settled

"Hi there, how're you doing?"

Grace said, "Oh, I don't know. I spend Friday night doing unspeakably wonderful things with you, find out that my friend has been sleeping with my husband, run away from home the next day, and am now living at Mum's place. And have no idea where my husband is."

"And here's the proof about Ted," he said, sliding the envelope of photos across to her.

"Tomorrow I'll get Ted to serve Claire with the divorce papers and the divorce settlement agreement. Either he persuades her to accept the deal, or I ruin him. Now today you have to change all the bank accounts into your name. Is the house in your name?"

"I can do the bank accounts, I handle all the bills and money anyway and, yes, I own the house."

"Okay, go do it right now, and change the house locks while you're at it. And call Cynthia Sharpe tomorrow. Here's her card. She knows you're going to call. If you want some fun you could bag up all his clothes and crap and pile them on the front lawn. If you need anything, call me."

"And Grace, Friday night was really wonderful."

Grace blushed as she picked up her coffee cup.

Steve called Sharon again and asked what she wanted for supper. Knowing that Sharon's eating habits usually defied understanding, he wasn't surprised when she answered, "Whatever."

He stopped on the way to her apartment and picked up the makings of a ham and cheese omelet, and a couple of bottles of wine. He also picked up some cereal, milk, some flavoured coffee whitener, and a bouquet of flowers.

At her apartment, Steve first organized his clothes, hanging up what he could, then cleaned up Sharon's kitchen. He knew from previous visits that the apartment

The Price of Success

was clean, but she didn't keep it organized, in spite of her extreme organization at work. He set the table and set up everything in the kitchen to make supper. Pouring two glasses of wine, he sat down to read the paper.

When he heard her come in, he went to give her a hug before starting supper. Holding him very tightly, she said, "Supper can wait, darlin'. Come with me, I've been ready for you since noon."

Later, after supper, lying beside each other on the couch and having fortified themselves with more wine, Sharon brought up the subject of the new building. "The Barchettis sent over all the building papers including the heating, power and tax bills. They also included a building survey by the architect Gabriel Abetelli, you know him, he's our building guy too. His latest survey for that building was completed only two months ago, and it recommends the windows be replaced, the roof be reinsulated and recoated. And that's just the minimum; he also has a full building reno plan roughed out. Lia included it with the other paperwork. So that's okay. Now, that second floor is really interesting! There's a ramp up to the second-floor area from the rear parking lot. The floor is an open space except for two immense square pillars in the middle. Apparently, the building is about 50 years old and was originally built as a farm implement dealership, with the top floors for grain and parts storage, so the second floor is reinforced to carry heavy loads, and the top floors are well built too. So, what we could do is use that floor for the courier and light truck business and leave the heavy trucks at the main warehouse. That would really help the heavy truck traffic; the damn courier vehicles are forever in the way over there. There's certainly lots of room on that floor for a manager's office, dispatch office, drivers' lunch room, bathrooms and a mail and package sorting facility. It would definitely solve most of the operating problems we have at the warehouse and in the office."

"So, for your needs it works?"

"Sure does!"

"What about the fifth floor?"

"Well, it's just a big empty, dirty space with lots of windows. There used to be an office for Abetelli up there, but he moved out and the Barchettis took the office down but never rented out the space. It sounds like Frank was supposed to do it, but I guess his illness interrupted the effort. But it's a lot of space. You could easily put our transportation and the consulting divisions up there and still use only part of one half of the floor space."

Steve was quiet for a moment, then asked, "How about another office for Quinn Enterprises itself, including an accountant and his staff? And living quarters for me?"

Sharon lifted herself up and, looking down at him, said, "And here I thought you'd live here with me."

"If I did, I wouldn't last long. You'd kill me in short order."

"Yabut, I'd get some decent meals for a change. And I'm not sure about killing you; I think I broke something tonight."

Quickly sitting up, Steve said, "Are you okay? Why didn't you tell me to stop?"

"And interrupt the best fuck I've had since the last time we were together? I don't think so."

"Are you okay?"

"I'm fine, or will be tomorrow. Now come back here."

Steve sat there looking at her and, apparently satisfied that she would be okay, lay back down. "How do you feel about taking on the building project? I'm thinking that we could hire Abetelli and have him design and supervise the redoing of the building? Let's talk to him and see if he's interested in actually doing this project. And he reports to you."

"Damn it Steve, what do I know about buildings?"

"Doesn't matter. Just wave the girls at him and he'll do whatever you want!"

She reached over and gently punched him. "That reminds me about what happened today when I was looking at the building. We, Toni and I -- he was in front -- were walking into Lia's office when he suddenly stopped and turned to say something to me. And I smacked him right in the face with my right boob! I damn near knocked him down! Lia laughed and laughed and couldn't stop, while Toni sat down with a dazed look on his face."

Steve started chuckling and laughing, said, "What a way to make new friends!"

"I was so embarrassed! But Lia said that she wished she could do that, it would certainly keep the assholes out of range. Apparently, it's the one thing she really hates about being small. And from that and other small things, I don't think the Barchettis get along as well as they would have you think. And, you know, I like her. She's a tough little broad and isn't afraid of me."

"Well, that's new! She's one of only a few. In the morning, see if you can find that architect and set up a meeting. I'll talk to Lia and the bank about buying the building. I think I'll start at about $350,000, but I'm going to need a ballpark number for the windows and roof. And I guess I'm going to need a new corporate lawyer. What do you think about using Lia for that? And I guess we'll need another law firm to handle the purchase of the businesses from Lia and her dad."

"As I said, I like Lia. And I think she likes you too."

"Go away, she hardly knows me!"

Sharon smiled a knowing smile and said, "Are you really sure about going ahead with this? The building I can see, we badly need some more space, but you don't even know what you're looking at with the businesses."

"Well, I'm going to prolly irritate you again no end when I say that my feeling on this one is very strong. I know you have trouble with my being fey, but that's the way she be. And I really don't know what this deal will bring, but I do know that it's something we must look at. Will you arrange to get all the Barchetti paperwork

The Price of Success

on Cheryl's desk in the morning? And get Cheryl to start sorting them out. I won't be in 'til later."

"Listen Steve, I'm okay with it. I've never seen you make a wrong move listening to your fey voice, and all we're doing is looking at this deal, so let's do it."

And on that note, they went back to bed.

The next morning Steve called Ted and set up an early appointment. He made a quick stop to pick up the new photos and video tapes from his investigator, and to be told that Ted and Claire had been very careless about who saw them in Calgary. Claire had parked the kids with her sister and spent the weekend with Ted. Then, after picking up the divorce agreement from Cynthia's office, he stopped at Timmy's, picked up a double-double and went to see Ted. Ted's office coffee was terrible.

"How was the weekend?" he asked.

"Good! Got back late last night so I stayed in town."

Steve threw the agreement on Ted's desk and, leaning back in his chair, said, "Open that up and read it please."

Ted picked it up and read all three pages. Looking at Steve, he reread the agreement and with slightly trembling hands, carefully placed it back in the center of the desk. "And so?"

"You're taking that agreement over to Claire today and getting her signature on it. All three copies, please."

Ted got up to pour himself a cup of coffee. As usual, Steve could smell its burned flavour and hoped it didn't ruin the taste of his Tim's brew.

"And why should I do this? I wouldn't -- or even couldn't -- ask anyone to agree to this. If you're actually divorcing her, then it's your job to persuade Claire and her lawyer to agree, if it's even possible. Hell, I could probably be disbarred for getting involved."

"Actually, the interesting thing is that you aren't surprised, nor are you wondering who prepared the documents. So," he paused, "Did I forget to mention that I have some rather revealing photos and videos of you with Claire in Calgary this weekend, here in Regina, and actually even in my house? The main bedroom to be specific. I also have hotel receipts and copies of phone bills. Plus sworn statements from some impeccable witnesses. Oh, did I also mention that some of the videos are of women other than Claire?"

He paused, "If you fail, I'll forward copies of everything to Grace and the other guys whose wives you've been porking. Remember, one is a judge and another is a lawyer."

Ted, now very pale, slowly stood up and walked over to the window. He bounced on his toes, gently banged his head on the glass, then turned and collapsed, sitting on the window sill. "Okay, what do you really want?"

Steve stood up and, with an ugly smile, said, "You've got until 2:00 this afternoon to return the signed agreements." He stopped at the door and said, "I hope it was worth it."

Back at the office, Cheryl had sorted out the Barchetti papers into roughly similar businesses and further sorted each pile into least to most profitable. There were six piles; specialty grocery stores including C stores, auto dealerships including both cars and trucks, auto repair shops including auto parts stores, small fabricators and welding shops, all manner of construction companies including electricians, plumbers, and roofers and a lone dentist. Steve grinned, "I knew you'd find a way to look at this mess! Which is the least profitable group in total?"

Cheryl blushed and said, "I'm not sure, but the welding/fab shops don't look very good."

"In addition, did you come up with a ballpark number if we were to purchase each pile?"

"Actually, the welder/fab pile has no value. Last year's net income from this group is negative. They have little capital and it doesn't even come close to their debt load. Barchetti should pay us to take the fab group off their hands. And I suspect, after a quick look, the other piles are not much better. Except the construction group and the dentist. Among the other groups there are a few individual businesses that are profitable. Very, very loose guess, $175,000 absolute tops for all of them."

Steve sat down and just looked at her. "That's all? For all 43 businesses? You're kidding, right?"

"Nope, basically most of this stuff is just crap. If you'd asked me about any one of them by itself, I'd probably tell you to throw it in the garbage. I'll bet Frank kept most of these businesses going out of his own pocket."

Steve sat back in his chair, thought for a moment, and said, "Well Christ! No wonder the Barchettis don't want them. So what the hell are we supposed to do with them? Play bail out doctor?" He stopped. "Any ideas?"

She picked up the pile of fabricators and suggested that with four shops in Regina and one in Saskatoon, it would probably make sense to combine the Regina shops and sell the Saskatoon shop. There were no big integrated welding/fabricator shops in Regina, so the market was wide open. She looked at him and asked if he remembered talking about the coming big resource boom. If so, there would be a hell of a demand for fab shop services. Also, the funds from the Saskatoon shop sale would provide the capital to combine the Regina shops. She reminded him they already owned a welding shop and that it was finally quite profitable. She liked the shop manager and thought that he was capable of doing much more than just managing one shop. She suggested bringing him on board.

She continued, "Then, if we did what I suggest, I think we could create a viable business. Then we could either sell it or, if the cash flow is big enough, keep it and

The Price of Success

use it to finance the other fixer-uppers. Particularly if we could buy them without paying for the debt. Then the debt work-out would allow us to absorb the incoming cash tax-free."

Steve just sat there looking at nothing. Cheryl had seen this before and knew he was thinking furiously. "So," he said coming back into focus, "You're suggesting that we can buy them for next to nothing, including the debt, work like hell to close, combine or whatever, and then reap the profits tax free?"

"Basically."

"Damn, you're good! That might work! Okay, Cheryl, keep going. Do you need any more immediate help?"

She shook her head. "But," she said, "It'll take lots of cash, and people I don't now have, and a place to work."

"Give me a list of what you need, and I'll see what I can do. The space I'm working on. I'll be back later. I must go see the bank."

Steve called Sharon and said, "Sharon, I'm off to the bank, then I'll get some lunch. If Ted shows up, ask him to wait. I'll try to be back by 2:00. And if you get a moment you might talk to Cheryl, she's found some great stuff. This deal is actually looking interesting. Gotta run, I'll be late for my meeting."

At the bank Steve outlined the Barchetti deal and asked for a $200,000 line of credit. The bank suggested they approve $300,000 to allow him some negotiating wiggle room. And to give him some working capital. Steve also asked for another $350,000 to purchase the building. He told them that he had enough cash to repair the building and to modify the second and fifth floors. Again the bank suggested he take up to $600,000, or more if required to cover a complete building rehab, the unexpected, and to be able to capitalize all the rebuilding costs within the mortgage. Steve promised to have Larry Baines, his accountant, submit all the paperwork the following week. Steve left, realizing he had yet to talk to Larry about the Barchettis. Steve laughed at his haste. He needed Larry to begin structuring a favourable financial arrangement for both the bank and the Barchetti deals.

Steve managed to get back to his office before 2:00, in time to find Ted waiting for him. Without a word, Ted handed Steve the signed agreements, then turned and left. After checking them over, Steve let out a rare wild whoop, high fived a surprised Betty, and called Cynthia. Cynthia didn't believe his success and suggested he wait for a couple of days to let everything settle down. She would then file the divorce papers in the courts.

By five, Steve had talked the deals over with Larry and had asked Lia for a meeting for the next morning. He also asked her if she was interested in taking over his business legal work, and if she would recommend another law firm to act for him in the business and building sales between the two of them. He left for Sharon's place, well pleased with the day's progress.

21

At Sharon's apartment, making a supper of pork chops sautéed in blue cheese salad dressing, with red rice and corn with a touch of red wine, he reflected on the day. Everything had gone as planned, in fact better than planned. And above all, his fey sense was now quiet. There were some loose ends and lots of work ahead, but this looked like the break he'd been looking for. The only big issue left was his own business' organization. Quinn Enterprises was his holding company with three divisions, Transportation, Consulting, and everything else. But the divisions had no formal structure other than being companies owned by Quinn and were getting too large to be managed in such an informal manner. With the additional companies and business volume, he had to do some rearranging. And Larry wanted a job. Steve hadn't seen that coming, but it looked like Larry was sick and tired of working with his overbearing, controlling wife and daughters, and wanted out. Well, Cynthia could always use another client! Steve knew that Larry wasn't the biggest stick in the wood pile, but he was a damn fine accountant. Most important, he would tell Steve the truth, no matter how unpalatable. Steve now realized that Larry was one of those men that needed to have a solid management structure around him in order to feel comfortable.

Just then Sharon came in with a bottle of expensive Chianti in hand saying that she understood celebrations were in order. Over supper Steve brought Sharon up to date on the divorce shenanigans, leaving out Grace's Friday night visit. Or that Claire had not called to ask where he was.

"Okay!" she exclaimed. "I'm glad to see the end of that prick, Ted. I never told you he pestered me for dates, did I? And Betty had problems with him too. How about you release those pictures anyway?"

"If I'd known that, I would have. But I think Grace will take care of him for us. I understand that Cynthia is already talking to her."

"Hmmpppfff! Maybe the next time I see him, I'll punch the bastard."

Steve knew that Sharon regularly attended a gym and he had also introduced her to the sensei at his martial arts dojo. She and Steve had practised and sparred together and Steve knew that she was a formidable opponent. Not only was she big, very strong and quick, she fought dirty!

Steve laughed and said, "Now that I would like to see!"

"So what does this actually mean? What happens now?"

"In a day or so, Cynthia submits the divorce papers to the courts, along with the settlement, and, presuming the judge or Claire's lawyer doesn't object, in a year or so the divorce becomes final."

"And then you're done? What about child support?"

"Yes, I'm done. Child support is paid from the $50,000 per year. And informally, I'll pay the kids' tuition fees at university or wherever else they wish to go."

Just then the phone rang. Sharon answered it and said, "It's your daughter, Samara." (Samara is Steve's oldest child and his only daughter. She is 20.)

The Price of Success

Steve said, "Hi there, Charley Brown, how're you doing?"

"You're divorcing Mom? How come you didn't tell me?"

"I assumed that you'd have figured out long ago that it was coming!"

There was moment of silence, "Yeah well, I guess. Especially after I saw Ted and her doing it in the kitchen last summer."

"What!"

"I came home one day early and they didn't hear me coming. I saw them in that big mirror in the hallway, so I snuck downstairs."

"Where were the boys?"

"Watching TV upstairs, I think."

"Son-of-a bitch!" he said. "I'm sorry you saw that. I hope the boys didn't see anything."

"I don't know, but Sergio (Steve also has three sons, the two oldest are adopted. Sergio is 14, Shaun is 12 and Skip is 8) has asked me several times why Ted was upstairs with Mum."

"That dumb fucking broad! Someday I'll tell you about the divorce, but for now, I'm looking after both of those bastards. Do you need anything? No? Everything's going okay? What about the boys?"

"I don't think it's sunk in yet. Mom is so often bad mouthing you that if you're not there, it just means you're not fighting. But if she keeps drinking, they may change their minds."

"Well, okay, I can't do very much about that. I suggest we just let things settle down for a week or so. If you need to talk to me, call Sharon and ask her to pass on a message. Let's have supper next week and I'll bring you up to date about the business. Interesting times are upon us!"

"Dad," she said in her warning voice, "What are you planning? I know you can be a mean bastard but this is, after all, still my mother. Ted, I don't care what you do to that prick."

"Hey, hey, whoa, this is your old man! Don't talk like that; I'm not supposed to think your poop stinks." He paused. "Basically, I'm giving Claire the house, all the furnishings, or at least most of them, her car and 50 grand a year for 10 years. And if you kids want to go on to higher Ed, I'll pay for that too. So don't worry about your university tuition fees."

"Does this mean I don't have to work for you anymore?"

"Nice try. See you next week."

Steve hung up and turned to Sharon, "You heard that? Those two assholes are so finished."

With an obvious mental effort, Steve changed the subject and began to outline what Cheryl had found, and the results of his bank visit. He then went on to outline a possible course of action. Sharon told him that she'd found the architect and they were meeting tomorrow. He was still angry when they went to bed. Sharon liked it when he was annoyed.

The Price of Success

Chapter Four - A New Home

Wednesday morning Steve went directly to the Barchetti offices where Lia suggested they take a quick tour of the empty spaces in the building, First they took the elevator down to the empty second floor. It was as Sharon had described, and Steve saw immediately why she liked it. He made a mental note to have a closer look at the ramp; it seemed a bit steep and rough for a loaded truck, and the door was going to have to be replaced too. They then went up to the top floor and it did indeed have a lot of windows, another point Steve liked. He hated the feeling of being confined, especially in his storage room office. However he thought, the original single pane windows were prolly proving a challenge for the environmental control systems. With no tall neighbours to break the wind, a minus 40C windy winter day up here was not going to be pleasant. That was prolly why the architect had moved out. Note to self: Triple pane windows all around! Back in Lia's office, he asked her to show him the rest of the building. The Barchetti offices were on the fourth floor and had just about as many windows as did the fifth. He noticed the heavy curtains, now drawn back, and asked Lia about the heating and cooling.

"For a building this age, it's reasonable, but in the dead of winter or July, the systems struggle."

"How long have you been here?" he asked.

"Dad moved here about 30 years ago when he knew we were all going to be lawyers, and the client who owned the building needed some financial help."

"Have you done any remodeling?"

"We haven't. I don't think Dad did either. I do know that all the windows and doors as well as the mouldings are original. The furnace, boiler, and A/C units were replaced about 10 years ago. Each floor has its own hot water system, and our tank was replaced last year. Why they did it that way, I don't know. The bathrooms were redone about 15 years ago, and they need it again. The wiring I don't know."

Back in her office with its view over the city, coffees in hand, Steve asked about the building's financing. Lia replied that it was clear of encumbrances. She went on

The Price of Success

that if Steve were to finance the purchase he would have to pay for a building survey because it was more than 50 years old.

"If," he said, "We decided to replace all the windows and to reinsulate the roof or, prolly better, insulate the walls and upgrade the bathrooms and elevators, could you still work in here? Then you'd have to redecorate. Or better, if we reno'd the top floor first and set up temporary offices for you there, could you do that?"

"Shit Steve! Sorry, that wasn't called for. You're talking about rebuilding the building!"

"Well, what better time than when I buy it?"

Trying to buy time, Lia said, "But you don't even own it yet! Wow, I see now why Dad was so positive about you. Do you always steamroller through problems like this?"

"Would you be surprised to know that the mortgage is already arranged? Judging by the look on your face, the answer is yes."

Weakly, Lia asked, "And how much are we selling the building for?"

"I'll give you $350,000 cash for it. I know Toni said it was about $450,000, but he didn't mention the improvements required."

Lia laughed. "We figured you'd start at 325 and we could close at about 360 or so. Three hundred and fifty we can do. Now, who pays for the redecorating after doing the renos?"

"You do. I'm assuming that the other tenants also will. Yes?"

"Probably. Shake on it?"

Steve sat and looked at her for a few seconds. He didn't sense any foolishness coming from her, so he stood and shook her little hand. "Got a law firm for me?" he asked.

Getting up, Lia said, "Follow me, there's a firm we use down the hall. I've talked to them, and they'll look after you." Looking over her shoulder she asked, "What about the businesses?"

"We're still looking at them. It's a much bigger problem than we first thought, and we haven't worked out a way to tackle them yet. I've got several analysts working on it but so far we're stuck just trying to get our heads around them to see what we actually have."

Lia stopped and looked up at him. "Are you setting me up for some bad news?"

Damn, Steve said to himself. Note to self: She's quicker than I thought. "How much do you want for them, package deal?"

Lia looked troubled. "Dad wants $500,000, but our accountant has said that's much too much."

Steve looked at her, shrugged and said, "At that price we might as well return the papers to you and stop wasting each other's time. But I haven't been into the office yet today, and last night someone may have had a bright idea."

After introducing Steve to Jamie Price of Price & Company, Lia headed back to her office for some quality seat time. Checking with Maria, her assistant, she told her to hold everything for a while, she had to think. Maria giggled and said, "He got to you, did he?"

"What do you mean?"

Giggling again, she said, "Everyone in here is drooling. Who is he anyway?"

Lia blushed. "Steve Quinn. He's buying this building, among other things."

Lia escaped into her office and started pacing, something she did when troubled, or needed to think. She was shocked to realize that Maria was right, Steve had gotten to her. She was going to have to be careful that she didn't screw up the sale. Shit, she thought, stopping, I already did! I gave that bastard at least 10 grand! God damn it!

She resumed her pacing, now moving at a furious rate. Now, what about fixing this place up? She looked around her office and saw perhaps for the first time that it really was Frank's office. And it was rather shop worn. If it were reno'd, then maybe the company would really begin to feel like hers. If Steve installed new windows, insulated the walls and installed new drywall, then all she'd have to do would be to get new flooring and ceilings, new lighting and some new furniture. Presumably Steve would rebuild the electrical wiring and install completely new bathrooms. But should she get a renovation agreement out of him before they sold the building? Or just trust he wouldn't screw her and the other tenants around. She stopped dead, then resumed pacing. Shit! She'd already shaken hands on the sale. Perhaps she could arrange to have some input into the reno plan. Smiling, she thought that might work. Maybe even Toni could ramrod that little project. As long as Sharon wasn't involved.

Okay, now the businesses. Their accountant had said they'd be lucky to get $100K for them. In total. Then they simply would have to write off the outstanding debt. And would that put a huge hole into their balance sheet! Steve probably wouldn't even want to touch some of them. Damn Frank anyway! She didn't want this problem or to be forced to take over the support program her father had set up. The firm, in the long run, couldn't support the cash drain. She stopped pacing and decided that she was just going to have to wait until Steve came back with a proposal.

Sitting at her desk, she pulled up a blank two way confidentiality agreement and started work.

Steve, needing some time to think after meeting with Jamie Price, decided to try the food in the first-floor restaurant in Lia's building. He went in and immediately loved the smell and the décor; it was mid Italian and specialized in Avezzano cuisine from the hills above Rome. Steve sat down to think and enjoy some great food. The meal finished and, inspired by a glass of old Chianti, he suddenly had a great idea.

The Price of Success

After lunch Steve called Sharon and Cheryl into a meeting to discuss the Barchetti package. Neither one had come up with a new idea on tackling the Barchetti problem, so Steve said with a crooked grin, "I've got the solution. In fact, I've got two solutions, and one for a problem we never even talked about."

They looked at him. "Usually," he went on, "We start looking at a company from the inside out. We look at the people, the systems, the facilities, the product, and the market. We then fix what's broken or out of kilter, and then push the rebuilt company to prosper. Right? Okay. How about we turn it around? What if we look at the businesses from the outside first?"

They looked at him, not understanding.

"Cheryl, you had the right idea. Let's look at each pile, not individually, but as one big possible business. If we were to consider the totality of each pile, we could then decide if we could make one or more viable businesses out of the pile of pieces, or not. If we can't see how to make a pile go as one or two businesses, then we decide how to dispose of the parts that don't fit. If we think it can be made into something, then we continue to look at it from the outside and decide how to put the various parts together in order to make something. Then we look at it from the inside as usual and make it into a profitable entity."

They both looked at him, and Cheryl got it. "Yes," she said, "Yes! Then we could blitz each pile separately and solve this whole god damn problem of knowing what we've got fairly quickly. But what's the problem we missed?"

Sharon laughed and slapped the desk, "How much to pay for each pile!"

Steve continued, "Exactly. If the pile is not viable, we pay nothing for it; if the pile works, or if we can make several businesses from each pile, then coming up with a price will be easy."

As the two women sat back to think about it, Steve continued, "And we buy the piles one at a time, conserving cash. Buy the junk first and get it out of the way."

Steve sat back and waited. Cheryl finally leaned forward and said, "Yup, that'll work. And now I suppose you want a viability report and a suggested purchase price for the first pile?"

"Yes. While you're doing that, Sharon and I are going to argue with an architect about our new home. The sooner you're finished with that report, the sooner you can help us design all that new office space you're going to need. And hire all those new bodies."

Steve called Lia and told her what he had in mind. He'd buy the businesses in groups over a period of six months. At the moment it looked like there would be six groups, and the first one was the welding/fabricating shops. They were prepared to buy it for one dollar. As he expected, she was not happy. But, he continued, they didn't need a decision just yet from her and, besides, they had to discuss how the entire group of companies was going to be advised of the proposed change in ownership. He suggested she think about having a general meeting of all concerned, introducing him and getting all the objections out into the open. Perhaps they could meet on Monday next? He hung up, well satisfied with the project's progress.

Lia, on the other hand, was very troubled. She'd just been backed into an unpleasant corner. Frank was not going to be happy with the emerging financial picture. Between them, they had approximately $780,000 in loans (hah, she thought, more like gifts) tied up in the 43 businesses. She knew that most of the loans were "non-performing" that is, no payments had been made on them for years. But on the plus side, most of the loans had been in place for years and the lack of payments was not impacting current Barchetti LLP or Frank's operations. The loans made the Barchetti LLP balance sheet look like hell but, thanks to having a significant amount of cash in the bank, as a practical issue it didn't really matter. She wondered if, when they sold the businesses, they could also write off the loans and give the company some big tax loss credits. Frank's personal financial picture didn't look very good either but, again, he did have enough cash on hand to carry on. Lia decided that perhaps Barchetti LLP should buy the businesses from Frank. This would clean up Frank's finances and his estate, another worry. She knew that Frank's will gave the bulk of his estate to the three kids, with about 25% being split between a number of Italian community organizations. Their mother had died many years ago, and Frank had had no other companions, except his sister. And she had lots of money so didn't need any more. Lia sighed. She better call their accountant and lay it on him. And then she was going to have to talk to Frank. Shit, she thought, shit, shit, shit!

Steve and Sharon's meeting with the architect, Gabriel Abetteli, was short and to the point. Abetteli had already created designs for the building's renovation, a project that he'd been trying to sell to the Barchettis for several years. He indeed was the architect that had moved out and, yes, it was because of the poor climate control on the fifth floor. He loved the building though and thought he could add at least 50 more years to the building's life through the improvements. Steve asked him to prepare a package that included the windows, roof, insulation, electrical wiring, and plumbing. And an evaluation of the heating and A/C systems if the building were rehabbed. The packages to include costs. Gabriel pointed out that Saskatchewan Power had building energy improvement grant packages and loans that effectively would make much of the insulation upgrade free. The City of Regina also had grants and loans available for this type of work. Then Steve wanted a second package for rebuilding the second and top floors. Steve suggested that he could also talk to the renters about redoing their space. But first he had to buy the building! Gabriel gave them a delivery date of about two weeks or so. Steve made sure that Gabriel knew that his contact person was Sharon, a point that didn't seem to bother Gabriel at all.

It was still early in the afternoon, but it was a slow day in the transportation business, so Steve persuaded Sharon to head home early. They stopped at the market and Steve bought the ingredients for a seafood and pasta supper. Once at home, each

The Price of Success

with a glass of wine in hand, they sat on the couch for some down time. Sharon put on her new Pink Floyd album and they both sat back to listen.

"Do you know that I can't remember the last time I came home early?"

Steve laughed and replied, "See, I couldn't live here. I'm a bad influence on you."

"Yeah, and I'm putting on weight too."

Steve looked at her, "After just a few days? Where?"

Sharon swatted at him and said, "Go make supper, jerk."

As he got up, he didn't see the fleeting expression of loss on her face.

After supper, Sharon, who'd been uncharacteristically quiet during the meal, dug out two joints and went to have a long soak in her tub. She too needed some time to think. While having Steve live here was a real gift from the Gods, it was going to present some problems. She knew that with him around, they would rarely take time just to sit and recharge. He just never sat still and worse, he did not sleep very much. Although it was nice to have him doing the shopping and cooking, and having breakfast ready when she woke up, Sharon wasn't sure if sometimes he even came to bed! The bottom line was that she knew eventually he would, but not on purpose, run her right ragged.

But he did treat her right. From the beginning he didn't treat her as a freak, or look at her boobs, or even feel her ass. He treated her, and Betty, Cheryl and the others too, as real people. He expected her to think and contribute, something most men didn't do. Privately she joked that her boobs got in the way! It had taken a while but Steve was one of the very few men Sharon now trusted and there was no getting over just how safe and secure she felt when he was around. She blushed slightly as she remembered that she had initiated sex with him. The first and only time she had done so! After talking to the other woman about him, she knew that they felt the same way. Fuck, she thought, he simply was too much of a good thing.

Steve took his share of the weed and went to sit on the balcony. It was time to get his thoughts in order again. Lighting the joint, he started with the building purchase. The actual sale could now go ahead, and the architect was putting together a renovation package. So that's okay. He was going to have to be involved, but Sharon knew what she wanted on both the second and fifth floors, so all he was going to have to do was keep an eye on things. And keep an eye on the building rehab costs. This was going to be the most expensive project they'd ever undertaken. Cheryl could oversee the consulting office layout, bearing in mind that they should not overbuild. Betty, with her eye for detail, could supervise the actual minute by minute construction. Everyone would enjoy having the three women around!

Getting a whole bunch of new clients all at the same time was a one timer. On the other hand, he expected them to double or even triple the number of businesses they owned when this deal was finished, and that would require additional management staff. Or maybe not; it depended on how the businesses were organized. And that led to the last unresolved issue. How was this organizational mess supposed to be managed? One thing he'd learned was that the management of a business was everything. Shit, maybe he should call in a consultant. At that he laughed out loud and said to himself, consultant heal thyself!

Going back inside, he got a pad of lined paper and returned to the balcony. Drawing a series of lines across the paper to represent the various management levels, he started by putting himself at the top of the page. On the first line on the right-hand side he put Sharon's name and the title, Vice President, Transportation Operations. On the second line below her, he put two titles side by side: Manager, City Express, and Manager, Rayner Freight Lines. The courier operations would include all second-floor activities, courier sales, and new courier distribution methods. Which reminded him that he should talk to Sharon about the pickup and delivery routing article he'd read last week. That new package collection and distribution system looked like the future direction of the courier business. The freight manager would supervise the warehouse, cross dock and the heavy truck operations. To the left on line two he listed Cheryl Letti, Vice President, Merit Consulting. She would be in charge of all consulting, analysis of new businesses and the ongoing oversight and analysis of their existing businesses. As well as all their contract accountants, computer analysts, and market researchers. Then, again to the left, Betty Cookston, Vice President, Administration. She would have Payroll, Benefits, Building Operations, Staff Relations, Publicity and Parking. And finally, on the extreme left, Larry Baines, Vice President of Finance. Rereading it, he added below his own name, New Business Operations. He wanted a direct hand in orchestrating the success of the new businesses. He also wanted to have the deciding vote on staffing, selling or combining these new businesses. Okay! This would work. Now to find those two people for Sharon. He hoped that she'd been thinking about having subordinates, as he'd suggested several times over the past few months.

Now the fifth-floor layout. They could designate the south end of the building for Sharon's and Betty's offices, a computer and communications operations area and an office for Cheryl and space for her analysts. The north end past the elevator entranceway could contain the Quinn Enterprise's office including Larry's office and space for his staff, Steve's office and, at the back, his apartment.

This would also work. Now to talk it over with Sharon. He cleaned up the dining room, did the dishes and set out the coffee makings for the morning. And discovered Sharon sound asleep in bed. He picked up her clothes, cleaned up the bathroom, and, since she was sprawled over most of the bed, went back to the living room. Getting a blanket and a pillow, he lay down on the couch for a short sleep.

The Price of Success

Chapter Five - Growth, Promotions and Repercussions

Monday morning, Lia called; she told Steve that she'd talked to her father and had devised a plan of action. Barchetti LLP would buy all the remaining businesses from Frank, then when Steve was ready to buy a group of them, she would call the owners into the office and she and Frank would explain to them what was going to happen. Then she would introduce Steve, and he could explain to the group what was coming.

Steve asked, "And who do I negotiate with? And who am I really buying from?"

"You're buying from Barchetti LLP, and you negotiate with me. Frank will no longer be involved. In fact, Barchetti LLP, by lunch time, will be the sole owner of everything and Frank will be retired."

"Okay, we're ready to buy the first group, the welding/fabricating shops. I'll have Price & Company send over an offer for one dollar. The purchase price includes any debt. The owner of the package to be Quinn Enterprises."

"Other than giving away the debt, we've got a deal. I must talk to my accountant first, but, okay. See you after I've talked to him. Oh wait. Can I send Price the sales agreement for this building?"

"Okay, but you better send a copy to me so that Larry can look at it."

"Who's Larry?"

"Larry Baines. He's my business accountant. He's starting here full time next week."

"See you later."

Lia then called her accountant and was told that the debt really, to Barchetti, had no value. Since no one would repay it, they might as well clean up the Barchetti balance sheet by including it in the sale price. Besides if they didn't include it in the sale, Steve would probably demand they pay him to take the businesses of her hands. He was sure that Steve would find a use for it, and it may even generate Lia some personal goodwill with Steve. Lia wasn't happy, but she saw no way out of the pit that Frank had dug.

The Price of Success

Steve called both Price and Larry to warn them the building sale agreement was coming. Now to talk to Sharon about the organization. With this new structure, he'd be removing himself from day to day management; well actually, minute by minute management would be closer to the truth. But first he'd had to think about it. Last week, he decided to practice not managing, so after waking up on the couch and finding Sharon gone, he'd put on his work clothes and gone over to the warehouse to organize the bay into a shop. No one seemed to need him, so the next day he went back to continue the job. The first requirement was to have the walls framed up so that he could have them spray insulated and drywalled. After framing the walls he'd been there every day organizing all his tools and supplies, buying a new work bench and sorting out the jeep and its parts. He'd also had the electrician come in to rewire the bay, adding a 200 Amp service, lights, heaters and a circuit for his welding machine. Every evening he returned to Sharon's apartment, made supper, and listened to the office events. He was a happy camper.

Now it was Monday again and time to get back to work. Lia called and asked if, on short notice, he could come over for the welding/fab shop sale meeting. He grabbed Cheryl and they went to the Barchetti office, met the shop owners and outlined the plans for the businesses. Without much choice, they all agreed to the sale. The sales concluded, the existing fab shop manager was introduced and Steve turned the floor over to Cheryl.

Later they returned to Steve's office with Steve and Cheryl each feeling completely reenergized. Cheryl had a huge challenge in front of her, exactly as she liked, and Steve had just made great progress with his new shop and Jeep rebuilding plan. Now for the organization to support all the corporate fun and games! He called Sharon and asked her to come up to discuss the plan. He began by repeating the drawing on a large whiteboard and asking for her opinion.

"You're making me number two in the company?" she asked.

"Yup. You've earned it, and you're the best one for the job. This position will give you almost as much authority as I now have. I'll go over the exact details later, but basically you get all the authority required to run the company on a day-to-day basis. And a new office. And a raise."

"In the event of an emergency you can assume whatever authority is required to deal with the emergency. And, although Peter Thayer (Steve's personal friend and Managing Partner of Thayer LLP, Regina's largest law firm. He was also the lawyer Steve turned to for major issues, leaving Barchetti LLP the routine legal tasks) hasn't figured out yet how to do it on paper; he's working on it."

Sharon sat looking at him, stunned. Not saying anything. Steve began to get a bad feeling that something was wrong here. "But I know nothing about the other businesses! Or finance. Or the people. And what about the managers? How will they feel reporting to a woman?"

"Well Sharon, you're the Boss; you simply will tell people what to do, and if you have a problem you talk to Larry, Peter, Cheryl, or me. You prolly don't realize just how respected you are around here, but believe me, I think most like you more than me. Besides you're better to look at!"

Sharon drew a ragged breath and said, "Truckin' Ted can do the heavy trucks and Jason Lapointe is ready to move up on the courier side. Both are going to need support, but they can do it. And I have people to move up into their positions as well. When do you want to talk to them?"

Steve wanted to ask what was going on, but the moment had passed. He said, "How about tomorrow morning? After the morning rush? We'll make all these changes effective the beginning of next month?"

Steve, with a puzzled look, stopped and asked, "Wait a minute, who the hell is Truckin' Ted?"

"You probably don't remember but he was the manager of that specialty reefer trucking company we bought last year. He's about 50, always wears broken down cowboy boots and a ridiculous cowboy hat. But I've discovered he really knows his stuff and seems to know everyone in the business. The best part is that I've never seen him get pissed off or upset or even raise his voice. Although I don't care, all the guys like him too."

Changing the subject, she said, "Gabriel will have the building designs and costs by Friday. He won't design your office or apartment until he talks to you, but there's no rush for that. Everyone else's office is blocked out. We'll do the details later. But I did tell him that the priority is the fifth-floor offices, especially work space for Cheryl and her analysts."

"Okay. I can't wait! But don't forget the Barchettis have to have a temporary place up there as well."

Steve yelled for Betty. Betty stuck her head in the door and said, in a scolding voice, "Don't yell, Steve. That's not cool."

Steve had the humility to blush and mutter, "Sorry, I guess I'm kinda excited."

In minutes Steve had explained to Betty what he had in mind. She sat there, shocked and speechless. He went on that he knew she didn't know everything about the job but that she'd proved over and over to him that she could do anything he threw at her. He outlined the raise he had in mind and that if she wanted to take courses on anything, he would pay for it. Betty just sat there, and then tears started down her face. Steve looked at Sharon with a question on his face, but she gave him a little shrug and shook her head.

Betty finally said from behind her hands, "I came in today to quit. Rusty punched me again last night and it's just been getting worse and worse. I was going to leave him and go back to Calgary tonight."

Steve jumped up and yelled, "That fucker did what? Hit you? Son-of-a-bitch! I'll beat the crap out of him."

The Price of Success

Sharon moved over and held Betty. She looked at Steve and said she'd arrange something for Betty until she could find her own place. Steve, nearly jumping out of his skin, clearly enraged, muttered that he'd find a place for himself if she thought Betty would be better off with her. Sharon smiled gratefully, and they both knew this development would also solve another problem. Sharon also hoped that Steve would calm down before he met up with Rusty. Steve was a big man in remarkable condition, a trained martial artist, quick as a cat and brutally strong. He also had a vicious temper, and if he chose, she thought, shuddering, he could, without any remorse whatsoever, easily kill someone.

"Betty, you're not leaving Regina. You're a very important person to me and I'll not let you go." Stomping up and down the hall, hitting the walls with his open hand, Steve said, "You and Sharon take a few days off and get your new place organized. I can stagger along without youse (another of Steve's speech oddities) two for a while. And Sharon, take her over to see Cynthia Sharpe. I'll pay for it."

"I'll go over and pack right now. Get Cheryl to find someone to look after the front desk and the phones." Still in a rage, he stormed out, violently slamming the door.

After packing his stuff at Sharon's, he had most of it moved to the warehouse and arranged to stay at a small B&B outside of the city. The owner, Ann Bazvsky, owed him a large favour and was happy to have him stay as long as he wished. They both knew no bill would ever appear. Steve had saved Ann's life a number of years ago, in an accident where her husband, Janos, who had been a good friend, had died. Ann from time to time also served as Steve's psychiatrist.

The next day, back in his supply room office, Steve, Larry and Jamie Price reviewed the building sales agreement and, with minor changes agreed to by Lia, Steve signed it. Price and Larry agreed to drop a copy off at Lia's and go over to the bank and finalize the mortgage. Okay, Steve thought, that's done. Now for Cheryl.

He called her in and showed her the organization's new management diagram. In addition to being surprised at the new position and the increased salary, she wasn't sure she could handle the increased responsibility. Steve assured her that with him and Sharon as backup, she'd do just fine, especially as Steve wanted the final say on any major plans for the new businesses. As she was getting ready to leave she said that they now had a detailed plan for the welding/fab shops, and she suggested they look at the dentist next. She suggested that they get the dentist to buy back his shop, or if they had to keep it, it could provide more cash for the fixups. Steve asked her to put a price on the dentist and get back to him. And to keep going with the others. He also asked her about the existing clients, and she assured him that they were being looked after, but that new client inquiries were being put on hold. She was also hiring three new staff. Steve asked to see the welding/fab shop plan ASAP. Cheryl told him it was being typed up right now.

By Thursday, Betty and Sharon were back at work, and Betty had a new place to live. On Friday, Steve had Price prepare a purchase agreement for the dentist, and the plan for the welding/fab shops had the approval of Larry, Jamie, and Sharon. He asked Lia to arrange a meeting with the dentist for the following week.

After lunch, an angry, drunken Rusty appeared and tried to drag Betty out of the office. Steve, hearing the commotion, came out of his back office and, cutting in front of Rusty, told him to let her go. Sharon, also hearing the fracas, came running and yelled, "Steve, don't hurt him!"

But it was too late. The sudden aura of violence coming from Steve was almost visible, and he chopped at Rusty's head with a closed fist hammer blow. Rusty, shaken, dropped his hold on Betty, and Sharon pulled her to safety. Steve then kicked Rusty in the chest, and down he went. Steve turned to make sure Betty was okay, and as he did so, Rusty came staggering back up with a knife. Steve barely dodged Rusty's first slash, and that move gave him time to grab Betty's chair. Steve swung the chair and caught Rusty on the left hip and, stumbling ass over teakettle, down the long front stairs he went.

As Rusty hit the main entrance floor, Truckin' Ted was coming through the front door. Steve ran down the stairs and grunting loudly, proceeded to kick and stomp Rusty in every major muscle mass on his body, slowly reducing him to a whimpering, crying pile of broken flesh. Except his face; he left his face alone. As a final move he stomped on Rusty's closed right hand, breaking and splintering the bones. As he did so, he yelled, "Pull a knife on me, you fucker! This'll teach you!"

Ted, in his usual unflappable drawl, moved toward him and said, "Uh Steve, if you keep that up, you might kill him."

Sharon, having run down the stairs, shouted at Ted, "Don't touch him! Stay away!"

Sharon slowly and cautiously approached Steve. She grabbed his shirt and slowly pulled him away from what used to be Rusty. She told Cheryl to call 911 as she then dragged Steve back up the stairs and into his office. Steve, breathing heavily, sat down and muttered, "Another fucking asshole taught to stay away from my people."

"Shit Steve, you could've killed him!"

Steve, with an air of disassociation about him, shrugged, and looking at nothing said, "Shit happens."

Sharon went back to the front to see how Betty was. She found her sitting in a chair shaking and crying with Cheryl comforting her. Sharon told Ted to clean up the blood and broken furniture and then get lost. Rusty was still lying in a heap, unable to move, crying and cradling his smashed hand. Cheryl was telling Betty that it was about time one of these assholes got straightened up and that it was great to watch Steve tearing Rusty apart. Cheryl, eyes shining, was clearly excited with what she had just seen. Sharon called Cynthia Sharpe, explained exactly what had

The Price of Success

happened and asked her what to do. Cynthia told them to call 911 and tell the cops, if they bothered coming around, that Rusty had attacked Betty, Steve had come to her defence and Rusty had fallen down the stairs. Leave it at that.

And that is exactly what they did.

Sharon sent Betty home with Cheryl and asked Ted to come back to see her. She said, "Ted, I want you to drive my car and follow me. I'm taking Steve home in his car, and I'll bring you back."

Steve remained quiet in the car, and he remained quiet and unresponsive as Sharon took him inside to Ann. She said to Ann, "He needs help", as she explained what had happened. Ann led Steve into his bedroom and asked Sharon to help get him into bed. While Sharon undressed him, Ann went to get a sedative. Neither woman was embarrassed to see Steve undressed, and Ann commented on how healthy he looked. She gave him the sedative, and after a few moments of watching him, they left him to sleep.

Ann asked Sharon how she'd known to bring him out here. Sharon replied that Steve had told her about Ann, that she was a shrink and that he was now living there. She figured that Ann would help; she didn't know what else to do. And she knew that he needed help.

Sharon finally relaxing, sitting in Ann's kitchen with a glass of wine in her hand, said, "Okay, what happened to him? Will he be okay? It looks like he went crazy, then just shut down."

Ann, who in a former life before her husband died had been a practising psychiatrist, answered that that was pretty much what had happened. She explained that Steve was a towering genius who was forever struggling to function in what he saw as a kindergarten world and, sometimes under severe stress, would lose control. Ann, who knew Sharon, but not that well, also commented that she was a very lucky woman. She continued that when Steve lost it she thought he could become horrifically destructive and attack and smash anyone and anything around him. By grabbing his shirt, she had taken a huge risk. Sharon said that she hadn't thought, she just wanted to stop him from killing Rusty. Ann agreed with her; she too thought he could easily kill someone.

Ann went on to explain that she thought Steve was forever trying unconsciously to solve all the problems he encountered in life. Whether they be business, or his life, or his kids' lives, it didn't matter. He was so intelligent and wired to solve problems that it didn't seem to matter who or what the issues were. And that was another struggle he faced daily. He was always trying to sort out the necessary solutions to immediate problems and discard the extraneous problems and issues. It was a very difficult struggle for him as he considered all the problems he encountered, required solving.

Both women sat quietly. Sharon broke the silence by asking what she was going to do with him. Ann told her that he'd now sleep for 12 hours and then should awaken hungry and hopefully ready to resume life. All he really needed was a break from the stress. She explained that a number of years ago she'd measured Steve's mental acuity and the test results were fantastic. He not only was the smartest person she'd ever seen, but his other abilities were also off the chart. But he was paying a price in that he was not a stable person. She wasn't sure just how unstable he really was, but today's violence was not a surprise. It was no surprise to her that his marriage had broken up and that he'd withdrawn into his shell. She said that even though he appeared unaffected by the breakup, it was the original trigger to today's violence. He'd only partly worked off his anger through the punishing divorce. But the additional stress of buying all 43 businesses and the building had just ramped up his tension again. In fact, she continued, what probably saved everyone was his work on the Jeep. She continued that she wished he'd talked to her, because she may have been able to prevent today's violence. Ann said, with a head shake, that in many ways the fight with Rusty was fortuitous. Otherwise someone else or something else could have triggered a terrible accident. For example, if Rusty or anyone else attacked you, Sharon, probably nothing would or could stop Steve from killing them.

Sharon said, horrified, "What are you saying?"

"I think he loves you, Sharon, and has for a long time, but he won't or can't admit it to himself. And because he does, he feels very, very protective toward you. When you left Dan, it was all I could do to stop him from going out there and destroying him. I don't know why he can't admit it; so far, he just can't. I don't know anything about his childhood, but the answer is probably back there somewhere. And a word of advice: Don't ask him about himself; let him bring up the subject. There may be something very horrible back there that he's trying to forget."

She paused, "I guess you know that I too have feelings for him, but he ignores me."

Ann continued, "I suppose you also didn't know that whenever he feels overly stressed, every couple of months or years or so, he comes here and we talk it through. Even Claire doesn't know." After a pause and with a wistful look, she said, "He really, really is a remarkable person. I wish he'd let me study and write about him."

Sharon hesitating, remarked, "You know, from time to time I feel a force about him - I know it sounds crazy - but I swear I actually see his eyes blaze. Is that his anger or his feelings?" In a moment she continued in a small voice, "Is it safe to live with him or work for him or even be around him?"

Twisting her hands together, Ann said, "I don't know how to answer that. This is the first time in 15 years or more that this level of violence has happened, and breaking up with his wife was a monstrous event. I'm going to say that as long as his life is reasonably orderly, those around him are safe. And as long as he gets to do enough of those things that calm him down."

The Price of Success

Sharon, looking at her watch and standing up, asked, "Can I talk to you some more? I have feelings for that man, and I don't want to fuck us up."

Ann replied, "Come on out next week and we'll have a coffee."

After a hug from Ann, Sharon left and found Truckin' Ted beginning to fume. As she started the car, she said, "Ted, you never saw this, you never did this, and you will never ever say a word to anyone about where he is. Or I swear I will kill you."

Truckin' Ted simply nodded.

Chapter Six - Family

By the middle of the following week Steve, after finishing the jeep, was back at work. Betty came in, gave him a full hug and thanked him for saving her life. Betty held him very tightly and told him that she owed him. And would do anything for him. Steve kissed her very lightly on the lips and felt her shiver. Steve apologized for perhaps going too far with Rusty, but Betty told him to hush; Cheryl had opened her eyes and that whatever Rusty got, Rusty deserved. He was going to be in the hospital for weeks, and then rehab, and that was just fucking fine.

On Friday, Gabriel and Sharon presented the building plans. After several hours of discussion, the only changes he wanted were to make Sharon's corner office larger and move Betty's office into another corner. His apartment space was blocked out and would be addressed last. Gabriel left to organize cost estimates and get approval from Sask Power for rebates. But he did say that Steve was looking at more than a million dollars in renos. However, with rebates from Sask Power and the City, the bill should not exceed half a million. After seeing him out, Steve asked Cheryl to come in and join them.

He asked Cheryl where she was with the dentist. The dentist wanted to stay with Quinn, so that made everything easier. Cheryl had called Lia and they'd agreed on a price for the dentist. All he had to do was write the cheque to Barchetti. Steve laughed and told Cheryl he knew she was the right one for the job. Next, he wanted to know about the construction group. She replied that it was next but was going to take time, it was so large. Steve told her that he needed the group organized as soon as possible to give them a crack at the building rehabilitation contract. Might as well keep it in house.

He then went to see Lia and Price & Company. He explained what he wanted to do to the building and that he needed their cooperation to get it done. He also explained just what they would be left with, and if they wanted to update their own decorating, he would have the architect work with them. He'd pay for the architect's time, but they'd have to pay for the materials and labour. Both enthusiastically agreed. Cold winters and hot summers were no longer acceptable. Both understood the rent would probably increase but were willing to discuss that too. After all, the current rent was only slightly more than half the cost of new space. He finished the meeting with the reminder that Sharon was their contact for the project. He then asked Lia to arrange a meeting with the other tenants.

Steve returned to Ann's B&B, changed into his working clothes and went to spend the rest of the day testing his Jeep in the mud out behind Ann's farm. The jeep was an ass puckering performer, lots of fun to be in while easily able to churn through the mud and wade through the water. Steve soon was covered in mud and the jeep looked like it had been rolled, it was so dirty. It was very noisy though; the performance mufflers rattled and howled, especially when he had his foot well into it. When the turbo spooled up, the noise was absolutely horrific. Steve loved the racket, it added to the thrill, especially when he lifted his foot from the gas, then the engine would bang and pop and occasionally shoot blue flames from the mufflers. It wouldn't do for the street though; the cops had already warned him about the noise. But that short run on the street, drag racing a local street rod, had been thrilling! Laying 100 feet of smoking rubber while in four-wheel drive, with the turbo howling and the mufflers playing arpeggios, was gut wrenching! Steve had just about peed his pants. He'd even managed to burn some of his tension away. Nothing could beat the fun of driving a lightweight noisy open 4x4 truck with a super abundance of turbo power to play with!

Sunday afternoon he and Ann went for a long single-track mountain bike ride through the hills around Ann's farm. Twice Steve came off, once in deep mud, the other after missing a jumping turn. Ann finally called a halt and, checking Steve over, said the ride was done, he'd punished himself enough. They rode home slowly, with Steve covered in mud and looking much the worse for wear. After a shower and having PlastiSkin (a plastic spray product when sprayed on injuries forms a clear film. It prevents infections and deters scars. But it hurts like hell to apply) applied to his cuts and scrapes, they sat down to supper with Janet, one of Ann's daughters. Janet and Ann did the talking; Steve did the cooking, the listening and the supper dishes.

After Steve had gone to an early bed, Janet asked Ann if he was okay. Ann replied that she hoped so; he was just recovering from a bad time. Janet then asked if Ann was sleeping with him. Ann was shocked and embarrassed. Janet went on to say that it was obvious that she liked him and that Janos, her father, had been gone a long time now. If Ann wanted a boyfriend it was okay with Janet and her sisters. Ann sat there with her mouth just hanging open. Janet laughed and said that the three girls had had a long conversation about her and decided that she needed a boyfriend. In fact, that was why Janet had come out for the weekend. To have "the talk" with her mother. Ann, to cover her amusement, embarrassment, and confusion, went to get another bottle of wine. Then later went to Steve's room for the night.

The Price of Success

When Steve went in to work on Monday he'd regained some of his good humour, thanks to the bike and jeep, and decided that he had three priorities: Getting the new building completed including his office and living space, making the new organizational structure work, and finishing the purchase of the Barchetti businesses and integrating them into Quinn Enterprises. And keep an eye on Claire and the boys. And finish tuning the jeep!

Steve decided that Sharon really could handle the building. He'd noticed that Lia was taking an interest in the project and that perhaps he could mention to Sharon to use her, if she felt comfortable doing so. Otherwise Steve had confidence that Gabriel knew what he wanted, and that Sharon and Betty could easily keep an eye on him. So, other than having a weekly progress meeting and being available for problem solving, that would work. He had another meeting tomorrow to get the other tenants on board. Lia thought the others, except for one, would be enthusiastic.

The new organisation was going to be much tougher, and Steve knew why too. He was going to have to step back and let people fumble the ball as they learned their new jobs. Sharon would be okay. Cheryl he would have to work with, but he would do that anyway. Betty he wasn't worried about either because she would have Larry and him to lean on. She was a hell of a lot smarter than she even realized. And Larry would be a rock. He was a brilliant accountant and manager and only needed a strong structure to work within to perform at his peak. It was the new junior managers coming up behind them that would require watching and mentoring.

The big problem was the Barchetti companies. Perhaps it hadn't been such a smart idea to have Cheryl start on the construction group when the other groups prolly needed more attention sooner. But why waste the building construction money? Gabriel had indicated that he'd used most of the construction people on other jobs and had been satisfied they knew what he wanted. Steve concluded that he'd have to devote the largest part of his time to the Barchetti problem. But that was okay, that was what he enjoyed most anyway, and it was his company, right? Okay, time to get this dog's breakfast organized!

First, he called in Sharon and Betty and asked them what they thought about having a general meeting with all the staff. Or, better yet, renting space and throwing an open buffet party for all the staff and partners. And then explaining what was going on with the company. Betty looked at him and laughed and said that she was about to suggest having a general meeting but he beat her to it. Steve told her that she was already thinking like a VP! Betty thought she could get the party arranged on short notice at the hall they usually used at Xmas, as this was the off season. She asked how much she could spend and Steve suggested she talk to Larry and double whatever that skinflint suggested. Giggling, she asked him if he knew just how many people would be there. He didn't, so she told him that the employment number, including the contract experts in the consulting division, stood at 124. Double it and he was looking at about 250 for dinner. Both he and Sharon were surprised. Neither one realized they'd moved past 100 employees and contractors.

Later that day Samara came in and asked if he had time to talk. His tough as nails daughter looked troubled, so Steve was quick to close the door and move away from his desk as he asked what was up.

Samara said, "Have you talked to Mum lately?"

"No, why?"

"She's drinking heavily and I had to look after the boys this weekend because she couldn't get out of bed. I think you better do something."

Steve, making a face of disgust, said, "What would you suggest? She's turned the boys against me and I doubt they'd welcome my interference. How about you call her sister Margaret? Tell her that I'm thinking of applying for full custody. She'd come down from Calgary so goddamn fast she wouldn't need a plane."

"Well, that'll work, but Sergio (Steve's oldest son) asked if they could come and talk to you. I think he's starting to see that Mum has just been spinning him a line. Besides, for some reason he really doesn't like her drinking. He's asked her to stop and even has started hiding the bottles. Unfortunately, it hasn't done much good."

"What about Curly (Shaun, Steve's second son) and Skip (the youngest son)? What do they think?"

"Skip is all confused and not very happy and Curly doesn't seem to be bothered. You know how he is."

"Yeah well, don't be fooled by Shaun, he's one helluva lot smarter and aware than he appears."

Steve hesitated, and then asked slowly, "How are you doing?"

Samara looked at the floor and, fighting tears, told Steve she wasn't doing that well. She continued by telling Steve about the fight that Ted and Claire had had and that he'd not been back. She'd also overheard Claire, drunk, yelling at Grace, Ted's wife, that she didn't want him anymore. Samara looked up at Steve and said that she didn't think it'd be this bad. She'd figured out that it was coming but also assumed that Ted would move in and the altered family would continue. But now she didn't know what was happening. Or what to do. She sounded very lost. Steve moved over and gave her a hug.

Steve said, "I knew a long time ago that we'd divorce, but I also didn't plan on your mother being as stupid as she's been. I think she's slipped a cog or something. But anyway, call Margaret. My problem is that I've nowhere to keep us, and I won't until the new building is finished."

"Where are you living now? With Sharon?"

"You're not supposed to know that! And for the record, no, I am not. I'm staying at a B&B. Here's the phone number."

"Well, it's common knowledge that you and Sharon are really good friends. For that matter, Betty and Cheryl and half the women here would keep you!"

At that she saw at once that she'd gone too far. But being his daughter, she wasn't going to back down. Or apologize. Visibly controlling his anger, he said, "Call Margaret and keep me posted."

Samara got up and left. Steve called Cheryl and asked her if she needed his help on the construction group. Cheryl told him to get his ass over there.

The next day, Cynthia Sharpe asked him to come over. She wanted to discuss the divorce and she had an idea for him. Sitting in her office, he listened to her outline the changes that the courts were going to require in the agreement. It was mostly housekeeping, but they were going to have to change the support for the kids, making Steve's obligation to their higher education part of the agreement.

As Grace had agreed, she wouldn't start divorce proceedings until the courts had approved Steve's divorce. This way, the door would not be opened for Ted or Claire to renege on Claire's agreement, at which the courts had already cast a jaundiced eye. Ted had few friends at court though, as it was suspected that he'd been dallying with another lawyer's wife. Cynthia, laughing, said that the tightly knit Regina law community had already figured it out and were laughing at what Steve had done. Ted was finished. He just didn't know it yet.

However, that wasn't what she wanted to talk about. She fiddled with the papers on her desk and appeared to be suddenly nervous. Not looking at Steve, she asked him just how badly he'd be upset if she meddled in his private life. She went on, before Steve could say anything, that she'd already talked to Sharon and that Sharon had thought what she wanted to say would be okay.

At that, Steve objected. "Damn it!" He paused and sat back saying, "I guess that's what I get for having a bunch of women around me. They run my goddamn life!" He calmed down, shrugged and said, "Okay, what've you guys come up with now?"

Cynthia said, "Grace was in here the other day complaining about being in that big house alone. She missed having people around. I understand that Claire is turning into a problem and that the kids aren't doing well. I know you don't have a place for them yet, so why don't you move them and yourself into Grace's house? The house is close to your old place so they wouldn't have to change schools or friends," she finished with a rush.

Steve sat back and thought about it. "What about custody of the kids? That hasn't been settled."

"We can get around that by having Samara, at the appropriate time, request an emergency visit by Children's Aid and then you'll apply for emergency custody. If Samara times it right, what the worker sees will seal the deal. I know just the worker to request." At the look on Steve's face she asked, "You didn't know we have our own unofficial aid network?"

"What about Grace's divorce? Or even her neighbours for that matter? The idea of a guy and his four kids moving in with her is a bit much, don't you think? And to think about it, I'm not ready to play house with Grace or anybody else for that matter."

"Look, do you have a problem with Grace looking after the kids? No? Okay why don't you talk to Samara and see what she thinks about this idea. And leave the details and Grace to me. If the kids go for it, I'll arrange everything."

Steve, after sitting and thinking about it some more, borrowed a phone to call Betty and have her ask Samara to call him as soon as she came into work.

A couple of days later, he arranged to take all the kids out for supper. While they were happy to see him, it was clear that the boys had some reservations about Steve. They weren't happy that he'd moved out and wanted to know why he hadn't tried to work things out with Claire. The idea that Claire had deliberately broken up their marriage wasn't one they liked. But they had to agree that her having Ted around raised lots of questions, and meeting him in Calgary hadn't been very smart. Now her drinking and pills were making life at home very tough. They were beginning to understand why he'd left. They also understood that they couldn't live with him just yet, because he didn't have a permanent home.

Steve let them talk; they needed to get it out. Shaun in particular seemed to have a clear grasp of Claire's problems and disagreed with her actions. He thought that she didn't want them around, she really just wanted to party instead. Sergio and Samara reluctantly agreed. They were all adamant however that it was now time to live elsewhere, anywhere away from Claire. Steve was shocked at just how upset the kids were. He had no idea that Claire had been so blatant about her fooling around and so obvious that she didn't want the kids. Keeping custody of the kids had been a point she'd defended tenaciously after he'd left. It was now clear that she'd done so simply to piss him off.

He raised the idea of living somewhere else in the neighbourhood, maybe with someone else. To his surprise they jumped at the thought; they didn't want to leave their friends or school. They begged him to get a house in the area so they could all move in together. He promised to look into it immediately. Before Samara drove them home, he took a few moments to ask her privately about Cynthia's plan. While startled, she saw the benefits and agreed to make the call whenever Claire next was drunk. In the morning he called Cynthia and told her it was a go. He'd bring Samara down to meet her so the two of them could proceed.

By the end of the week, the welding/fab shops had been folded into Quinn's existing welding shop, complete with an analyst on site full time to oversee the development and installation of the new business control systems. The manager of their existing shop turned out to be even a better manager than Cheryl had thought and took to the amalgamation plan with enthusiasm. Within days he'd produced a plan to expand his building for the additional men and equipment. The Saskatoon shop owner managed to raise enough money to both pay off his now non-existing loan and buy the shop back. One of the old shop owners turned out to be a better

The Price of Success

salesman than a welder and proceeded to call on every engineering operation in Regina. The first grouping was well on its way to success and profitability.

The following weekend, Steve hosted the company general meeting and supper party. Betty had done her usual superb organisational job and all 240-odd attendees ate and drank their fill. After supper Steve stood up and introduced himself and all the senior staff. He then thanked everyone for coming and pointed out that there was still some food left! He then went on to thank them for all the hard work they'd done to make all the companies successful. He continued on to outline the company's growth plans and the changes in the management organization. Finally, he wanted them to know that the company's culture and way of doing business was absolutely not going to change. Everyone's number one task was to do whatever it took to make Quinn Enterprises successful. In the future, as in the past, they would be well rewarded for their efforts. He sat down to a prolonged thunderous applause.

CJ Vermeulen

Chapter Seven - Another Deal

Three months later Steve needed another holiday. Many of his plans were well underway, but the stress was getting to him again. Thanks to Ann, he was still functioning at a high level, and now she had another weapon to help him. She'd discovered Zopiclone, a new sleep assistance drug. Zopiclone was different; it didn't dope you to sleep. Rather, it slowed overactive brain activity, which was exactly Steve's problem. He was so intelligent and able to think in parallel on so many levels, his brain simply would not slow down enough to allow him enough sleep. Turn down his brain activity and presto, sleep was immediate. But the drug was somewhat addictive with daily use. However, Steve seemed to be able to handle a small dose every four to six weeks, which then allowed him to crash for 10-12 hours and then to run slowly for the next 24 hours as the drug wore off. The drug also had an unexpected side effect that, at least in Steve, was very welcome. The drug had absolutely no hangover effect, as did most other sleep aid drugs. But he still needed a break, and Sharon and Ann were determined to get him one.

The building renovations were well underway. The courier and light truck operations had moved into the second floor, and the top floor offices were only a week away from completion. Steve's living quarters had been designed and would be completed last. The third and fourth floor renovations were well started, and the plans for the stores and restaurant on the main floor were finished. In all, the building was an orderly mess, but now, with all the exterior windows and doors replaced, and the brick siding cleaned, it did look very presentable. Even the newly placed shorty radio antennas on the roof didn't detract from the building's classic appearance.

The new management plan had slowly come together with only one surprise. Lia, who'd been spending more and more time working with Steve, Cheryl, and the consulting group, had come to realize that she enjoyed the variety and complexity of this work rather than being a lawyer. Her brothers, after much complaining, suggested she move to just half time and they hire another lawyer. Lia decided to invite Steve home to supper, feed him some of his favorite Italian food and wine, and see if she could persuade him to hire her. While Lia had vague plans to have Steve spend the night (she'd changed the bed sheets), after supper he reluctantly left to pick up Samara at the airport. She'd been at a volleyball evaluation camp in Winnipeg, trying out for the national junior team. Steve did promise to come back for more wine later in the week. He also would talk to Sharon and Cheryl about bringing her on board. But privately he wasn't sure about staying the night. Lia was a very tiny woman and he had some concerns about them being able to play together.

The absorption of the rest of the Barchetti businesses was proving to be much more difficult and complicated than Steve or Cheryl had anticipated. The main problem was the original owner/managers' attitude toward business. Most were mom and pop shops and didn't see the need for financial control systems. The common attitude was that if there was money left over at the end of the month, everything was just fine. Nor did they want to grow or be part of a larger business. Many were threatening retirement with some already moving that way. Fortunately, with Lia working closely with the old owners, and Frank brought in from time to time to convince the hard cases, progress was being made. Unfortunately, as a result, Steve was having to find many more new business managers than he'd anticipated.

It was worth it. Not all the businesses had been purchased yet, the auto and truck dealers were still being discussed, and the auto parts stores deal had not yet been finalized. But the groups that were done had proven to be very profitable. Between the efficiencies and growing profits from combining operations to the sale of some of the revitalized operations, Quinn Enterprises had a large amount of cash in the bank. He couldn't wait to see what could be done with the auto dealers, auto parts stores, and the completely reorganized construction company.

To Lia, the whole process was an eye opener. She was used to working in a world where rules and procedures were well established and the job of lawyering had become basically a slow paper shuffle. Here the sky was the limit, with new ways of doing business discussed and implemented every day at a dazzling speed. Lia stood in awe of Cheryl and Steve as they tackled the organization problems and directed the analysts, accountants and computer programmers toward finding solutions. She watched and listened as Steve and Cheryl almost seemed to have one mind, one telling the other what to do as the other agreed and both instantly understanding the direction they had to follow. Everybody loved the fast pace and challenging work. Lia could already see that alone she never would have been able to do even a small part of what Steve and Cheryl were doing. And that Frank should have done this long ago. She suspected that Steve was going to make a ton of money from their work.

Steve's kids, with some connivance from Children's Aid, had been moved to Grace's house. Billy, her six-year-old son, had welcomed the three boys, and Samara and Grace had decided to get along. Steve had offered to pay for a

The Price of Success

housekeeper to do the cleaning and laundry and a yard service for the yard, and he contributed to the household costs, but otherwise Grace was a happy camper. Steve usually managed to have supper with them at least three nights a week and usually took them all out for supper on the weekend. He and Grace fell into an easy relationship, with him spending the odd night with her, but he still lived at Ann's B&B. Claire had been in and out of a detox center and had been living in Calgary with her sister for the past month. But Steve knew from a back channel to her sister Margaret's husband that this arrangement was wearing thin and he expected her back in Regina any day. Meanwhile, Claire's house was beginning to look rather shabby and neglected.

Several weeks later, on a Friday afternoon, Steve took a call from a Louis Finkelman. Finkelman was a lawyer and the managing partner of Barber LLP, one of Saskatoon's leading law firms. Finkelman wanted a meeting in Regina at Peter Thayer's office. Whether Finkelman knew that the managing partner of Thayer was a personal friend of Steve's, no one knew. Finkelman wouldn't discuss the reason for the meeting over the phone. Steve, who was going "age-class" bike racing again with Sergio this weekend, decided that he'd just wait and see what Finkelman wanted. He asked Sharon to be ready for the meeting on Monday and left early to get his bike and motorhome ready to pick up Sergio and leave early Saturday morning.

The Saturday races went well with Sergio coming in second in the open class in the downhill category, and Steve qualifying for the cross-country final in his age category. However, on the last lap of the final race, just prior to crossing a small log bridge, another racer slammed into Steve, sending him flying. Steve, this weekend performing well above his usual level, was lying second overall and was just about to catch the leader when the accident happened. He was travelling at a very high speed and was violently hurtled into the ravine below the bridge, ruining his $9,000 bike. The racing had to be stopped while they frantically dug him out of the muddy ditch and the ambulance took him to the local hospital. Steve's looks weren't going to be improved by the 14 stitches required to close a nasty cut from his forehead down to the corner of his chin. The real damage, though, was a jagged tear in his back from a broken tree branch. The local doctor was able to close the cuts with lots of tape and staples, but advised Steve to see a Regina surgeon as soon as possible to make sure his back muscles also didn't need repair. The local ambulance was busy elsewhere so, like the dumb man he could be, full of pain killers and with Sergio's help, Steve packed up and drove the motorhome back to Regina. At Ann's B&B, where the rig was usually parked, Steve gave Sergio the keys to the big Mercedes and told him to drive himself home. Sergio, shocked that he was being allowed to drive the Merc, quickly took off. Ann took one look at Steve's injuries, berated him long and loud for being the stupidest man she had ever seen, and rushed him to

Regina General Hospital. He was in surgery for three hours having his back properly repaired. A cosmetic surgeon was also called in to redo his face.

Late Monday morning after begging for a set of blue scrubs and with Anne's reluctant assistance, he left the hospital in a wheelchair. He promised to go home after the Finkelman meeting and to see his own doctor in several days to check for infection. They were late arriving at Thayer's office, mostly because when Sharon found out what had happened, she also harassed him about not staying in the hospital. Sharon also wasn't very happy with Ann for letting him out but refrained from saying very much about it. After all, she realized that if Steve wanted to leave, he would just leave, regardless. While Peter Thayer was taken aback at Steve's appearance, he knew him well enough to be able to temporarily overlook his scrubs, bandages and the wheelchair. They met in Peter Thayer's office, with Peter carrying out the introductions; then he left them to proceed with the meeting. Finkelman had two other men with him, and they were introduced as his sons. The three Finkelmans were upset at Steve's appearance and asked him if he was competent to have a business discussion. Sharon told them that was why she was there. The oldest son, Mark, the tallest Finkelman at about 5'10', was not impressed with Sharon being in the meeting or being able to look down on him. The younger son, Abe, stayed in the background and seemed to be favouring his left leg. It wasn't until much later that Sharon noted that the Finkelmans, while concerned and wishing him well, hadn't asked what had actually happened.

Louis opened by complimenting Steve on the Barchetti deal and the work his company was doing in the consulting field. He too mentioned the Marcella project. He then asked Steve if they'd ever worked in Saskatoon or if they'd ever planned on expanding into northern Saskatchewan. Sharon replied that it had come up, but their hands were full in Regina. Louis went on to say that they had a client, a large freight company that was in financial trouble through unluckily expanding into the oil field service business just as the price of oil had collapsed. Louis was trying to find a solution for them that would entail their being either purchased or managed back to good health. Louis went on that there were two companies involved and that one owned the other. Either was for sale as the owners also wanted to retire, or the smaller of the two was open for a management contract. Steve asked a number of questions, particularly concerning the volume of sales and state of the buildings and equipment. Sharon took over as Steve was beginning to wilt and asked for all the financial and tax documents for the two companies. She also told Louis that if he'd arrange it and the financials warranted it, she'd have their Vice President, Consulting and a freight expert come up in a few days and have a look. There would be no cost to Finkelman or the freight companies. Based on that preliminary look, Quinn Enterprises would decide what could be done.

Mark, ignoring Sharon, asked Steve what he thought. Steve, looking at him with a slight, tired smile on his face said, "In this company, Mark, we work from the

The Price of Success

bottom up. First you have to convince someone like a supervisor, division manager or one of my vice presidents of the value of your project to Quinn. If you can interest them, then if they can interest me, we'll look at it. Otherwise you're wasting our time."

Sharon, taking her time and looking at a red-faced Mark, said, "I'm interested enough to send a crew up to have a look, but the idea of expanding northward is something I'll have to think about. Send the papers down, Louis, please. Now if you will excuse us, Steve is bleeding on the floor."

All three Finkelmans started at Sharon's words. As she wheeled Steve out, she apologized to Peter for messing up his floor and told him to send her the cleaning bill. Peter just stood there with his mouth open. In the car, where Ann was waiting, they discovered some staples in Steve's back had let go. She debated with herself and then, with Sharon's concurrence, decided to take him to the B&B. Ann had a better chance of grounding him than any hospital! Once at Ann's B&B, Ann butterfly taped the wound closed, gave him a shot of Zopiclone, and they put him to bed. Ann threatened to beat him if he so much as lifted a finger until she said he was ready to do so. And Sharon offered to help her. Before Sharon left, she asked Ann if there was any way they could slow Steve down some more. Ann shrugged and said that the only other thing Steve liked to do was long distance bike touring. Possibly they could talk him into taking a long ride. Sharon said she would work on it, then went back into the city to check on Sergio and Steve's big car.

Three days later, Steve was getting restless. His injuries were beginning to heal and he was asking about business and the Finkelman deal. Sergio came to see him, bringing the other kids out with him. While the others had seen him hurt, this was the first time for young Skip, and he was very upset. Ann distracted him by taking him out to see all the farm animals and to feed a pair of baby goats in the barn. The kids had come out in two cars, with Sergio driving Steve's big Mercedes sedan. Several hours later, Samara took the two younger boys back home while Sergio stayed to continue talking to his dad.

Sergio appeared somewhat nervous. He asked Steve if he remembered how the crash had happened. Steve replied that he didn't remember anything; he hadn't even seen any sign that the other rider was so close. Sergio, fidgeting, told him that he had seen the crash and he thought it had been deliberate. As Steve looked up at him with suddenly wide-open eyes, Sergio continued.

"The guy that hit you was an Abe Finkelman," Sergio said. "His older brother Mark was the outright race leader and needed that win to hang on to his national ranking. Besides, I think you'd have caught him, he was fading fast and he didn't need to have an old guy to beat him. Several other people who also saw the crash have complained to the race authorities, so I don't know what's going to happen. Unfortunately, the race steward didn't see it, but the buzz is that you might be declared the winner and Abe Finkelman will get his licence yanked. No one is sure about Mark, but he might get disciplined too. By the way, did you know that your helmet was actually broken in half? No one knows why you weren't killed."

Steve shrugged and made a brushing-it-away gesture, "You're sure it was the Finkelmans?"

"Yes."

"Motherfuckers! Well, now I know who owes me nine grand!"

After a pause while he calmed himself down he asked Sergio about his bike. Sergio said the carbon fiber frame was broken but that the running gear was okay, apart from the front wheel. Steve asked him if he'd order another frame and wheel, and Sergio said that he already had done so. Sergio offered to rebuild the bike when the new frame arrived. Steve reached out and shook his hand, a rare gesture between them. Steve asked him how he liked the Merc, and Sergio replied that he liked it, but it was too big and expensive for him to feel comfortable. Steve asked him if he would rather drive the smaller Merc toad (RV speak for a towed vehicle) and when he nodded, called Ann and asked her to give Sergio the toad's keys. With a grin, he asked him to try and not wreck it.

Friday came and Betty, Lia, Cheryl, Truckin' Ted, Larry and Sharon came out to the B&B for the weekly management meeting. When the subject got around to the Finkelmans, Cheryl began to explain the results of their research. It appeared that Finkelman had taken all the shares of a company called Oilfield Service Company as collateral for a loan. In turn it appeared that they had granted a loan to Oilfield Service for $1.2 million. That money was mostly used to purchase two very special truck-and-trailers. The trucks could be used only to move drilling equipment without having to break down the equipment as much as otherwise required. This saved a ton of money and time and, for the first several months the trucks were available, they ran them 24/7. When the price of oil went south a couple of months ago, drilling stopped and the trucks hadn't turned a wheel since. Of course, all the other servicing work also evaporated, and ever since the company has been burning through cash at a hell of a rate. They'll be out of cash in another month or two.

"So," she said, "I don't think there's any way to save it." She shrugged. "With no market and the equipment so specialized, unless the price of oil recovers, they're done."

Steve said, "Which bank has the loan?"

Lia answered, "Well that's a bit of a mystery. We don't know and we didn't talk to the accounting guys." Seeing the look on Steve's face, she hurried on, "Don't get me wrong, we just didn't have the time to really get to the bottom of it. We have other questions too. But when we realized Oil Service's problem, we decided there was no point to look further, so we went to look at the main company, Douglas Terminals."

Ted took over. It's a pretty well run operation. The trucks are fairly new, the shop is clean and I know the head mechanic, and he's okay. They have a good cross

The Price of Success

dock, a nice big heated warehouse, and a large fenced compound. The offices are in good shape and the people I talked to seemed to be happy and think highly of the Douglases. Their business has dropped off because of oil prices, but they service a huge area of northern Saskatchewan and have a diversified business supplying the mines and backhauling ore concentrate and grain from the northern grain Terminals. Oilfield and Douglas don't seem to work together; operationally they almost appear to be separate companies. I'll need more time to see what can be combined and what sold. Cheryl then took over. The offices are also clean, organized and appear to be well run. Finkelman also owns about 55% of Douglas stock, but other than that the company is debt free. The payables and receivables look okay, but they're very short of cash. The computer equipment and software need upgrading, and the phone system is old. They do run a good truck location system though.

After a few questions, Steve asked for the bottom line. Lia, Ted and Cheryl said they wanted to finish analyzing the paperwork, but it didn't look good. Sharon took over by saying that if Quinn could get Douglas alone at a decent price, then all we have to do is decide if we wanted to start a hands-on northern operation. Oilfield Services is not worth looking at, and if we have to take both, then the current price of oil and the debt load of Oilfield Services would make rescuing them impossible.

"If we're looking at this then, Steve, we better have a very heavy-duty session about northern operations. I'm not convinced that we need to go that route just yet. We're also going to have to do something about Brian Patterson at Patterson Freightways in Saskatoon. Cutting off his work delivering our stuff up north is not going to go over very well. We discussed this on the way in and didn't come to a conclusion."

Sharon paused, took a deep breath and said, "I think, Boss, this one is going to have to be your call."

They all nodded.

With the entire management team present, Sharon changed the subject to a holiday for Steve. In spite of Steve's protest, she polled the group to get their need of Steve for an extended period. While they all indicated they could use his help, other than the Finkelman deal, everything was under control. Sharon told them and Steve to be ready for his coming holiday; she was determined to get him some free time.

Steve spent a quiet weekend with Ann and her daughters until Grace and the kids came out with supper for everybody on Sunday afternoon. The kids were happy to see him and were even happier that he was getting around by himself. Samara complained about Sergio being given the Mercedes toad, but Steve reminded her that he'd bought her a car on her sixteenth birthday and that four months later she'd wrecked it. And that he had replaced it. Besides, he hadn't given Sergio the toad; he'd just lent it to him. Samara continued grumping until Steve reminded her that she also didn't pay for gas or maintenance on her car. Grace took Samara aside and suggested that she quit while she was ahead, and that was the end of that.

In a quiet moment, Sergio got Steve aside and told him that it looked like the Finkelmans were going to be disciplined and that he would be declared the race winner. The racing stewards had wanted to talk to Steve but Sergio had told them he remembered nothing of the crash. The association was also looking at some previous races where Abe had been involved in accidents and re-interviewing those involved and outside spectators. The racing association had promised to make their ruling public by Wednesday of next week. But the word was, even with the Finkelmans threatening to sue, Steve was to be declared the winner, the Finkelmans were to be disqualified, and for good measure they were going to be tossed out of the cycling club. This would be a terrible blow to them because Mark, who was leading in the national cross-country point's race, without a club membership would be stripped of his national standing.

Next Wednesday at 3:00 p.m. that is exactly what happened.

The Price of Success

Chapter Eight - Another Way Forward

After the Sunday family supper, a very tired sounding Lia called Steve and asked if she, Sharon, Cheryl, Larry, Truckin' Ted and Peter Thayer could come for an early Monday morning visit. They'd found something and had an idea to present to him. Steve, who'd planned to try riding on that Monday and then afterwards get caught up on his company's ongoing projects, reluctantly agreed.

Ann, who hadn't wanted him to go back to work for a few more days, carefully removed the bandages. She suggested that he could leave his face wound open as the cut was healing well. If he wanted, she could remove the stitches, trim his beard, give him a shave and spray the injury with PlastiSkin. He'd have a scar, and for another few weeks wouldn't look very friendly, but eventually the scar might even improve his craggy looks! He agreed.

His back was another matter. The long jagged rip from the tree branch, in spite of the cosmetic surgeon's efforts, was not pretty. The fact that his back had a number of old scars on it already, didn't help. It was healing well though, and it was time to remove the stitches and staples. Ann removed them and redressed the still slightly weeping wound. It would be a few days yet before she could cover it with PlastiSkin. Even though it was early, Ann fixed him a stiff nightcap and put him to bed. It had been a long, tiring day.

The next morning, after Steve had barely had time to get ready, the crowd appeared. Everyone stared at his face until Ann said defensively, it'll get better; I've never shaved a man before! The crowd laughed, the tension broken. It was evident that while the crowd looked ragged and tired, excitement gripped them. Lia began by saying that they'd found something. In fact, it had been Larry who'd seen it and asked them to check it out.

Lia, who couldn't contain herself any longer continued, exclaiming, "Douglas Terminals doesn't own Oilfield Services!"

Steve just looked at her, not yet understanding.

The Price of Success

Peter took over, "It appears that Oilfield Services is a company that Finkelman set up four years ago for Douglas when Douglas wanted to expand into the oil business. Since at that time most of the work was in Alberta, Finkelman registered the company in Alberta, with the shares owned by Terry Douglas personally and not his company. Why it was done that way we don't know. At some point about three years ago Mark Finkelman came across pictures of this huge special truck that could move entire drilling rigs while minimizing the need to tear down the rig. With all the drilling going on in Alberta, he decided that this looked like a hell of a good idea. He talked Terry Douglas into buying two trucks and operating them through Oilfield Services. Mark even talked his dad into fronting $1.2 million to buy the trucks, taking ownership of all the shares in Oilfield Services and 55% of the shares in Douglas as collateral. At this point it gets a little tricky. We think from what we see is that sometime later the Alberta Corporate Registry of Oilfield was supposed to lapse and the assets sold from Terry Douglas to Douglas Terminals. We suspect that with all the new drilling work in Saskatchewan they figured it would be easier with just one province's rules and regs to follow, but again, we're not sure. Up to this point, the new trucks were a gold mine, operating 24/7."

He paused to refill his coffee cup. "But that never happened! It looks like some anonymous clerk at Finkelmans just kept submitting the annual reports and fees to Alberta. As the price of oil dropped, the idea of Oilfield Services being collapsed and the assets sold slipped through the cracks."

Steve interrupted, "So if we bought Douglas, we'd avoid all the debt from Oilfield."

Lia interjected, "Bingo!"

Peter said, "And here's where it gets tricky. Cheryl, it was your idea, you explain it."

For once Cheryl looked a bit flustered but carried on, "If we offered to buy the 55% of Douglas that Finkelman owns for, say, $300,000 but never mention Oilfield Services, we could get a controlling interest in Douglas for 10 cents or less on the dollar. Finkelman would think we're also taking over the responsibility for Oilfield debt and that he'd eventually be repaid. Actually, we'd be leaving Finkelman with Oilfield Services, its special trucks and its $1.2 million in debt. This all hinges on Finkelman not realizing that Douglas Terminals does not own Oilfield Services. And if we can persuade Terry Douglas to walk away from Oilfield."

Steve sat there stunned. It was the most audacious legal business robbery plan he had ever seen. Cheryl started to explain more, but Steve waved her to be quiet and got up to pace back and forth furiously. The group had seen this before and sat forward on the edges of their seats, sweating with tension. Steve stopped in front of Cheryl, pulled her up and gave her a huge hug and a giant kiss right on the lips. Cheryl was totally flustered while the group whooped and hollered. Even staid Peter cheered. Ann hurriedly stuck her head in the meeting room to check that everything was okay.

Steve turned to Peter and said, "Can we really do this? Can you put together an offer in such a way that we're not bidding on Oilfield Services but don't actually say that?"

Peter hesitated and then replied, "Yes. I have to advise you, though, that this is remarkably risky. What are you going to do if they catch wind of this scheme?"

Steve answered, "Plead ignorance! But really, once the sale goes through and it's completely paid for, is there anything Finkelman can do?"

Peter replied, "Well regardless, they can always sue for misrepresentation, but since they're selling their asset to you, that won't get very far. I'd say that the odds of their being able to have the courts reverse the sale are slight to nil."

Turning to Truckin' Ted and Sharon, Steve asked, "How well do you know Terry Douglas? I know him, but not that well."

Ted said, "He's a straight shooter and good to work for. I think he wants out, but that may be just because of the debt load thing on Oilfield Services. I don't think that he's aware that he never did sell Oilfield to Douglas Terminals."

"How about I call Terry, swear him to secrecy, tell him what we're doing and ask what he thinks of our owning 55% of his company? Think he'd go for it? If he does, how about sometime in the future I offer to buy the rest of it?"

An immediate uproar ensued. Sharon stood up and seized the floor. "So that means you've decided to expand into the north?"

Steve hesitated, then said, "This feels right. Apart from the bandages, the fey itch is gone." He hesitated again. "I guess the same way we decided to expand into a bunch of companies when Lia came to see us the first time. I'm not 100% sure this is a good idea, and we'll have a few management issues to organize, but if we can carry this off, it's a gift. Just like the Barchetti deal." He stopped and looked at them, "I know you've all talked about this move. Does anyone know of a concrete reason why we shouldn't do this deal? Speak up; this will be the last chance to have a dissenting opinion." He waited. "No? Okay, we go."

They all cheered again as Steve continued, "Peter, can you have an offer ready for Finkelman by Wednesday morning and arrange a meeting in your office for, say, 10:00?"

"Why the rush? I'd be happier with a few days more."

"Sorry Peter, I have a personal reason." And with that his facial scar went white, his eyes flickered, and the group felt his anger.

The group left and Steve called Terry Douglas. After asking for his word about keeping a secret, except from his wife, Steve outlined what he had in mind. Terry, after asking some questions, said that he didn't have a problem working with Steve and his crew, but who actually would run Douglas? Steve said that it depended, then broached the idea of Terry selling the rest of the company. Steve offered to pay a

The Price of Success

fair price for it in the near future and to consider hiring Terry as his general manager of northern freight operations. Steve would also keep as many of Terry's staff as possible. Terry wanted to talk to his wife first, but he liked the idea of selling out and possibly retiring. Fucking up the Finkelmans would be an added bonus.

Steve then called Louis Finkelman and suggested Quinn would be interested in offering $300,000 for their 55% share of Douglas Terminals. But that was the most Quinn would pay. The deal was going to be difficult enough to make work. If Louis was interested, then perhaps they could get together on Wednesday morning in Peter's office? Louis indicated that such a deal sounded interesting, but that he'd have to get back to him later in the day. Meeting on Wednesday was possible as they had to be in Regina anyway.

After lunch Steve got out an old mountain bike and, with Ann as company, rode slowly around the farm. The exercise felt good and his back didn't complain at all; the damaged muscles were little involved in the effort of riding. Ann, looking for another way to divert him from business, asked him about doing a road trip and Steve was all for it. When he had the time.

When they got home, there was phone message that the Finkelmans would meet him at Peter's office at 10:00 AM Wednesday.

The next morning, he got on the phone to Sharon to check on operations. Everything was rolling along and the building was nearly complete. At least the construction portion. The redecorating of each renter's space was taking longer than expected, but that wasn't Sharon's concern. All the new mechanicals were working as designed and the renters were very happy with that outcome. Steve's apartment would take a little longer; the roofers had to come back to install the new skylights he wanted in the kitchen, living and dining rooms. She asked about decorating the apartment and he asked her for some suggestions. Steve had just acquired a few of David Dasse's paintings and was anxious to hang them. He didn't have much furniture, or anything else for that matter, except his Eskimo artwork, some rare Eskimo carvings and antique office furniture. And his music collection, including many rare vinyl LPs. Sharon said she really didn't want to make those decisions and would rather he talk to Gabriel. Steve chuckled and agreed it had been an unfair request. He'd wait to see what Gabriel suggested.

Steve then called Larry. Larry reported that the renovation costs had come in over budget, but nothing serious. The rebates from Sask Power, as expected, had reduced the cost by half. He expected to recoup the overages in the construction company profits. He wondered if Steve had considered paying off the building mortgage. They now had a large cash reserve thanks to excellent courier and freight sales and the sales of some of the Barchetti companies. Steve asked him to hold off; he might need the cash for the Douglas Terminal's purchase.

Cheryl was next. She reported that the final moves with the Barchetti companies were proving difficult. The used car businesses didn't want to work together and, as they had little or no assets other than the cars, there was little leverage available to force them forward. Steve, who'd been hearing this crap for several months now, asked what the cash situation would be if they closed them down. Cheryl replied that, if they sold off the inventories, they'd recoup their cost. Everything else was rented. If one of the operators wanted to buy, then they'd make a few bucks. He told her to give Barchetti one dollar for them all, then get rid of them; the trouble wasn't worth the gain.

The auto parts stores were a different story. They'd paid Barchetti $50,000 in total, plus taken on their large debt and had an unsolicited offer sitting on the table from one of the big auto parts chains for $250,000. The chain had told her it was willing to overpay just to get into the Regina market with established stores. Steve scoffed and told her that was way too low. He told her to get a replacement value for each store, including inventories, and then offer to sell them in total at 75% of the replacement value for cash. As is, where is. She replied that was going to be, at about $250,000 for each of the seven stores, a sell price of about $1.3 million! Steve laughed and said remember, you can always drop the price, but you can never increase it. Cheryl agreed to go that route.

The construction companies were last, and they were giving her staff the biggest hassle. No one - but no one - wanted to work together in one big company. Steve asked her to get them all together and he'd talk to them. He had in mind first working with the main company only. To everyone else he'd say that he was giving them three choices; they could either join up with the main company or buy themselves out, or if they wanted to join up with another contractor doing the same thing in the group to make another larger company, that was a possibility too. First Steve wanted to visit the manager of the main company to see what he was made of.

He then asked about Lia. Could Cheryl use her as an analyst or organizer or something? Cheryl replied that Lia didn't have the experience or training to be any of those, but she seemed to be a very good lawyer. She was quick to find solutions to legal problems that stumped her brothers and was able to persuade others to do her bidding. She was able to do something that Cheryl has seen only him do better, and that was to be able to see solutions and work across corporate division lines to implement them. Cheryl added that Lia wasn't afraid to think, and think big too. She certainly wasn't afraid to work and she wasn't afraid of Sharon! Cheryl suggested that he bring her in as the in-house legal counsel. That would save money too. And she had to straighten out a misconception. It hadn't been her idea about buying Douglas Terminals, it had been Lia's. Peter got confused because Cheryl talked to him first.

Steve then called Betty to see how she was doing. She sounded a bit frazzled but said all was under control, she just had a new receptionist she was training. It was Marcia, Lia's assistant from Barchetti, and Marcia was having trouble adapting to the pace and variety of duties at Quinn. Betty was glad to talk to him though and

The Price of Success

bring him up to date about all the inner goings-on at Quinn. Betty was particularly concerned that they didn't have a good central handle on the computer systems and equipment. She repeated that they had better make an allowance for both more space and money for computer operations. She reiterated that this was the way forward in the business. While Steve didn't disagree, he simply had not yet taken the time to fully understand the machines and what they could do. Steve suggested that she get Lia and Larry to see about organizing a computer division or, if they had a better idea, he wanted to hear it. He let her talk and then asked what she thought he should do about his apartment. She suggested they take next Friday after the weekly managers meeting and visit some furniture stores for ideas. At the very least they could buy some dishes, pots, pans and cutlery. Betty also told Steve that her mother in Calgary wasn't doing well and that she might have to take some time to help her out. Steve told her to do whatever was needed. Sharon called back and said that she'd arranged for Steve to go to the construction company office to meet the manager Thursday morning.

With a sigh of relief at being caught up and everything under control, he accepted a pre-dinner drink from Ann, and they then spent a long time discussing Steve's kids and Claire. The kids were doing fine, their school work was improving, and Grace was a happy camper. The topic then switched to the Finkelman meeting. Both agreed that tomorrow was going to be fun, although Ann didn't like the look on Steve's face or the aura he was emitting. Sex that night with him was extended, rough, and very satisfying.

Wednesday morning Sharon, Lia and Steve met at Peter's office, and Peter was impressed with Steve's improved appearance. Steve quipped that at least the possibility of his bleeding on the floor was much reduced. Peter suggested that he conduct the negotiations, all that Steve had to do was sign the offer and the cheque if it were accepted. Sharon and Lia were to remain quiet. The Finkelmans then appeared and they got down to business. Again, no one asked about his face or other injuries. It was soon clear that the Finkelmans had something else on their collective minds. Peter was about to ask, Steve could see, so he kicked him under the desk to get his attention and almost imperceptibly shook his head. The Finkelmans' examination of the documents was cursory, questions were few and they quickly signed their acceptance of the offer. They didn't even check the effective date. Steve signed the cheque and everyone shook hands. It was done.

Then Steve said, "Ahh, one more thing, Abe. I believe you owe me $9,000."

"What the hell do I owe you money for?"

"One wrecked bike, asshole."

As Abe opened his mouth, Steve, really stepping into it, hit him right on the side of his face, breaking his jaw and nose and knocking three teeth out. Abe flew backward and, on his way down, smashed into the chairs and knocked over a plant stand holding some of Peter's prized roses. As Mark turned toward Steve, he'd half pulled out a gun when Sharon hit him with a solid overhand right and then a chopping left. He too had a broken nose, cheekbone and broken teeth. Mark also went flying, taking more chairs with him. Sharon then stepped over the chairs and kicked him in the groin. Both men were down hard and weren't getting up. Steve grabbed Sharon before she did any more damage, then stepped over and stomped on Mark's right hand, smashing his fingers.

"That's for pulling a gun on me, asshole."

Peter, who'd been seated with his mouth hanging open, seeing the gun on the floor, started yelling at Louis about guns. Louis, becoming increasingly pale, closed his eyes and was dead before he hit the floor.

Sharon grabbed the signed papers and shoved the cheque into Louis' jacket pocket. Meanwhile, Peter's secretary had burst into the office and, seeing that Peter was okay and bodies scattered about, turned to call 911. Sharon handed the completed contracts to Peter, told him where the cheque was, and asked him to deal with it. Mark and Abe were alive, but badly hurt. Steve checked Sharon, who was still shaking with anger, grabbed her and Lia and left, telling Peter they were going to the hospital to get their hands checked. All the way to the hospital, Lia could only mutter over and over, "Holy fuck, holy fuck, holy fuck."

It had not really been a fair fight. Both Sharon and Steve were bigger, taller, and meaner than the Finkelman boys and had been primed for the brawl. Steve didn't really care; as far as he was concerned they got what they deserved. In any event, in Steve's approach to life, anyone who fooled with him better be ready for the consequences. Period.

At the hospital Lia took charge and soon had their hands x-rayed. She also ordered them both to keep quiet and say nothing, she would handle whatever came up. Sharon had cracked fingers in her left hand, Steve had a fractured bone in his right hand, but neither one needed a cast, just heavy taping. After they were taped, Lia herded them out to the car and drove back to the office.

Several hours later, congratulating themselves and waiting for the police, Betty called the hospital and found that the police weren't interested. The hospital had advised everyone that Louis had simply suffered a fatal heart attack. Abe and Mark had declined to discuss their injuries with anyone.

That was the first they realized that Louis Finkelman was dead. Steve called Peter and asked him if he knew about it. Peter replied that he'd wondered; the way he passed out didn't look right. But Peter, ever the lawyer, continued that the sale was good. All the papers were signed and the money had changed hands. Peter would register the sale that afternoon. But Peter wanted to know why he'd hit Abe. And why are they not screaming "assault" to the police? So Steve reiterated the bike race story and what was going to happen to the Finkelman brothers as a result of the deliberate crash. And that is also why they were so distracted at the meeting. Peter's response was to ask Steve to never let Sharon get mad at him! Peter added, "Just before they took Mark away I slid his gun underneath him on the stretcher. So he's going to have another distraction to worry about!"

Steve then called Brian Patterson of Patterson Freightways in Saskatoon. Patterson was Rayner's agent in Saskatoon and distributed all of Rayner's northern freight. He told Brian of the purchase of Douglas Terminals but wanted to assure him that they didn't intend to make any immediate changes to northern operations. Brian was irritated. He said, "Well shit, Steve, if you wanted to expand into Saskatoon why didn't you just buy us? I'm pissed that you didn't ask."

Steve gave Brian an abbreviated and sanitized version of the Douglas deal, and Brian laughed and laughed at the Finkelmans getting their comeuppance. Apparently, Louis Finkelman had few friends in Saskatoon. Steve then asked if Brian was serious about selling out, and Brian said he'd consider it if the details and his future were right. Steve asked him if he'd accept a "Right of First Refusal" and a cheque for $1,000 with a time limit of one year. This meant that Steve had the first right to refuse to match any other offer made for Patterson. If Steve matched the offer, then Brian was obligated to sell to Steve. Brian agreed, and Steve told him to expect a call from Lia. He instructed Lia and Cheryl, both of whom were sitting listening, to do their usual trick on Patterson and try to figure out how best to use them.

Quinn Enterprises now had another major direction in which to expand and had the people, money and now assets to accomplish the task. Steve thought it was time to celebrate. He leaned back and asked who wanted a drink.

CJ Vermeulen

The Price of Success

Chapter Nine - More Progress

Ann and Sharon, at their now regular weekly meeting, decided that now was the time for Steve to take a long cross-country bike ride. They knew he liked to do these rides and somehow, when he returned, he looked and acted like a new man. They decided that a ride from Vancouver to Trail, B.C., a distance of about 400 miles over the rugged B.C. mountains, would be perfect. Steve hadn't done this stretch before, along Hwy #3 but had talked about doing it. The ride should take five to seven days and provide an excellent workout. If the business didn't need Steve and he felt like it, he could continue on over the highest main highway pass in Canada to Creston, or farther to Radium and even Calgary, if he wanted to spend that much time on the road.

The next concern was who, if anyone, would accompany him. Ann, Grace and Lia all were accomplished long distance cyclists, but only Lia could free up the required time. A bigger question, if he even wanted someone with him. Steve had often commented on the challenges of surviving alone on the open road and just how revitalizing the experience was. And was Lia even interested?

The two women decided that Ann would pick a time to talk to Steve. They agreed that this time they wouldn't accept Steve's refusal. If Steve wanted company, then Lia was a possibility. Neither one was too happy at the possibility of Lia spending a week with him, but they conceded Steve needed the holiday. And maybe, with luck, he'd want to go alone.

On Thursday morning, Steve went to see the owner/manager of the Barchetti construction company. His excuse was that he wanted to say "Thank you" for the job well done on the building. However, the meeting didn't go well. The owner was obviously irritated with Steve's efforts to combine companies and resented the fact that Steve would own his company. He also didn't want a woman, Cheryl, organizing his operations. Steve, pissed that this idiot wouldn't listen to his people trying to help him get bigger and more efficient, called Lia and asked her to come over to the meeting. With Lia watching, Steve asked if the owner knew that when Barchetti had sold the company to him, he now owed Steve the nearly $270,000 Barchetti debt. And that the company shares were the collateral for the loan? The owner, who figured that his loan was so large that Steve wouldn't do anything about it, made a big miscalculation by suggesting that Steve take a hike. Steve told him that this afternoon he would have a written demand on his desk for full repayment of the loan. If the loan wasn't paid within 24 hours, Steve would then take full management control of the company and he would be out in the cold. With nothing.

Lia and Steve got up and walked out.

That afternoon Lia received a call from Frank, her father. He was very upset at the story he was getting from the construction company and suggested he might give the owner the money to pay off the loan, at which point Lia went ballistic. Lia, without thinking of the consequences, for the first time in her life openly disagreeing with her father, told Frank that he was wrong and that when he sold all the companies to Barchetti LLP he had forfeited any right to interfere with what happened. Lia went on to say that if he did interfere she was resigning immediately from Barchetti LLP and he could find someone else to run the damn place. Frank, shaken, realized that his little daughter had truly grown up and was now completely in charge. He promised to back off and interfere no more. After Lia had repeated the essence of the call to Steve, he told her it was in her hands now. Acting as an agent for Quinn, if no payment appeared, she was to fire the owner and take over the company.

By the following afternoon with no payment having been received, Lia proceeded to take over the company. Including firing the ex-owner.

That Friday morning, though, after the management meeting where the big news was the removal of the blockade from the construction company takeover, Steve and Betty went shopping. They had fun buying a whole kitchen's worth of dishes, pots, pans, cutlery, small appliances and all the little stuff that makes a kitchen. Steve being an accomplished cook, dragged Betty through every cook ware store in town. They had a driver deliver it all to the new apartment, then Betty took Steve to her place for a good Ukrainian lunch. After lunch, as Betty had planned, one thing led to another and they were soon in bed. Betty was inexperienced but a willing and enthusiastic partner. After making her come twice with his hands and tongue, he flipped her over and entered her from behind. Holding her down so that she couldn't move, he slowly brought them along until they both came with a satisfying ferocity.

The Price of Success

When he came back from having a quick rinse off, Betty was quietly crying. As he lay down beside her, she kept repeating, "I didn't know it could be like that, I didn't know, I didn't know."

When she'd stopped crying and had visited the bathroom, Steve slowly moved her down until he could tuck his penis between her breasts. He moved back and forth, also massaging her nipples. He moved her farther down until she got the idea and took him in her mouth. Then he pulled out and slid down to enter her from the front. He told her to pull her legs up, and he rolled them both to the right. Her left leg fitted easily under his side, and by leaning back, he could drive as deep as possible into her. Moving faster and faster, he made them both cry out.

Betty, shaking, whispered, "I'm done, I'm done, please, no more."

Later, after they both again had a rinse off in the shower, she shyly asked him about anal sex. He told her that some liked it, some didn't. She replied that she'd thought about it but wasn't sure, she didn't want to get hurt. Steve assured her that if they did it again, they'd do only whatever she was comfortable with, nothing more. After a short nap, Steve got up and got dressed. With a final kiss on her right nipple, he left her in bed falling back to sleep. He headed back to the new apartment to put away their purchases. The apartment was nearly finished and he reminded himself to get Sharon to arrange moving all his stuff from the warehouse to his new home. Then out to Ann's for supper and to get the motorhome ready for another Saturday of bike racing with Sergio. This time it was Sergio's turn to win the cross-country race outright, and Steve's to win his "age-class" downhill race. But Steve suffered. He knew his back would prevent him from doing the cross-country race, so he'd entered just the downhill. Even so, his back hurt from the pounding of the downhill course and, as his training rides had been interrupted, his conditioning had slipped. When they got back to Ann's he and Sergio soaked in the outside hot tub to relieve their aches and pains.

On Sunday, Ann decided that it was time to broach the subject of the road trip. She asked Lia, Cheryl, Betty and Sharon to come out for the afternoon and warned them she wanted to talk about Steve's road trip. When the subject came up, Steve of course said he didn't have time, with too much going on. Each of the women showed him that everything was under control and that all road blocks to finalizing the Barchetti deal had been removed. The Douglas deal was well underway and the Patterson deal was also organized. All of Cheryl's staff, Sharon's staff and Larry had a ton of work before them, but it could and would get done without his presence. The building reno's were just about complete, and all that was needed was for him to finalize his apartment's decorating. Lia and Betty were deep into researching a computer division, and Sharon said she was sitting around just picking her ass, the way it should be.

The resulting hilarity sealed Steve's fate. He sat for a minute looking at these women who ran his life and decided that life was pretty damn good, he was a fortunate man. Besides, this break would allow him to move back a bit further from the day-to-day management of the organization. Tomorrow he'd service his road bike and pack up everything he needed for life on the road. Betty told him she'd get an airline ticket to Vancouver for Wednesday. Sharon reminded him that the new apartment would be ready when he returned, that is if she and Ann could organize it? Steve agreed.

The Price of Success

CJ Vermeulen

Chapter Ten - Bike Ride #1

Steve, wearing his usual gaudy Quinn promotional track suit, carrying his pannier bags, helmet and feeling somewhat conspicuous, deplaned in Vancouver and headed for the baggage area. At the special freight window he retrieved his disassembled bike in its hard-sided shipping case and carried it to a quiet corner. With several interested passengers watching, he reassembled the bike and remounted the panniers. He then arranged to send the shipping case back to Regina. Wheeling the bike outside, he donned his helmet and gloves and headed for the water.

Vancouver airport bordered the Pacific Ocean, so it was easy to find a spot where he could dip the bike's rear wheel into the water. That ritual completed, making the ride official, he headed east toward the city, slowly getting used to the traffic and watching for heavy trucks. While Vancouver was generally a bike friendly city, even having its own bike lanes on most streets, heavy trucks and bikes don't mix well. With truck drivers being unable to see all around themselves and a truck's need to make wide turns, Steve's policy was simply to stay away from them. Steve, riding down 56A Ave, then onto Hwy 1A toward Aldergrove, slowly progressed toward the east side of the city. Once past Aldergrove he began looking for the motel where Betty had made his overnight reservation. It had been only about 30 miles from the airport, but Steve figured that was enough for the first day while trying to stay alive in heavy traffic.

The next day at 6:00 a.m., which was to be his regular waking time, he was up and packing. The attached restaurant opened at 6:30 and he was first in line for a carb loaded breakfast. He got the kitchen to half fill his water bottles with apple juice and, finishing his coffee, went back to his room. He topped up the half-filled bottles with water and headed for the highway. As he was rolling east out of the city, traffic wasn't too bad as most of it was heading west to work in the city. When he got to Trans-Canada Hwy #1, he made sure his flashing tail light was working, and headed for Abbotsford. Steve wasn't sure that bikes were allowed on this freeway,

The Price of Success

but he decided to try it and, if stopped, plead ignorance. However no one bothered him and once past Abbotsford he was on his way, Abbotsford being the last major coastal city on the highway. Sixty miles later he arrived in the city of Hope, where Hwy #3 split off from Hwy #1. He found another motel and gratefully settled his tired legs and sore back into a tub full of hot water.

That established his overall daily routine. His riding routine was to stop every hour, possibly eat a handful of trail mix, have a drink and rest for five minutes. It was a standing cycling rule that if you didn't have to pee every hour, you're not drinking enough fluids. Not drinking enough fluids was a slow route to real trouble, particularly if it was hot and you were sweating profusely. Often, if it was a particularly difficult cycling day, if he could find a restaurant or even a service station, he'd take a break and drink an extra bottled fruit drink. At day's end, Steve would stop at 4:00 p.m. or so, find a motel, soak his tired legs and sore back for a half hour and then have a carb loaded supper. After an hour of reading or watching TV, washing his clothes and servicing his bike, he'd be in bed by 9:00 p.m.

On day three he headed up Hwy #3 and the first serious climbing of the ride. Hwy #3 was the old Trans-Canada and was not a modern highway. Particularly this beginning section. It was rough with broken pavement, and was narrow and very winding, with many posted 10 mph corners. And bloody dangerous. Cars coming toward him that had pulled out to pass usually didn't give a rat's ass about a cyclist in the way. Steve had driven this road many times, even in his 40-foot motorhome, but a bike was something else. Several times he was brushed by passing semi-trailers, and the rough road was not doing his back any good. The road finally climbed into Manning Park where the highway opened up and became much safer to ride. He was happy to get to East Gate alive and in one piece.

The next day's run was virtually dead north, but again rough and winding with continuous climbing and some long, fast descents. The descents were exciting but also dangerous. Coming up on a posted 10 mph corner at the bottom of a descent where his speed had reached 40 or even 50 mph had his hands sweating and his heart pounding. But he loved it! His brain forgot about everything except survival. He was sorry when the day ended with a long descent into Princeton.

From here the highway became a regular mountain highway with long flat runs along valley bottoms, long flat runs along the tops of the mountains, the whole being connected by long climbs and fast descents. It was fun, peaceful riding, with little traffic and with time to pay attention to the mountains and wildlife along the highway. One advantage of being on a bike was that it was dead quiet, and he could ride right up to sheep or deer before they noticed him.

After seven marvelous days on the road he'd arrived in the mountain ski resort town of Rossland. From here it was a 10-mile descent to his destination, the smelter town of Trail. And what a descent it was! The highway was four lanes wide, smooth and fast, but did have the odd stone and some patches of loose gravel near the edge.

There were few straight stretches, the grade was never less than 6% and at times exceeded 14%. Every serious B.C. cyclist knew of this stretch of highway and either had done it or dreamed of careening down it. There were even some whose challenge was to ride up the highway! The descending speed limit was 30 mph for cars and only 15 mph for heavily loaded ore and wood chip trucks. This meant that cyclists had to pass the trucks and cars on the outside, even if they didn't move over! But most motorists were used to bikes flying down the hill and they would give the bikes passing space.

After stopping at the top, tightening his helmet strap and gloves, he took a deep breath and rode around the right hand corner and then left over what appeared to be the highway's edge. Steve's speed rapidly approached 55 mph and he prayed he wouldn't see a cop, or hit a stone or a hole. The RCMP had been known to follow a bike to the bottom and hand out speeding tickets! Most bikers considered these tickets a badge of honor. At this speed, braking was not feasible and a high-speed wobble and crash a real possibility. He soon had to start cutting across the traffic lanes; he was going far too fast to stay in one lane. He swooped down the road, slicing and dicing around the cars and heavy trucks, his heart rate climbing past 180 bpm and a maniacal gleam in his eyes. As he rode, he thought of the stories of the high school kids riding shopping carts down this highway to Trail, one in the cart, the other with roller blades on his feet, hanging on and steering. Nearing the bottom, heart racing, hands sweating, Steve let out a whoop as he leaned into the last corner.

It was very exciting and bloody dangerous. And he loved it.

Once down in Trail, Steve found a street bench in the Gulch and stopped with his heart rate monitor blinking like mad and his hands trembling. As his breathing slowed, he got up to find a phone and called the office. Betty answered and was glad he was okay; they thought he'd have called sooner. He told her that he was just checking in and would get back to her when he was organized. He then called his friend Mike Benson and Mike immediately asked him to come over. Steve climbed back on his bike and slowly found his way to Mike and Myrna's place.

The Price of Success

Chapter Eleven - More Family Problems

In Regina, Quinn Enterprises was rolling right along. Gabriel the architect had assigned his interior designer to look at Steve's apartment, and she had a tentative layout and decorating plan ready. The building was nearly finished and the new furniture had arrived for the fifth floor offices. The individual renters had also made progress with their renovations, and soon the building would be free of construction noise and mess. They were planning on moving the City Express offices into their new home this weekend. Cheryl had completed the construction company reorganization plan, and it too was well under way. They'd end up with a large, well equipped construction company and several smaller plumbing, heating, and electrical contractors. Hopefully all under one roof. The rest of the construction material and equipment would be sold. The auto parts stores had been sold for $1,250,000 and the money was in the bank. The several leftover businesses would be sold within the next 10 days. All in all the Barchetti deal had produced a mountain of cash and a new solid, steady source of profits. Larry was a happy camper. Cheryl was planning on a long holiday when Steve returned. The only unfinished piece of business was the creation, funding, and finding the personnel for a computer division. Lia and Sharon had discussed the issue at length and agreed that it sounded like a very good idea, but they didn't know just how to go about it. They came to the conclusion that they could open up their own computer division or hire an outside data management company or buy an existing data management company. They favoured buying an existing company as they thought that might include more in-house analysts. Both agreed to wait until Cheryl had completed some of her projects and then they'd discuss it with her. Meanwhile they'd look around for a suitable company.

Terry Douglas had come back and, dealing with Sharon, had agreed to sell his 45% share of Douglas Terminals. Then he wanted to retire. Truckin' Ted had worked with one of Cheryl's analysts and completed a detailed analysis of Douglas, and they'd developed a modernization plan that mostly centered on office equipment, including a new computer system. Brian Patterson had been negotiating with Lia, and after she'd visited and had a good look at Patterson Freightways, she had the glimmering of a brilliant idea. Brian and Lia weren't too far apart in their assessment of Patterson's worth and had, as well, established a good working relationship. Lia thought that Brian was a rather bright young fella and that he'd already figured out that, when Rayner took over Douglas Terminals, the competition for business would become very rough. Lia wanted to talk to Sharon first though. Perhaps, she thought, I can figure out the details of my idea on the way home.

In other words, at the moment they didn't need Steve. Everyone's hands were full, both completing the plans Steve had left them and running the resulting business organization. When he called back, Sharon told him so. She also told him that in another week, the entire company would be in their new home. Everyone was so excited!

After Steve got settled at Mike's house, he called Grace to see how the kids were doing. And found a problem. Claire was back in Regina and, high on something, had tried to break into Grace's house to drag the kids away. Grace had called the police and Claire was in custody. Grace had also called Cynthia and had obtained a court order to keep Claire away. Fortunately, this happened when the kids were in school. She had also asked Cynthia to proceed with the divorce from Ted. He was apparently now again living at Claire's house.

But a bigger problem had arisen at the school. The school bully had been picking on Shaun about what his mother was now doing. Sergio had found out about it, waylaid the kid on his way home and had given him a black eye. The kid's father, himself a bully, had complained to the principal and threatened to beat the crap out of Sergio. Sergio, without telling Grace about it, had asked Sharon for help. Apparently, she had a meeting with the principal, and all 6'1" of stunning good looking, very vocal and angry lawyer-woman had convinced the principal to look more closely at the situation. Especially when she'd threatened to bring a lawsuit against the school for negligence with regard to the safety of its students.

But the real problem happened as Sharon and Sergio were walking down the hallway on their way out. The bully and his father were coming in and the bully pointed Sergio out as the reason for his black eye. The father tried to grab Sergio, but Sharon stepped into him and, with a right cross, decked him. When he tried to get up she stepped around him and, with her pointy shoe, kicked him in the liver. Meanwhile, Sergio hit the kid in the other eye, and he too was down. The final indignity was that both father and son had peed their pants. As they stood there watching the two groaning, Sharon told Sergio something she'd learned from his father. When the other guy was down, a kick to the liver will keep him down. There was no point letting him get back up and having to knock him down again. When Sergio looked at her with a question on his face, Sharon told him t
win the fight in the shortest time possible, not to be nice about it.

The fracas had occurred when the halls were full of students, and many had seen what had happened. With the bullies down, they cheered, particularly the girls. After the police had taken the two injured bullies away, (both were well known to police) the guidance counsellor asked Sharon if she'd talk to the bullied students. Sharon had agreed and, after meeting with them the next day, was the talk of the school. The girls loved her, the boys were in awe, and everyone envied Sergio and Shaun.

But Grace wasn't so sure that the right thing had been done. She didn't condone violence, and here it had landed on her doorstep. Steve convinced her that sometimes it was the only answer, although he agreed that Sharon could be a little quick with the rough stuff. He suggested that Grace keep an eye on the boys to make sure that they didn't let it go to their heads.

He had to laugh though. Sergio had figured out that a volatile 6'1" Sharon who was always angry when it came to bullies would be a hell of a lot more effective than a 4'9" Lia! Grace laughed, and he knew it was going to be okay. She admitted that Sharon had been far more effective than she'd have been. She laughed again, ruefully.

He then called Ann to make sure all was well. She told him she missed him, especially his cooking! She didn't tell him about the long meeting she and Sharon had had, with him as the main topic.

The Price of Success

Chapter Twelve - Bike Ride #2

So, Steve decided to carry on. He was feeling good, his back was finally fully healed, he had ridden himself back into top shape, the bike was performing as designed, and life was good. After staying at Mike's for two nights, getting all his clothes properly washed, resting and refilling his stock of trail mix, he hit the road again. This was the day he had to climb the Creston-Salmo Pass, the highest pass on any major highway in Canada. At just under 6,000 feet in elevation, it was not going to be easy. It started at a 6% grade, halfway up increased to 7% and, toward the top, increased again to 9%. The road was winding and climbed relentlessly; there simply were no flat areas to take a break from the climbing. It was windy up there and even in the summer could be damned cold. Then he had to descend the other side to Creston, also on a never-ending slope carved into the mountainside.

Steve hoped for a cool day, but it looked like it was going to be warm and sunny. He got nicely warmed up by climbing up out of Trail to Montrose and then continued east toward Salmo. There he found an open restaurant and, because it was about 9:30, he stopped to have a plate of pancakes to top up his carb levels. Besides, he needed a crap and there simply was no privacy on the coming mountain climb! As he parked his bike and locked it up he encountered a surprise. There were 18 other cyclists having breakfast, all belonging to a supported cross-country touring group. This meant that a van accompanied the tour and carried all the cyclists' luggage, spare parts and full water bottles, a mechanic and more road food. The tour riders were surprised to see him travelling alone, unsupported. They were also impressed that he'd travelled from Vancouver as quickly as he had. Particularly when he'd actually cycled the beginning of Hwy #3 and survived! As a group they'd taken a bus from Hope up to Manning Park, the road being considered just too dangerous for a group of cyclists.

When he left the restaurant, he was at the tail end of the touring group with the van and it's flashing lights just ahead of him. The group rode spread out in a single line on purpose, mostly for safety. This allowed traffic to pass and hopefully no one

The Price of Success

would get brushed off the road. Within three miles the road started up to the pass with the mountain on his left and the river valley to the right. Steve had warmed up again and, selecting a lower gear, settled into his normal high rate pedalling cadence. The miles went by as Steve passed the slower members of the touring group. This surprised him as he was generally a poor climber and hated climbing. Steve was simply too big and even though he was heavily muscled, his power-to-weight ratio was much lower than a shorter, smaller man. The best climbers were generally less than 5'6" tall and weighed less than 150 pounds. He surmised that the answer was that he had ridden himself into better shape than the tourers and was riding better equipment, even if he had to carry his own baggage. He made his normal one-hour stop and shed his track pants to ride in shorts and bare legs. Changing on the side of the road didn't bother him at all. After all, who was going to see him that he would ever see again? Another hour and another stop, this time to shed his jacket to don a colorful cycling jersey. It was getting warm; the sun was heating up the pavement and he was drinking a lot of juice. He was now high enough that it was a long drop on his right to the river below. And there were no more guardrails. He knew they hadn't been installed up here so that snow plows could easily push the huge volumes of snow over the edge. The shoulder was only about eight feet wide, so a slip or being brushed by traffic could be fatal. Some of the touring group had already gotten off their bikes and were walking on the mountain side of the road. He didn't blame them; the increasingly cold gusty breeze bouncing off the mountain side was becoming disconcerting.

Another hour and the heat from the sun was starting to get to Steve. He'd passed most of the tourers and was down to his last sips of juice. He'd already stopped to soak himself in a small waterfall and was soon going to have to do it again. The road was now at a 9% grade. The right shoulder had narrowed to some four feet wide and Steve could continuously see the drop from the corner of his eye. It was very unsettling, especially when the wind pushed him toward the edge. He was now out of water and, choosing an appropriate water fall, stopped, soaked himself again and refilled two water bottles. He knew he was running a risk of contracting the parasite giardia, but it was critical to be properly hydrated. If necessary, somewhere ahead he could always get a parasiticide at a local medical clinic to clean himself out.

The last hour was brutal. He refused to quit, or even to walk, he just kept pedalling. His pedalling cadence had also slowed to 60-65 rpm, and he was down to the lowest gear possible. Some of the walkers cheered as he slowly passed, barely moving faster than the walkers. And then suddenly he was at the top! He gratefully rode to the picnic area, stopped, and nearly fell off his bike. However, in spite of the bright sun, it was cool on top with a cold wind off the surrounding snow-capped mountains, so he changed back into his track suit. He walked over to the mobile food stand and bought two bottles of juice. After eating some trail mix and drinking the juice and not wanting to cool off too much, he was ready to go again. Tightening his helmet strap and his riding gloves, he headed for the east side descent of the Creston-Salmo Pass.

The east side descent slope was even steeper than the west side climb. The road was rougher too, and it had graveled repair patches. The road had been cut through the mountain and didn't follow a river gorge. It also had guardrails and, because it was sheltered, was not as windy. Steve knew that the trick to getting down safely was going to be to control the bike's speed. And stay out of the bloody gravel! That meant braking only where the road was clear and straight. He also knew that he prolly wouldn't be able to stop for a rest. Completely stopping from the high speeds that he expected to achieve was both simply too dangerous and too hard on the bike's brakes.

Steve planned to use a conventional cycling speed control method. He'd let the bike run until the speedometer read about 40 mph, or until a corner loomed, then brake hard. He could get down to about 20 mph before he could feel the brakes beginning to overheat, then he'd let it run again. Adopting this plan, he also sat up in the corners, creating more drag than when he assumed his normal tuck position, all the while avoiding the gravel, other riders and the odd slow-moving sightseeing passenger car. And the bloody trucks! The heavy trucks were all travelling very slowly, Jake brakes popping, and tail lights blinking. Steve could even smell their hot brakes as he sailed past them. He had to pass on the outside because getting between a truck and the guardrail and into the gravel was just too risky. It was great fun, exhilarating, and was becoming the highlight of the trip.

Partway down he slowly came up behind a fast running group of six tourers. He tucked in behind the last rider and slowed to watch if and when it would be safe to pass. He saw that the lead rider didn't like the fast corners and was slowing down for them more than was necessary. As the group approached the next corner, Steve shifted up into a higher gear and, approaching the turn, jumped out of line and quickly passed the tourers. He continued, strongly accelerating out of the corner into the next short straight. He left the braking as late as he dared, then briefly braked and, hoping there was no gravel on the road, rocketed into a blind left turn, hugging the center dividing line. In the center of the turn he just missed a head-on collision with an oncoming car and, whooping crazily, brushed the next oncoming car with his sleeve.

After some 45 minutes of heart stopping excitement, he could see the bottom of the pass. He was thankful; he wasn't sure his forearms could take much more of the pounding. His hands were cramping and the sweat was running into his eyes, starting to blind him. His breathing and heart rate had maxed out and his Polar heart rate monitor's display had turned red and was again beeping madly. Sitting up, he started coasting and cooling down. Slowly riding the last three miles of flat valley ~n, he found an open bar on the main drag and, carrying his bike into r a cold beer. His appearance stopped all conversation as the tourists

The Price of Success

and regular patrons all gaped at this sweaty, dirty, disheveled arrival. The bartender, though, was not concerned. He saw a steady stream of overheated riders every summer; they were good customers. The bartender asked where Steve was staying and suggested he ride another three miles down the highway to a quiet motel with an excellent attached restaurant. It'd get him away from the noise and confusion of the tourists in the downtown area. Steve finished his second beer and left to take the barkeep's advice. Later after supper, and after a rare celebratory glass of wine, he had to agree that the motel and restaurant were indeed excellent. He went back to his room to wash out his clothes and get some sleep. Today had been the best yet.

Chapter Thirteen - Bike Ride #3

From Creston the highway followed the Moyie River valley and adjoining river valleys all the way to Cranbrook. The highway was fairly flat and a welcome change from the climbing, something Steve didn't mind at all. He was too big and heavy to be a good climber and made up with grit and muscle for his lack of skill. On the other hand, his cat-quick reflexes, weight and strength made him a ferocious downhiller. On these flat roads however, he was really at home. He was able to record some decent daily mileages, one day almost getting to a century day that is, riding 100 miles in one day.

From Cranbrook he called Sharon, Ann, and Grace and with each call found that everything was rolling along as planned. Even the kids were doing well now that their place in the school's hierarchy had been firmly established. Grace thought Samara had a new boyfriend and asked if she'd been given "the talk." Steve laughed and told her that he'd had the talk with her when she was 15. Claire thought at that age she was too young and refused to do it. Steve thought she was just afraid to deal with Charley Brown. He told Grace that if she wanted, she could make sure Samara was taking her birth control pills and remind her to always use a condom.

Once he'd arrived in Cranbrook, he had a choice of the next highway. Since Steve had done Hwy #3 up and over the Crowsnest Pass several years ago, he decided to turn north toward Radium. The road, at least to Radium, was flat and fast, with little traffic. Before he got on the road again though, he looked up Cranbrook's leading bike shop. He had the tires reinflated to 110 psi each. (High pressure bike tires slowly lose air pressure over time.) He also bought two new glasses-mounted rear-view mirrors. They didn't have a very good mounting clip design and were easily blown off by the wind from passing vehicles. He'd lost his two days ago when a car passed him rather closely, and for highway riding they were highly desired.

The bike shop was intrigued by Steve's bike. They'd never seen one like it. It had the best Cannondale aluminum touring frame, but Steve had replaced all the standard road running gear with top of the line Shimano mountain bike running gear.

He'd even combined the lowest of the mountain bike gearing with the highest road bike gearing, front and rear, and as a result he could attack just about any road. A clever touch had been the use of heavier mountain bike shifter and brake cables. Even the hybrid wheels had been built to Steve's design by a custom bike shop using mountain bike hubs, heavy 2 mm spokes and heavy-duty axles laced to light weight Wolber touring rims. The tires were Kevlar lined, flat resistant with a rain-friendly tread. The bike even had a very rare set of Shimano handle bar end touring gear shifters. But he did use road type clipless pedals. His shoes were road shoes too, not really designed for walking, with built in clips for the pedals. The bike was light, rugged and very reliable. In fact, Steve had never had a breakdown while on a tour. Parts coming loose, yes. Two flat tires, yes. But never a breakdown.

After arriving in Radium, one day actually riding over 110 miles, he took a day off and soaked in the Radium Hot Springs pool. One of the unspoken things a serious biker took care of was his butt. Get blisters or actual splits in the skin and you were finished until they healed. Steve's butt that day had told him it needed a rest. Feeling much better the next day and smearing on his secret butt cream, Steve took off up Hwy #93. After a short but steep climb, he came to one of the greatest sights in B.C., maybe even in all of Canada. This was a turnout overlooking the valley of the Kootenay River. But along the other side of the valley, some miles away, from south to north ran the majestic snow-capped Rocky Mountains. It was a spectacular sight, one that Steve had seen before but one that never got old. Turning north, the highway now descended into Kootenay Park.

Some 60 miles farther on, at the north end of the park he had to climb the 3,000 foot high White Mountain and, very surprised, found a luxury lodge at the top. Originally built in the 1920s, it had been a CPR (Canadian Pacific Railway) area construction complex with staff cabins. After his shower and tub soak (in a high sided iron claw footed tub no less) he walked up to the main lodge for a beer in the great room. Sitting in front of the huge fireplace, drinking beer, talking to other guests while waiting for supper, Steve was in touring biker heaven. At 6 p.m. the small crowd was called to the dining room and shown to their tables. They were seated four to a table, each table having a candle and vase of fresh flowers in the center. Supper was a rack of buffalo ribs with a sweet bourbon sauce, dirty rice, fresh rolls, and peas smothered in butter, served by attentive waiters. With an excellent British Columbia red wine. On a cloth tablecloth with cloth napkins. And cherry pie with ice cream for dessert. The fresh ground Columbian coffee with real cream and raw sugar was the superb crowning touch.

The next day as usual he left early and found it was unusually cold, being just above freezing. Proceeding downhill at high speed, it was damn cold with, at his speed, actual frostbite possible. He even had to watch for icy road patches! It was a cold, cold rider with blue fingers that finally arrived at the bottom of the mountain. He saw a highway construction cook shack with smoke coming from the chimney,

The Price of Success

so he stopped, parked his bike and walked in the door. He asked a surprised cook for a coffee and sat down to talk and warm up. A half hour later, fully warmed up, he tried to pay the cook, but he wouldn't accept anything, saying that the conversation was enough. Steve shook his hand and took off again.

Two easy downhill miles later and getting cold again, he arrived at the junction of Hwy #93 and the Trans-Canada Hwy. Turning to the right, he continued downhill toward warmth and Calgary. Fifty miles on, he found a motel on the west side of Calgary and, after checking in, gratefully climbed into a steaming hot tub. He hoped that the weather would warm up; another day of riding in the cold was not something to look forward to. He called Sharon and, after being assured everything was on track, told her he'd decided that he'd complete what was turning out to be the longest road trip he'd ever undertaken. He'd finish the trip by riding to Regina, another some 400 miles away. It would be a fateful decision.

He was surprised to be asked if he wanted some company. Thinking about it, he asked who wanted to do the ride with him. Sharon, rather hesitatingly, suggested that Lia was the only one available and, even though she'd never been on a tour, was very interested. Steve asked her if that was okay with everyone for her to be away and was told of the meeting at Ann's B&B. Steve laughed and laughed and commented again just how much the women in his life guided his life. He was still laughing when he said okay, call him with the time of her arrival. He said that when she arrived he'd meet her at the airport. After being transferred to Larry, Larry advised that he had a too-much-cash problem and was working on somewhere to put it. Steve's calls to Ann and Grace also resulted in his being assured that the kids were fine but missed his jokes and cooking. Ann missed him too and told him that her cooking didn't have the zing that his did. And her bed was cold. Steve, reading between the lines, was slowly coming to see that he was developing feelings for Ann. Shit, he thought, life on the road is so much simpler.

The Price of Success

Chapter Fourteen - Bike Ride #4

What Sharon didn't tell him was that Lia's brilliant idea had been implemented. For that matter, Sharon hadn't told him about Lia's idea at all! By using Steve's new "outside in" analysis approach, Lia had an epiphany. She'd worked out that the entire Saskatoon operation could be rationalized. That would mean that all heavy freight operations should be centered at Douglas and all courier, light truck and local deliveries be assigned to Patterson. Douglas had a more appropriately located warehouse and cross dock with a rail siding, and their equipment was more suited to handling heavy freight. Patterson's warehouse, yard and handling equipment didn't have a rail siding and were better suited and located to handle smaller packages, smaller loads and local deliveries.

While Brian Patterson and Terry Douglas liked the idea, everyone agreed that Quinn Enterprises would have to complete the buyout of both companies before such a major reorganization could proceed. Sharon knew that Steve had tentatively agreed to buy both companies but that the price had not been finalized. She talked to Lia and Cheryl and they arrived at a range of prices they thought would work. Larry confirmed that they had the cash available to spend on the two businesses, and he also agreed that Sharon had the authority to proceed without Steve's explicit approval. And finally, Lia asked Peter Thayer for an outside opinion on the limits of Sharon's financial power. Peter, well aware of the internal dynamics of Quinn, told them that as acting President, she had virtually no limits on her authority.

So Sharon and Lia proceeded. Arriving at a deal with Terry Douglas had gone well, but Brian Patterson was being stubborn. Sharon, finally becoming exasperated, had flown up to Saskatoon with Lia to lay down the law. Either Brian sold at a reasonable price, as he had previously agreed, or the entire deal was off and he would have to deal with a revitalized and refinanced Douglas Terminals. And the first step would be to cut Patterson off from forwarding Rayner freight. Brian's response caught Sharon and Lia off guard. He laughed and told them that he'd heard that Sharon was a ball breaker, and now he believed it. He also saw that Sharon was getting pissed off and, remembering that he'd been told that that was not a good idea, hurriedly continued. He agreed to a fair price and offered to take the women out to supper to celebrate. Lia, privately thanking the gods for Sharon's not going ballistic, agreed. After a moment Sharon laughed quietly and, reaching over, gave Brian a crushing handshake. The deal was done.

Lia hurriedly packed up her bike in the travelling case that Steve had sent back from Vancouver. She washed all her cycling clothes and packed her saddle bags with two changes of outer clothing, plus what she would wear. She also packed her gloves, water bottles, wallet and ID cards including her medical and credit card, plus her sunglasses. She bought a plane ticket and asked Sharon to call Steve and pass on her arrival gate and time. Finally, she decided to simply carry her helmet as hand baggage.

The next day, excited as a little kid, and looking like one with anticipation at the coming adventure, she watched out of the plane's window as Calgary came into view below. At the arrivals gate she didn't see Steve and immediately worried that he wouldn't be there for her. Lia went downstairs to the baggage area and, with a sigh of relief, saw Steve waving at her. She ran down the stairs, rushed over, and he picked her up and hugged her tightly, telling her just how glad he was to see her. Steve apologized for not being upstairs but he couldn't take his bike up there and he couldn't leave it alone down here.

Lia was amazed at his appearance. He'd lost weight, at least 10 lbs. and his face was now finely drawn. The facial scar was noticeable only when he smiled and actually gave him an interesting look. He was also heavily tanned and the muscles on his arms and legs were now sharply defined. He also had the pattern of his cycling gloves tanned on the back of his hands. They retrieved Lia's hard case and reassembled her bike. Steve arranged to have the case returned to Regina while Lia went to the bathroom to change her clothes. When she returned, she was nervous but excited at the prospect of being on the road. Steve showed her on his map where they would ride down the Deerfoot Trail to 16th Ave, the Trans-Canada Hwy. This highway ran right through downtown Calgary; then on to the east side of the city where they would arrive at a motel where they had reservations. Steve suggested that she ride in front, and he would cover the rear. He reminded her to put on her rear-view mirror and keep an eye on him. He also warned her that Calgary was not a bike friendly city, so be bloody careful.

Three hours later they arrived at the motel, both somewhat traffic frazzled and happy to have survived several close calls with rowdy drivers. Steve explained his usual routine of a shower, a hot soak and then washing his riding clothes. He offered her the bathroom first, but she felt that a short three-hour ride warranted only a shower. Lia then took Steve's hands and nervously said, "I know there are two beds but we're going to sleep in only one, aren't we?"

The Price of Success

Steve, caught unware, answered, "Are you sure you want to? Because I'd like that."

Lia, now fully composed, said, "Okay, that's settled. Now for a shower."

Steve, while Lia had her shower, marveled again at these women in his life. One had once again set the rules and the path forward. He shook his head, smiling; they made life look so easy. He checked over the bikes, found a loose cable on Lia's bike and had it adjusted by the time she came from the bathroom. After his shower, as he was soaking in the hot water, Lia came in and sat on the edge of the tub. She was saying see, I can do it too! Steve, realizing that he had been one-upped, laughed and told her to be careful or he would pull her into the tub. She stuck out her tongue and told him to hurry up, she was hungry.

With the tension between them now much diminished, they enjoyed an excellent supper and a celebratory bottle of fine California Chardonnay. Back in the room, Steve set the alarm for 6:30 as the restaurant didn't open until 7:00. They then fell into bed, eager to explore each other. Lia, in complete contrast to Steve's hard hewn chiseled physique, was a perfect tiny doll. Her breasts and waist were marvellously shaped and firm. Steve slipped her on top of him so that she was kneeling on his chest and, holding both of her saucy ass cheeks in his hands, slowly moved her forward. He started gently biting the insides of her thighs and heard her moan as she realized what he was going to do. Steve held her tightly until she was done and then gently laid her down beside him.

When he returned to bed, Lia said softly, "Jesus, Steve, I came so hard it hurt!"

Steve didn't say anything and began to stroke her with his fingers. He leaned over and gently kissed, then sucked her breasts. Lia sunk her hands in his hair again and forced her whole tiny breast into his mouth. With his fingers stroking her, Lia slowly began moving and moaning, finally with another shriek, arched her back off the bed and came again.

Steve slowly let her go and she collapsed like a rag doll. With Lia now lying on her stomach, Steve spread her legs, kneeled between them, lifted her perfect ass up and slid into her. As Lia moaned and thrashed, Steve, being careful not to go too deep, had his own orgasm.

Later, after they had cooled off and were standing in the shower together, Lia said, "Nobody ever did that to me before, making me come more than once. I didn't know I could do that." She hesitated, then said, "I've only ever had two serious relationships and I guess they really weren't that good in bed. I just didn't know; I just didn't know I could do that."

Steve kissed the end of her nose and said, "We better get to bed or you just might see what else can be done."

They both fell asleep in moments and both slept the sleep of the dead. The alarm went off much too soon. In the morning, for several reasons, Lia was sore and stiff; she was going to have to do some stretching before they set off.

After breakfast, as they were donning their cycling clothes, Steve gave her some Lanacaine and suggested she might want to use it on her bum's sit bones and her vagina's lips. He was a little pink as he told her that those areas take a pounding when touring and, with riding day after day, nothing had a chance to heal. And they'd already been well used. Lia laughed and laughed and told him that was one of the things she loved about him, he wasn't afraid to talk about anything. She assured him that she'd already looked after her nether regions and she hoped his were going to be okay too. Steve, still pink, made the mistake of telling her about his butt calluses. Damned if Lia didn't want to feel them. With that, Steve knew they were going to have fun and get along just fine.

Once on the road, heading southeast, they found it was a magnificent day. The temperature was in the low 70s and the gentle wind was from the northwest, a direct tail wind. Steve had to keep getting Lia to slow down, reminding her that it was going to be a long day, with at least 10 hours on the road. The highway, as most Alberta highways are, was smooth with a paved shoulder for cyclists. At one point they came upon a pair of young cyclists stopped for a break, and they too stopped to talk. It turned out that they'd left Calgary that morning very early and were riding to Medicine Hat to attend college. It was obvious that they weren't ready for the trip, nor was their equipment in good shape. However, with the enthusiasm of the young, they thought nothing of it and were having fun.

Steve and Lia had an excellent day, one of the best days Steve had ever had on the road. The sun wasn't too hot, Lia applied sunblock early enough to avoid trouble, and the mild tailwind helped push them right along. One hundred and ten miles later they arrived in Brooks and found a clean motel with an outdoor hot tub. It was Lia's first road century so, after getting cleaned up, they went in and had a celebratory supper. The restaurant being Italian, Steve searched out the proprietor and, explaining the situation, asked him for a bottle of his best Chianti Ruffino. The owner actually had stored away a 25-year-old Ruffino still in its raffia wrapped bottle. Finding out that Lia spoke high level Italian, he gave it to them as a gift. The wine went perfectly with the spaghetti and meatballs, all covered in a fragrant garlic and herb sauce. A soak in the hot tub and they were ready for bed. Lia passed out again the moment her head hit the pillow, and Steve marvelled at this tiny 30-something woman looking just like a little kid in the big bed. Morning again came too early for both of them.

On the first day of the tour Steve had determined that Lia was a "spinner," that is, she liked to pedal at a rapid cadence, as he did. He showed her how to be an even more efficient cyclist by maintaining a steady pedalling speed by constantly shifting gears rather than varying her pedalling rate. Other than her pedalling, Lia was a well-trained cyclist and had obviously put in a lot of time on both the road and a cycle trainer.

The Price of Success

In the morning, Lia was again stiff and sore, and her bum was slightly sore. But she had the sunburn under control and said she felt like she'd lost some weight. Steve wasn't sure from where, but from his own experience he knew that he burned between 6,000 and 8,000 calories each riding day but could eat only about 5,000 calories each day; he simply couldn't eat any more. So he had a net loss of between 1,000 and 3,000 calories each day. Lia wouldn't have that kind of net loss, she was too small, but still, like Steve, would lose some weight every day.

It was going to be another nice day, but the wind had moved around to the northeast. It was still mild but would now mean they'd have to ride with a quartering or sometimes even a side wind. But it was all in a day's riding and they enjoyed the scenery and the silly gophers. With the bikes being so quiet they could ride right up to them before being noticed, and the gophers' antics trying to escape could be hilarious. They also saw a red-tailed hawk stoop on a gopher and then carry it away for its dinner. Riding slowly, they were also able to enjoy the wild roses and other wildflowers that grew in profusion along the highway. Lia was in seventh heaven. She hadn't imagined that the scenery, seen up close from a slow-moving bike, was so superior to that seen from a car. Whenever they stopped she wandered through the ditches marvelling at the roadside biodiversity, something she'd never imagined before. She even discovered that real cactus grew along the highway.

Tonight they'd stay in Medicine Hat, a shorter day's ride of about 65 miles. But with the wind it had been a full eight-hour cycling day. They were happy to see a shower, a good meal, and a wide, soft bed. That night Lia decided to explore Steve, and the feel of her tiny hands stroking and squeezing was a distinct thrill. After she'd cleaned him up, she was able to take him in her mouth. In no time he was hard again and she laughed as she slid back down on him and slowly put him completely inside her. For the first time they came together, then Lia collapsed on top of him.

The next day, Lia had worked through her stiffness, and both of their bums were problem free. Today's goal was Maple Creek, a town in Saskatchewan some eight miles south of the highway. It was only 60 miles away, but the wind had now swung around to the east, so it was going to be a headwind day. Even worse, Hwy #1 traveled down through Walsh, Alberta, right on the Alberta border, one of the windiest places on the prairies. The night before, Steve warned her that they'd have to leave as early as possible in order to get by Walsh before the daily winds fully developed. In the morning with it still dark they were able to find a 24-hour greasy spoon and were on the road just as it was getting light. The highway continued to be in good shape and traffic was light, so the early morning riding was easy. But the wind was building so Steve took the lead to break the wind. They even missed several stops in order to travel as far as possible as early as possible.

At Walsh, which is nothing more than a couple of gas stations and a bar, they stopped for an early lunch and had several large drinks to rehydrate. The wind was tough, but not too rough yet, nor was it too hot. The biggest problem was the violence caused by the passing trucks. The passing cars weren't too bad, but the truck turbulence combined with a headwind was bloody dangerous. Both Lia and Steve rode on the shoulder as far away from the traffic as possible, but still the flying stones, road dirt, turbulence and wind took their toll. Both were very happy to come to the junction of #21 and turn south toward Maple Creek. Here they stayed at a motel Steve remembered from previous trips, and both fell gratefully into a large bathtub full of hot water. They were both covered in road dirt, Steve had some stone cuts and they had fun scrubbing each other clean. Lia started playing with Steve, so Steve began to stroke her anus under the water. From Lia's reaction, no one had done that before, but when Steve stopped, she wanted him to continue. Steve turned her around and was able to stroke her anus, vagina and clit all at once. Lia started to move and shake, splashing water onto the floor, and Steve made her come again so hard she cried out, slipped in the tub and got a face full of water. They were still laughing about it when they sat down to supper.

The next day they experienced the full beauty and emptiness of the Canadian prairies. Their goal was Swift Current, or Speedy Creek as the locals called it, 85 miles down the road. The road now angled northeast by east and passed by some of the driest parts of Saskatchewan. North of the highway was the huge Great Sand Hills Desert, an ecological reserve, home to cactus and unique desert animals. There were no major towns or motels, nor any restaurants along this stretch; they'd have to carry all their supplies, including food and water. Steve found a gallon plastic jug at the restaurant and had it filled with water and juice then, along with a prepackaged lunch, strapped them onto his rear carrier. The restaurant cook asked him why the juice/water mixture and Steve told him that the water would be absorbed faster if it had a bit of sugar in it from the juice. With all the different kinds of water they had to use, it also masked the taste of the worst of them. It also seemed to protect them from getting upset stomachs from the harsh minerals in the water.

Fortunately, the weather had changed overnight with the temperature dropping to the mid-50s with a mild tailwind out of the northwest. With a high overcast, sunburn danger was also reduced to a reasonable level and the empty desert and minimal traffic made for a pleasant day's ride. With the tailwind, in spite of the distance, both of them did well. Lia was fascinated by the desert, the lack of trees and the lack of growing crops or even many cattle. In several places the highway gently climbed a thousand feet or more and the view from the top was amazing. The downhills with a tailwind afforded them time to rest by allowing them to stand up on the pedals and coast. This gave their bums a rest (and a chance to dry out!) and for their bodies to act as sails, pushing them along. Lia, though challenged by having to climb the hills, never complained, and Steve's opinion of her continued to rise. With a bike and load that was nearly as heavy as Steve's, but with her body weight being less than 100 pounds, she had to work harder than he did, but she never slowed them down. Steve was concerned though. She was so small that he worried her body

The Price of Success

wasn't going to have the reserves to continue to do battle with the continuing cycling rigors. He also worried that she really needed more sleep and rest every night in order to rebuild her energy levels. However, she was cheerful and still loved the adventure, so he kept his concerns to himself.

CJ Vermeulen

Chapter Fifteen - Disaster

As Steve and Lia rolled over the prairie roads, Sharon, Truckin' Ted and Cheryl and staff were frantically converting Douglas and Patterson into separate heavy truck and light truck operations. With the full and enthusiastic cooperation of the two companies, the conversion was rolling right along. Sharon's goal was to have both companies operational before Steve returned. She knew that the truck dispatching computer systems, office modifications, new accounting systems, and employee education would not be totally complete when Steve returned, but she was determined to have the company conversions far enough along for it to be a fait accompli.

Secretly she was a little worried that Steve would disapprove of what she'd done. After all, she'd taken control of his company when, up to this point, he'd been the only one to ever make final management decisions. She knew she'd acted within her authority, but she didn't think Steve had quite this in mind when he'd promoted her. After all, she'd spent over half of Quinn's cash reserve! On the other hand, it was a good feeling when everyone had willingly accepted her direction and were busting their collective asses to get the job done. She wondered how Lia was doing. Everyone had gotten used to this perfect, tough, smart, tiny woman being as good as or better than anyone in the company at whatever she did. Lia had even tried to learn to drive a semi-trailer tractor and had nearly wrecked the driver's seat because it couldn't be adjusted far enough forward for her to reach the pedals! But being on the road was different, especially with Steve. As a shot of jealousy coursed through her stomach, she too wondered if they'd figured out how to work with each other. She shrugged. She knew that Betty and particularly Ann both were not too happy with the situation with Steve and Lia, but it was what it was. Meanwhile they all had work to do.

After Steve and Lia arrived at Swift Current and were enjoying a final glass of wine after supper, Steve asked her how she was doing. Lia replied, "Well, that's physically the toughest day that I've had in a long, long time."

"Do you need a day off?"

"Never! Just another good night's sleep! Why?"

"The next stretch is kinda tricky. We can try for Moose Jaw, 110 miles away, or we can stop at Chaplin, about 55 miles away. Now, I know there was a motel in Chaplin, but I've never stayed there. I do know there's an RCMP district office there, with jail cells, so that's an alternative."

Lia, with an astounded look on her face, said, "Jail! I don't want to spend a night in jail!"

Steve laughed uproariously and said, "It usually isn't too bad as long as there're no drunks in with you."

"Are you serious? You've spent time in jail?"

"Well in my errant youth, I rather misbehaved a couple of times." He continued, "On Friday nights we used to take the train from Winnipeg out to Grand Beach for the weekend and, once there, get someone to buy us a case of beer. Then we'd hike way down the beach, set up camp in the dunes and have a party. Then on Sunday afternoon we'd stagger back to the train station. Sometimes, though, the RCMP patrolled the dunes and would catch us. Then we got thrown in jail for the rest of the weekend until it was train time."

"That's awful!"

"Well, in those days it was considered just part of the game. The cops wouldn't charge you if you behaved, and everybody was happy. It was actually considered a badge of honour if you'd spent time in the Grand Beach jail."

Lia just sat there, staring at him. Steve changed the subject and explained that tomorrow's weather forecast was kind of iffy. There was a possibility of rain with hail and gusting winds, although the wind would continue to be a tailwind. From personal experience he didn't want to get caught on the road in bad weather, especially hail, because it could hurt. Further, the country was rather bare and empty of places to take shelter if they did get caught. There weren't even any overpasses to get under if it hailed. If she agreed, he suggested they head out in the morning and see what developed. If the weather closed in they would stop in Chaplin, but if all was going well, particularly with a strong tailwind, they'd try for Moose Jaw. If they got caught after Chaplin, they could always stay at Caron Port, 20 miles this side of Moose Jaw. If they got up in the morning to rain, they would just go back to bed. Lia wriggled and said she liked that idea!

After a good night's sleep they woke to a cool, strong wind from the west and low overcast skies. It hadn't rained and the forecast hadn't changed, so away they went. Immediately they found the going was challenging. At their usual riding speed of 15 mph the wind was allowing them to roll along easily while not giving them enough of a breeze to cool off. Steve stopped and suggested that Lia lead and get up into the highest gear she felt comfortable with. If she could manage, she should make her speed just slightly faster than the tailwind. This would maximize the wind advantage while giving them a slight cooling breeze. He would follow but at a distance of 10 yards or so, so as to not block her tailwind. He told her that she'd control their progress by selecting the speed and stopping when she needed to stop; he'd follow her lead. He reminded her of the number one bike touring rule, "Don't waste the wind!" With a look of determination on her face, Lia quickly got them up to a respectable 25 mph, and from what Steve could see, she was quite comfortable. The odd gust pushed her around, but it did that to Steve as well. At the first stop, Lia was exhilarated. The wind and the speed were exciting and she wanted to keep rolling. After a quick pee they both rolled away again. At the two-hour stop they could see Chaplin in the distance, but the weather hadn't deteriorated, so they carried on. Four and a half hours later they'd passed Caron Port and had clicked off another century, one of the fastest Steve had ever accomplished. Lia, though now tiring, loved it. It was one of the most exciting days in her life.

And then trouble. An RCMP highway cruiser coming up behind them blipped its siren, pulled past them, stopped, and the officer waved them down. He told them that a tornado warning had been issued and they'd better get off the road. That was a problem; there was nowhere to go. They could go back to Caron Port which, with the headwind, would be nearly impossible. The officer offered to take them there in his cruiser. But Steve, looking at Lia for confirmation, said they were only about 15 miles from Moose Jaw, where they'd intended to stay the night. He told the officer that at the speed they were going, they'd be there in less than half an hour. If it looked like a tornado was imminent, they'd get off the road and down into the ditch. The officer wasn't happy, but agreed. Remounting their bikes, Steve and Lia, each keeping one eye on the sky, headed for Moose Jaw as fast as they could go.

Now Lia pulled out all the stops. She quickly got back up to 25 mph, then slowly cranked it up. Steve could see that she was in her highest gear now, rocking from side to side with the effort of pedalling. For the first time she was also using her arms and upper body to pull on the handlebars for added pedalling power. Steve again thought that whoever had taught her to ride had known what they were doing. Soon they were rocketing along at over 35 mph and Steve marvelled at Lia's guts and determination. At these speeds the wind was a bitch, and hitting highway potholes and stones was bloody dangerous. But Lia didn't quit. Even when a passing truck got a little too close, she gave it the finger. In minutes they could see the motel they wanted and Lia, boldly slicing across three lanes of traffic, coasted into the parking lot. While someone held open the front door, they rode right inside to the front desk.

Lia had given it her all. Her face was white, her breathing a ragged rasp, and if Steve hadn't caught her she would have fallen off the bike. He could hear her wrist-mounted heart rate monitor madly beeping, flashing red, and her pulse was well over 190 bpm. Her body was so starved for oxygen that she complained between gulps of air that she couldn't see properly.

Steve, who was on his own ragged edge, laid her down while he watched her heart rate monitor. As it slowed down he told her that it was okay, her eyesight would return. He'd been there himself many times when racing and all it meant was that her body was shutting down for lack of oxygen. It wouldn't harm her as long as her pulse started to slow down as soon as she quit, and it was slowing down. The front desk clerk, alarmed at the sudden intrusion of two dirty, disheveled, falling-down riders, wanted to call a doctor, but in moments Lia, still shaky, was sitting up and embarrassed at the commotion she'd caused. They checked in and had just started down the hallway toward their room when the storm hit. The desk clerk called Steve back and made sure they knew where the motel's mandatory storm-proof room was. He said the signal was three short blasts of the fire alarm. Steve thanked him and checked out the storm room. They then went and found their room and were thankful for showers and a tub soak.

The motel had been built in a triangle, with the front leg built around a heavily reinforced center section and the other legs enclosing the swimming pool and kid's playground. Their room was just four doors down from the front desk and the storm room was behind the front desk, so from their room they could reach the storm room in seconds. The raging storm, being a prairie storm, was accompanied by brilliant lightening, building-shaking thunder and heavy, gusty winds. After their shower, Steve, who'd been feeling increasingly apprehensive, suggested they get organized for a quick evacuation. They hung up their cycling clothes unwashed to let the sweat dry and put on their track suits. Everything else was repacked and reloaded on the bikes. After such a rough ride, Steve checked the bikes over very carefully but found no damage. Then they took their water bottles and headed down the hall to the restaurant. And were surprised at the crowded lobby. Apparently several tour buses, also concerned about the weather, had made an unplanned stop at the motel. Steve and Lia were glad they'd managed to get into the dining room ahead of the large crowd. They had another pasta supper, this time lasagna with a triple cheese sauce with garlic Italian bread. Meanwhile the storm did not diminish and, if anything, was getting worse, with the occasional power flicker. Later in their room they watched TV which had a continuous text overlay warning about the tornadoes; they were getting closer. Steve suggested they wear their track suits to bed and place their shoes, helmets and gloves right beside the bikes. They were asleep by 7:30.

At 3:30 a.m. the fire alarm went off, scaring the crap out of them. Groggy, they still managed to be among the first to get themselves and their bikes into the storm room. Cramming themselves into a far corner behind a steel support pole, Steve made sure everything was still secure on the bikes. Then they put on their helmets and gloves, tightened the Velcro straps on their shoes' and wedged themselves in ⸺ort pole. They could do nothing more except wait.

⸺ts they could hear an increasingly loud roar and the room began ⸺ginal warning, only about a third of the motel guests had bothered

The Price of Success

to get up and come to the weather proof lobby. Now with the fire alarm continuously shrieking, the tornado roaring ever louder and the building trembling, the panicked tourists started to stream down the hallways toward the lobby. But it was too late. With a deafening roar the tornado ripped into the west corner of the front wing, demolishing the west wing. It then smashed its way through the front wing and tore into the east wing. Screaming bodies and deadly wreckage filled the air, then the lights went out. No one had managed to close the storm room door. With the air pressure wildly fluctuating, the heavy steel door swung madly back and forth. Some tourists trying to get into the room were injured by the deadly door until the wind finally slammed the door shut. But it was too late even for some of those that had made it into the room. They'd been smashed to a pulp by the door and were little more than a red smear on the floor. Steve crouched over Lia in their corner and fought the suction until the wind finally smashed the door closed.

Moments later, the storm had passed and the motel was dark and silent. Steve dug out his small travelling flashlight, crawled over whimpering bodies and pried open the door. He was shocked to see bloody bodies and wreckage piled everywhere with the air full of plaster dust. The reinforced lobby area had survived, but the roof and foyer were badly damaged. The rest of the motel, now open to the rain, was just lumber, clothing, smashed furniture and more bodies. In the parking lot the tour buses had disappeared, crushed like pop cans and had actually been lifted and thrown over the motel into the swimming pool. As often happened in tornadoes, the pool had been sucked dry of water. Water fountained from broken pipes, and Steve smelled natural gas. To get out they had to crawl over the wreckage, dragging their bikes while trying to avoid debris still falling from the ceiling. All the while crawling over or pushing bodies and body parts out of the way. It reminded Steve of videos he'd seen of the carnage a car bomb could cause in a crowded market. By the time they'd gotten to the motel entrance, both were covered in plaster dust and other people's blood and Lia was in shock. Around them in the growing light, tourists wandered like ghosts, also covered in plaster dust, bleeding but seemingly oblivious to their injuries. From what was left of the motel came the screams and moaning of the trapped and dying.

Moose Jaw had taken a direct hit from a Category 4 tornado. The air force base on the city's west side had also taken a direct hit and dozens of planes were damaged. Hundreds of homes had been destroyed in the surrounding suburbs and the city's old classical business section simply didn't exist anymore. Even the highway itself had been sucked up by the winds and miles of it were just broken concrete, covered with torn up trees and building wreckage. Broken and smashed vehicles were everywhere. Broken city water lines and natural gas pipes were spewing their contents into the air. It was going to be only minutes before the gas ignited and Moose Jaw burned.

Steve had a tough decision to make. Did they stay and get in the way of the rescuers, or should they try to escape down the road to Regina? Lia, badly shaken, sleep deprived and dazed, had stopped talking. He realized that she was in no condition to help anyone and neither was he trained to assist the injured. Besides, he couldn't help with the coming fires. He also knew the airbase personnel would soon organize a rescue effort and didn't need him. He decided they would go. Even though both of them had not had enough sleep, or drink and they were still suffering from the previous day's prodigious energy output. They hadn't had enough to eat, not even getting any breakfast. And the biggest issue: they didn't have enough juice in their water bottles. It didn't matter, they had to go, even if it was just to escape the coming gas fires. It was just getting light, the rain was tapering off and the sky was clearing as they worked their way through the parking lot wreckage toward the highway.

The Price of Success

Chapter Sixteen - The Struggle Home

Meanwhile in Regina, tornado warnings were also sounding. The line of storms was headed toward Regina but the weather service was predicting they would soon turn north and miss the heavily populated parts of the city. Truckin' Ted, who'd stayed in his second-floor office for the night to handle a late critical hospital shipment, called Sharon for advice. She told him to pull all the heavy curtains over the windows, then get into the corner of his second-floor office and stay there. She wasn't too concerned about the building's ability to withstand a fierce storm; after all, it had been built to hold farm machinery. She told him she would come down as soon as the storm passed.

Her real concern was for Lia and Steve. She'd heard on the radio that Moose Jaw had taken a major hit and knew they could be in the storm's vicinity. But there was nothing she could do until the storm passed. She had faith that Steve would keep them safe, but even he couldn't beat a tornado. Access to the area would be restricted so she couldn't even send a crew to look for them. Along with thousands of others she'd just have to wait for news. After the storm had passed north of the city, she went down to the office and helped Ted mount plywood over two hail damaged windows. He hadn't heard from the riders either.

It took four hours for the riders to travel the broken roads to get within sight of Regina. It was a brutal ride with broken pavement, a gusty tailwind, rain, broken tree branches and crashed vehicles. Lia was still silent and operating as an automaton. Steve was very worried about her, but she would answer questions and follow directions, so they just continued on. Three miles from the junction of Hwy #6 and Albert St, Regina's main drag, another disaster. Steve, riding behind Lia, was clipped by a pickup truck dodging a downed tree and was sent flying. Lia, when she turned to look, hit a pothole and was dumped into the gravel. The truck kept going and traffic was so light that no one saw the accident or stopped to help.

Steve landed on his side and skidded into the ditch. His shirt and shorts were ripped and he collected a huge patch of road rash across his shoulder, back and butt.

The Price of Success

Lia hit the ground head first and also tore up her clothes. Her helmet took a heavy hit but saved her head and face. She too collected an impressive patch of road rash across her hip and right leg. They both lay there for a moment, stunned, then Steve rolled over and crawled over to Lia. She was dazed, but conscious and trying to stand up. Steve checked her over and didn't find any broken bones or bleeding from her head in spite of her broken helmet. She was bleeding but, like his own injuries, was not running with blood. It was simply oozing out and slowly running down her legs. He staggered up, checked their bikes and found them remarkably undamaged. He checked the loads and had to tighten a strap, but they too were okay. He guessed the truck had hit him, rather than the bike, and hoped he didn't have any hidden injuries.

Steve looked around to see where they were. He judged they had another three miles to go before he could use the phone he knew was in the gas station at the junction. He asked Lia if she could ride and, when she nodded, helped her up onto her bike. He pointed her down the highway and then climbed onto his own bike and wobbled after her. They rode down the highway to the gas station and it's inside phone. The station attendant was horrified at the mess that had just staggered into his store. Steve told him to shut the fuck up as he sat Lia on the floor, leaning her against the counter and called Sharon for help. She was happy to finally hear from him until he told her he needed a light truck at the junction for their bikes and a ride to the hospital. Sharon nearly panicked when she heard they were hurt but quickly organized a truck and said she'd meet them at the hospital. When the truck arrived, Steve, with the driver's help, put the bikes in the back and then the driver helped Lia and Steve climb into the truck's bed. Steve wouldn't sit in the front saying he would ruin the upholstery with his bleeding and, besides, he had to hold Lia.

At the hospital emergency entrance, Steve picked Lia up from the truck bed and headed for the ER doors. Sharon, who had been waiting and watching, when she saw how battered they were, began screaming for help. With both of them covered in blood, gravel, and dirt, Steve carried Lia into the emergency department. Sharon, still yelling for help, held the door open and instantly ER interns came running with a gurney. Steve gently laid Lia on the stretcher and watched her be rushed into a treatment room. With Sharon's help Steve made it through the next set of ER doors when he stopped, leaned on the wall and, leaving a smear of blood and dirt, slowly sank to the floor. The last thing he heard was Sharon again yelling at the top of her lungs at the interns to hurry, hurry, hurry. After the interns had rolled Steve onto another stretcher, Sharon remembered the truck. She told the driver to take the bikes to Steve's apartment and to charge the company for a truck wash.

After a few seconds, when he regained consciousness, Steve insisted they not bandage Lia's or his cuts and scrapes, instead after digging out the dirt and gravel, they must use PlastiSkin on both of them. If they used PlastiSkin, he explained, the scars would be minimized. Doctor Allenby, who was treating them, was a cyclist and knew just what PlastiSkin was and how to use it. Unfortunately, the ER didn't have any in stock so Sharon called the courier office.

When the phone was answered she said, "This is Two. Dispatch."

The dispatcher who knew Sharon was at the hospital, asked, "How is One?"

Sharon ignored the query and asked, "Who's on standby?"

The dispatcher looked up and said, "56."

Sharon said, "Give her $50 and have her go to the nearest drug store and buy six, or as many spray cans as she can get, of PlastiSkin. If she delivers them to the Regina ER within 15 minutes, I'll give her a $100."

The dispatcher said, "Done."

Fourteen minutes later the PlastiSkin arrived. Sharon dug out her wallet and gave 56 two $50 bills. She then rushed down the hall and turned the cans over to the charge nurse. When Sharon returned to the waiting room, 56 asked how One and Lia were. Sharon replied that she didn't know, but that both of them were still alive. 56 went back to her car and, with a heavy heart, returned to being on standby.

Sharon, taking a deep breath and returning to work mode, called Betty. She told Betty to make a general notice and distribute it companywide that Steve and Lia were in the hospital, badly hurt. Further notices would come as soon as they knew their condition. She then called Ann, and Ann immediately dropped everything and headed for the hospital. Then Grace. She asked her to break the news to the kids but to reassure the kids that their dad was going to be okay, he had just had another bike accident. Then she called the Barchetti law office. She told Toni that Lia was hurt, in hospital, and would he please call Frank and tell him that Lia had had a bike accident.

What Sharon had missed was a TV videographer standing on the hospital steps. The cameraman caught the photo and video of his life; Steve covered in dirt and blood, clothes torn all to hell, carrying Lia with her broken helmet and dripping blood, into the hospital. The video ended with Steve slowly slumping to the floor, leaving the grisly smear on the ER wall. From the anguished expression on Steve's face in the video, it was clear that he was on his last legs, operating on sheer guts and determination. The reporter assigned to the cameraman immediately recognized Steve and Sharon and in minutes the TV station had its day's lead story. The photo eventually went on to win the highest awards the national media association could give it. In the days following, as details of Steve and Lia's adventure and miraculous survival came to light, the story went viral and TV stations across Canada aired the photo, video and their incredible survival story.

Several hours later, the ER head nurse come out, gave Sharon their torn bloody clothes and suggested Ann and Sharon go home and come back tomorrow. In spite of the significant damage to their bodies, Steve and Lia would live. They'd been heavily sedated and would not be able to see anyone until tomorrow. Ann and Sharon went back to Steve's place, where Ann made supper while Sharon had a

The Price of Success

shower to remove the blood and dirt. Sharon, needing something to wear, swiped one of Steve's sweat suits. She then unpacked Steve's and Lia's saddle bags and threw all the clothes into the wash. They had supper, had a bottle of Steve's expensive Italian wine and talked until nearly midnight. Ann insisted that Sharon take Steve's bed while she crashed in one of the other bedrooms.

In the morning Sharon went to work and Ann went to the hospital. She looked up Doctor Allenby and introduced herself. Allenby though, not recognizing either Ann or her name, brushed her off. The brush off triggered the stress she had so far kept under control, and she exploded. She called the hospital Chairman of the Board and asked him to make a call. Since the chairman was also a psychiatrist and very familiar with Ann's history and work, the phone call was short and to the point. When Ann went back to his office, Allenby apologized profusely. The last thing he needed was a problem with the chairman!

Ann then told him to sit down and listen carefully. She explained Steve's enormous intellect and wide range of abilities. And her concerns for his mental state when he was allowed to regain consciousness. She insisted she be there when he came around. And Lia too for that matter. He simply must not be allowed to become agitated, as she didn't know how much of his own condition he understood. Lia had so terribly stressed herself that, combined with her concussion, made her mental health also very fragile. Finished, Ann told Allenby that as a safeguard she was moving into Steve's room. Lia was to be moved into his room as well. At the look on Allenby's face, she asked sweetly if she was going to have to make another call.

At the office Sharon had a continuous series of phone calls and visitors asking about Steve. The TV news last night and today's hourly media updates, as more and more of the story was discovered, were making Steve and Lia notorious. Particularly when it was announced that at the motel alone, 37 had died and 116 were injured, and the toll in Moose Jaw so far was 254 deaths and climbing. One peculiarity was the complete disappearance of one of the bus drivers. In spite of a wide area search for bodies, where six bodies were found scattered in the surrounding fields, no trace of him was ever found.

CJ Vermeulen

Chapter Seventeen - Recovery and Reorganization

Sharon finally escaped to the second floor and directed the Saskatoon integration and reorganization from Truckin' Ted's office. And it was going well. The speed of deliveries had improved with fewer hands involved in the deliveries, and that meant happy customers. Drivers and staff were also happier with the separation of the big and small trucks. The results achieved in Regina by the vehicle separation was mirrored in Saskatoon. The heavy trucks didn't have to forever try to get around the light trucks, and the light truck and courier vehicles didn't have to forever avoid getting run over. The cross docks, now each handling only similar sized shipments, were also more efficient. Cheryl's staff was well into building and installing the new computer systems, and Larry's staff had the new accounting and billing system under control. Truckin' Ted had visited most of the new northern clients and discovered no serious problems. But he and Sharon both had reservations about the overall organization structure. Sharon had some ideas, but they would have to wait until Lia and Steve returned. The computer division issue also remained unresolved.

A day later when Ann returned from lunch, she found a very groggy Steve sitting up, arguing with an intern and trying to remove an intravenous line. She interrupted his efforts and discovered that, while still very groggy, he just really wanted to get up and have a pee, and a poop. Like anyone lying in bed, having a nature call in bed was not something he enjoyed. Ann helped him remove the line and, carefully holding his arm, helped him to stand. With an intern's help she walked him to the bathroom, and when he assured her that he could manage, left him to it. When he was done Steve was ready to get dressed and leave. Here Ann had an argument. She finally persuaded him that since he couldn't walk without help, he wasn't ready to go home. Later in the afternoon Lia had been judged well enough to be taken off the sedatives and slowly regained consciousness. With Steve sitting beside Lia holding her hand, Ann slowly talked her back to full awareness. Over the next few hours, Steve and Ann walked a panicky Lia through what had happened and discussed her injuries. Lia slowly relaxed as she correlated Ann's words with her own memories and realized that she owed Steve her life.

The next day Ann asked Sharon to arrange a full-time nurse for Steve and Lia. Dr. Allenby approved their discharge as long as Ann promised to watch over them. He then thanked her for her help and apologized again for his unwarranted behavior. He continued that he had researched her work and had no idea that such progress had been made in her field. With Sharon's help, Ann moved them both to Steve's apartment. She and Lia had discussed where she could live while she recovered and had come to the conclusion that she couldn't live at her apartment or with her father. And her brothers' homes were full of kids, noise, confusion, and cats she didn't like. Besides, being close to work would get her brain going again, and the business did need her.

The next day while Lia slept, Steve returned to work. That is, he slowly limped down the hall to his office where he found Betty waiting for him. Steve knew instantly that something was very wrong. He closed the door and they moved over to sit on the couch with fresh coffees. Betty took a deep breath and told Steve she wanted to leave. Her parents in Calgary were ill, which Steve knew, and Betty said that it was now time for her to go and look after them. Steve didn't say anything. Running his hands through his hair, he knew there was nothing to say.

He asked, "When do you want to leave?"

She looked at him in surprise, and said, "No argument?"

"Betty," he said, "I know you. You're dead serious so I'm not going to be a jerk about trying to change your mind. Even though I want to chain your foot to the floor! When to you want to leave?"

"Tomorrow."

Betty stood up and Steve hugged her, very tightly. He said, "You know that there will always be a place here for you."

Betty nodded and, crying, left for her own office.

Steve then went to Larry's office to see how the bank looked. Larry was pleased with the company's cash position, even with the Saskatoon purchases. Steve asked, "What purchases?"

Just then Sharon, having heard that Steve was about, popped her head into Larry's office and saw a strange look on his face.

"Ahhh, Sharon, did you tell Steve about Saskatoon?"

Sharon came in, sat down, and said, "Ah fuck."

She looked Steve right in the eye and, taking a deep breath, said, "I bought the rest of Douglas, and all of Patterson. Lia then had the brilliant idea of making Douglas the exclusive northern heavy truck operation and Patterson the exclusive light truck and courier operation. So we reorganized them and it's working like a charm. Cheryl has been working like a dog to get the personnel, billing and accounting systems up, running and integrated. And all the employees are being

The Price of Success

trained now. Lia did all the legal work before she left and Peter double checked everything."

Steve said, "And she didn't say a word!" With admiration in his voice he continued, "That sneaky little broad!"

Turning to Sharon, he said, "How much did you spend?"

Sharon looked at Larry and he said, "About $650,000 so far, and maybe another $40,000 to finish relabelling the trucks, buy uniforms and develop new packaging. A little more than half of our cash."

Steve thought for a minute, shrugged and said, "Anything else?"

"We have to talk about two more issues. The first is creating a computer division. Lia, Betty and I have talked about it, but we need your input. The other thing is the company organization. We need to talk about that and decide where we want to go."

"And," Steve said, "That brings up a problem. Betty quit this morning, effective tomorrow." He looked at Larry and said, "Write a cheque for six months' salary for her and give it to me. And make sure you get her Calgary address so you can send her the yearend bonus."

Sharon and Larry were shocked speechless. Sharon finally said, "What the fuck happened? We can't lose her! Jesus H Christ!" She jumped up and smacked Steve on the shoulder. "You didn't try to change her mind? Fucking Christ, we need that woman, she can't leave!"

Steve defensively raised his arm and in a quiet monotone, said, "Her parents are very ill and she has to go back and look after them. I've told her that she has a job here if she ever wants to return. I don't want anyone trying to talk her out of it. I mean that. We respect her decision."

Sharon and Larry looked at Steve in silence. They hadn't heard him lay down the law like that, ever. They nodded silently. Then he turned to Sharon and said quietly, again in a deadly monotone, "Don't hit me again, I don't like it."

Sharon's face went white. She'd never heard that tone from him before and instantly recalled what Ann had said when she grabbed his shirt after he'd attacked Rusty.

He turned to look at Larry and said in the same dead voice, "I want that cheque ASAP."

Steve got up, limped out and took the elevator down to the street. He then found his corner seat in the restaurant, ordered a coffee and a shot of Bourbon and stared out at the passing traffic. He was dead quiet and Luigi called Sharon to ask if he was okay. Sharon said, "Luigi, for Christ's sake, stay away from him. Don't talk to him and try to keep your other customers away too. Please just leave him alone. I'll be down in a few minutes."

A short while later, Sharon came down. She stood beside him until she was sure that he knew she was there. "I'm sorry, Steve. I shouldn't have hit you. I guess I'm in shock about Betty."

Steve sighed. "I'm sorry too Sharon, I should never have talked to you like that. He turned to look at her, "Will you forgive me?"

Sharon sat down beside him and, crying, held his hand. She couldn't speak, she just nodded. A few minutes later they walked back upstairs hand in hand.

An hour later Steve tracked down Betty and gave her the cheque. Betty tried to refuse, but Steve told her he would put it down her bra if she didn't take it. A funny look flickered over her face before she took it, and she hugged him again.

The Price of Success

Chapter Eighteen - More Family Additions

Five days later Steve invited Grace and the kids for supper, even though his injuries were still very painful. He sent the nurse home for the weekend and made sure Lia was up to a visit from the kids. She was tired, but her headache was gone and the PlastiSkin had started to peel off. The road rash was infection free and looked smooth and scar free. Steve made a big pot of carbonara with lots of garlic. He also cut up some pork chops into small pieces and cooked them right in the sauce. With some bottles of his good Italian wine, it was a superb supper. Even Skip liked it.

Earlier Grace had asked him if he'd ever met Samara's boyfriend or Sergio's new girlfriend. He hadn't, and expressed his surprise at Sergio having a girlfriend. He thought that the good-looking Sergio, so aggressive on his bike but so shy with girls, would always be a bachelor. Grace laughed and told him that it took an aggressive girl to see what kind of guy he was and to take charge of their relationship. And one had found him. Grace said she rather liked her; she was mature beyond her years. Grace suggested that both Samara's and Sergio's partners be invited to the supper. Steve agreed without an argument.

Grace also asked him if he had had "the talk" with Shaun and Sergio. Steve told her not yet, but did Shaun need it now? Grace told him that he was a real charmer and the girls were already coming to the house in pairs to see him. She suggested he do it soon.

Supper went very well. Sergio's friend Penny was a cheerful friendly sort who immediately tried to pitch in and help with supper. She was impressed when she found out just how good a cook Steve was. She quickly made friends with Lia, and again was impressed and amazed when Sergio told her that Lia was a lawyer and worked for his dad. Samara's boyfriend, Micky, was quiet and rather withdrawn. But Grace had told Steve not to be misled; she'd seen him easily withstand Samara's aggressiveness, and he wouldn't be easily pushed around. Grace added that he was probably quiet tonight because he was in awe of him. She told him that to a 20-

The Price of Success

something male, Steve was a very commanding figure. Not only was he physically imposing, he was Samara's father, and in spite of being hurt he exuded a tough, unbendable aura. To any male, of any age, Steve was a perceived threat.

But the funniest part of the evening was when Samara told her dad that she'd overheard Grace suggesting that Steve have "the talk" with the boys. Samara told him not to worry, she'd already done it!

Steve said, "You did what!"

"Relax, Dad, it was no big deal. I just remembered what you said to me and changed it around. Anyway, I figured it wasn't Grace's job and I didn't know when you'd have time, so I just went ahead."

"And how did the boys take it?"

"Fine! I think they, especially Sergio, were actually trying to figure out how to bring the subject up. With the girls being so forward now, they needed to know what it was all about. And you needn't have that look on your face. You can forget about it, it's all under control."

Steve stood there just looking at Samara. Finally, shaking his head, and giving her a hug, he said, "Thank you."

Samara, now with a troubled look on her face, continued, "Have you seen Mum lately? I understand that she's now blaming Sharon for your marriage breakup."

Steve turned toward her and said, "That's foolish. Your mother arranged all that trouble by herself; I didn't deliberately break us up."

Samara said, "Actually I think it's mostly Ted's fault. Whenever he would talk about Sharon and Betty being so hot, she'd get upset and jealous. You know just how bad her temper is. I've overheard her talking to her friends last week about your harem and how she'd like to shoot them all!"

"Shoot them? She doesn't even know how to handle a gun."

Samara said, "I hope not."

After supper, with Lia getting tired, Grace took the kids home.

The next day the nurse was back and suggested it was time to remove the PlastiSkin. Working on Steve first, she slowly peeled the plastic film away. Except for a small patch on one shoulder, the skin was healed and scar free. The nurse sprayed the one small patch and rubbed skin cream into the rest of the uncovered area. The nurse told him he had the most interesting back she'd seen in a long time. The bike racing damage, the road rash and scars from other old accidents made quite a pattern on him. Then it was Lia's turn. She hadn't been as badly torn up as Steve and the PlastiSkin came off fairly easily. She too had a rubdown. But the nurse wouldn't let her return to work. Steve agreed. Lia was still underweight, not back to her normal feisty self, and her head still occasionally throbbed. The fact that Lia didn't argue very much sealed the deal.

This was also the first week without Betty. As the week progressed, her absence grew more and more noticeable. Steve, while he'd thought about replacing her, hadn't settled on anyone. When Sharon came to have a coffee with him late in the day and suggested that Lia be promoted into Betty's slot, Steve was surprised. But he soon saw the merits of the move. He added that perhaps we should consider her promotion to be temporary. With the continuous growth of the company and the existing problems with the company organization, they prolly could use her legal skills elsewhere. Sharon didn't argue; she could see that with the continued growth, Steve was right. Also, Lia in Betty's old position would see more of the company structure and its management requirements. Sharon also had the nagging feeling that company growth was getting ahead of their management abilities and that, she knew, could be disastrous.

Steve suggested that if Lia had a full-time position with Quinn then she should get Peter appointed as the full-time company external counsel, replacing Barchetti LLP. Steve agreed and asked her to call Peter and get the change underway.

Later that afternoon, Steve went to visit the high end jewellery shop they owned. With the manager's help, he picked out an opal, emerald, and diamond necklace for Sharon. Just before she left for the day, Steve gave her the small package and told her she couldn't open it until she was home. Sharon, who had grown up in a large, happy, but poor family, never had had anyone give her an expensive gift. She literally didn't know what to do. After almost refusing the necklace, she thanked Steve over and over again. She didn't have a clue as to what it was worth, but correctly surmised that if Steve bought it, it wasn't cheap. In fact it had cost over $9000 wholesale. The next time they went out, she wore it and discovered that it was from a well-known estate sale. She was the envy of every woman at the gathering, plus having Steve as her escort!

The Price of Success

CJ Vermeulen

Chapter Nineteen - It All Starts to Come Together

Three months later, the company had grown used to Lia taking Betty's place, and the northern operations were rolling right along. Steve and Sharon had decided that they shouldn't treat the north as a separate division, rather that they should keep the management of all the heavy trucking and courier companies together. This meant combining all the heavy trucking into Rayner Freight Lines with Truckin' Ted as the manager and all the courier/light truck/local delivery into City Express with Brian Patterson as the manager. This would also solve the problem of the current manager of City Express, who just hadn't worked out. Cheryl had returned from an extended vacation and was busy bringing all the reporting systems in all the now 31-odd companies into one single format. This would make Larry's job so much easier.

They'd thoroughly investigated the idea of an in-house computer services division and decided that they needed one. Steve had finally had time to investigate just what modern computers could do, and was enthusiastically pushing the idea forward. He could clearly see that they were the future of being able to manage what would certainly be a much larger and diverse company. As well the current piecemeal approach to the simple current computer services simply didn't work. Cheryl was in favour of buying a computer services company because this would also give her access to more analysts. Steve had given her permission to search, and Cheryl and Lia had been looking and had been talking to banks, credit unions and even some friendly lawyers. Finally they'd found a large enough company based in Saskatoon where the owners wanted to retire. Cheryl and Lia had been working the problem and were close to offering the owners a deal.

Steve continued on a regular basis, to have the kids visit him in the apartment. He was also getting to know Micky and Penny and approved of both of them. Samara and Micky had arranged a supper at a downtown hotel with Micky's parents, and Steve found his father to be a high ranking RCMP officer, based in the Regina Training Depot. He of course knew who Steve and Sharon were and was pleased to meet them in person. His mother was a cosmetic surgeon and suggested that she could easily fix Steve's facial scar, but Steve declined. He softened the decline by pointing out that the scar helped him keep the kids in line! Penny and Sergio had insisted on taking Steve and Sharon to supper at Penny's house and the meeting with Penny's parents had gone well. It turned out that Penny's parents were concerned over the apparent chaotic organization of Steve's family and insisted on meeting him to see for themselves what she'd gotten into. Penny's family were Mennonites, although they were not strict about it. They also did not approve of Sharon and Steve's relationship, but Penny had talked them into at least meeting them. Their household was always organized, quiet and industrious. Penny wanted to be free of the religious life restrictions and wanted to go to university to be an engineer. While the parents weren't happy with Steve and Sharon's encouragement, they quickly saw that in Steve's family, Penny had found a home and was a happy camper.

Shaun always had a different girl in tow (and sometimes two!) and they were still young enough to be bubble-heads, but they were tolerable. Skip and Billy usually behaved themselves better than the older kids! It was getting expensive to take the crew out for supper every weekend, but Steve, Grace, Sharon and occasionally Ann enjoyed being part of the sometimes rowdy gatherings. Samara and Grace though, were now both becoming more concerned about Claire. Steve's big Mercedes had been "keyed" while outside Grace's house, and Sharon and Cheryl had both reported getting harassing phone calls.

Larry had also been working a problem. He, as Steve's personal accountant, wanted Steve to start building up a formal personal financial structure. The company, thanks to business sales, had millions in cash in the bank, and every month the businesses were generating tens of thousands more. Larry introduced Steve to several bank-based financial managers and personal wealth managers but Steve decided in the beginning to spread out the money across the banks. Larry so far had been able to move more than a million dollars into Steve's personal financial structure at the lowest tax rate possible, and there was a lot more to go. Larry also was working on an improved financial structure for Quinn Enterprises. Having millions in the bank sitting in savings accounts was a waste of money. Basically he wanted only as much money in Quinn as was required for operations, with a small reserve. Steve should have the rest in his accounts. If the company needed funds, they could always borrow them from a willing bank, with Steve's estate as the collateral.

Steve's apartment was finished with all his artwork hung. He'd spent a great deal of time with the interior designer in order to get his display of Eskimo art exactly right. He'd installed a large TV in his home office and a monster surround sound system in the living room. Gabriel Abetteli, the building architect, had his designer work closely with Steve, and they both liked the end result. Even conservative Sharon liked it, and the kids enjoyed giving Steve a rough time about his taste in furniture. Steve had broached the subject of the kids leaving Grace's and moving to the apartment but, surprisingly, the biggest objection came from Grace. She liked having the kids around and wanted Steve to continue his occasional late-night stays. Grace had also become a good friend to Samara, something Samara needed. Sergio enjoyed being mothered by Grace, even though he spent a lot of time at Steve's apartment. So that arrangement continued, and everyone kept a weather eye out for Claire. More than once Steve thought he was being followed when he left Grace's place after a late night. Even Sergio reported that Claire had accosted him on the street in front of Steve's office building, yelling at him to be aware of the she-devils working upstairs. Claire still lived in her house, but it was looking more and more run down. She was not looking good either, was very skinny and unkempt, and Ted had moved elsewhere.

Another three months passed very quickly. Samara had graduated from university and had gotten herself a position working as an accountant for a local car dealership, and Sergio and Shaun now both had part time jobs at Rayner Freight Lines. Sharon and Lia had effectively divided up the company between them and jointly handled the day to day operations. Truckin' Ted and Brian Patterson had worked out how to get the two divisions to cooperate and to share facilities and customers. Rayner Freight Lines, with its new acquisitions, was now the dominant heavy truck carrier in Saskatchewan and had additional terminals in Manitoba and Alberta. Cheryl and Truckin' Ted were looking for more local heavy freight companies in those provinces that were for sale or in operational trouble. City Express had grown into the largest privately-owned courier company in western Canada and was following Rayner with its expansion. While both companies were now bumping into other regional operations in their expansion drive, Cheryl's Merit Consulting was their secret weapon. With TT providing the aggressive push and Merit analyzing new customers and markets and with Steve supplying the cash, Rayner and City Express were formidable competitors. No one had a well-financed analytical arm like Merit to run intelligent interference in the various markets. By following Rayner, City Express had an immediate source of freight to deliver locally, which in turn introduced them to the local delivery customers in each new market. Brian Patterson, though at times a pain in the ass, also had the drive to keep the company expanding. His only drawback was his being, at times, reluctant to try the new methods and the innovative thinking that were one of Quinn's strengths. However, he'd heard what had happened to the Finkelmans so was very careful to do as Sharon instructed. But he was too late; Sharon and Lia had decided to replace him at the first opportunity.

Cheryl's Merit Consulting continued with its two-pronged mandate, to support the existing companies and to seek out new customers through banks, lawyers and credit unions. It had been decided in the beginning to place the new computer services company under Cheryl's wing, and they too were looking for new

The Price of Success

customers. With their existing customer base when purchased, plus the computer demands of Quinn, they'd been able to upgrade their equipment and services to the point they were now capable of being a major service supplier to both industry and governments. With their government work they'd also been able to move all their equipment down to Regina and into a new dedicated high security building. The only problem Cheryl and Steve had was that they were too successful. Quinn now owned 36 thriving separate businesses in a number of fields, each of which was being driven to expand and grow. Cheryl and Lia wanted to set them up in their own division with their own VP. This would allow Quinn to allocate adequate dedicated management resources to their maintenance and continued development.

The decision to expand into the other prairie provinces, Manitoba and Saskatchewan, had just snuck up on them. As they acquired more freight companies, it had seemed that it was a no-brainer. One day Steve and Sharon woke up and discovered they did indeed have full blown freight and courier operations across the west. However, they decided that acquiring and operating the other mish-mash of non-freight businesses required a bit more thought.

CJ Vermeulen

The Price of Success

Chapter Twenty - A Bill Comes Due

This growing management requirement was the subject of a morning meeting Steve was holding in his office. Lia, Sharon, Cheryl and Larry were there, deep into a discussion of who would be the new dog's breakfast division VP, when Marcia, who was talking to Truckin' Ted at the front desk, let out a scream. Steve, looking through the glass wall of his office, saw Claire standing in front of Marcia's desk with a gun in her hand. Sharon, who was closest to the door and who probably didn't see the gun, ran out and was hit by two shots to the chest. Lia, right behind her, caught a shot in the leg, and Truckin' Ted, trying to tackle Claire from behind, went down with a bullet in the arm. Steve, scrambling out from behind his desk, running into the foyer as the screams and roar of gunshots continued, also took two shots to his chest. Claire, looking at Marcia, calmly asked her if she too was one of Steve's lovers. Marcia, shocked into dumb silence, could only shake her head. Cheryl, who'd gotten tied up in her computer power cord, pushed out of the door just as Claire said to Marcia, "Your lucky day then." Those still alive watched in horror as Claire put the barrel of the gun into her mouth and blew her brains out. The deflected bullet shattered the glass wall behind her, while her brains were blasted all over the wall and ceiling. She fell into a combination of shattered glass, splattered blood and jellied brains.

For a few seconds there was a profound silence, then total chaos. Larry, finally getting his legs under control, burst out of Steve's office, tripped over Steve, took one look at what was left of Claire and promptly turned away to puke. His tough young assistant, Topaz, coming the other way, pushed him into a corner and turned, with Cheryl beside her, to help Steve. Truckin' Ted called 911 and, dragging his broken arm, crawled over to check Sharon. She was dead. Next was Steve, and he was dying. His two chest wounds were bubbling, so TT grabbed some tissues from Marcia's desk, and Cheryl stuffed the paper into the holes, slowing the air leaks and bleeding. Cheryl then ripped off Steve's shirt and wrapped his chest with it. Marcia was trying to stop Lia's leg from bleeding as more of the office staff came running and tried to help. To complete the confusion, two crews of medics came rushing out of the elevator following the police, who had guns drawn. One crew of medics confirmed Sharon was dead and the other immediately tried to stabilize Steve. The first crew then turned their attention to Truckin' Ted and Lia. In minutes all the wounded were on their way to the hospital, and the police had begun their investigation. Just before the medics took her away, Lia told Cheryl, "It's all yours now; you'll have to run the show until we get back."

Cheryl, her clothes and hands smeared with Steve's blood, shocked and paralyzed, sat at Steve's desk and shook uncontrollably. People stood around or wandered aimlessly, crying. Lia's words and the horror of what she'd just seen finally sunk in. Cheryl knew she had to do something, but her brain had slipped out of gear, and she was unable to move. Topaz, with Lia's blood staining her blouse, came in and said weakly, "You'd better call Grace. Steve's kids can't hear this on the radio. And call Ann to come help us. And call Betty."

Cheryl just looked at her and asked her to do it. Topaz nodded and, supporting Larry, left.

Then Marcia, still smeared with Truckin' Ted's blood, came in and said, "There's a police captain here."

Cheryl, fighting panic, asked Marcia to show him in. He gave Cheryl his and those of the mayor their condolences and asked her who was in charge. And just like that Cheryl's brain reconnected and she was in charge. He asked a few questions, but it was pretty obvious what had happened. After answering the captain's questions Cheryl realized that she immediately had to invoke one of Steve's management directives, "It doesn't matter if you don't have a clue, you always must show 'em you're in charge." She called for Marcia. She told Marcia to get the managers of all the companies, plus Larry and Peter, to be at a meeting in the boardroom at 2:00 p.m. After the police completed their initial investigation, the captain came back and said that he'd been directed by the chief to do whatever was required to help. He offered to station a police barrier in front of the elevator to keep the media away. He also gave her the name of a company that would come in immediately and clean up the lobby.

She then called Peter Thayer, told him what had happened and asked him if she could legally take over as Quinn's president until they knew how Steve was doing. Peter, horrified and speechless for a moment, didn't see why not, Steve had made the terms of each of the senior manager's positions deliberately open and expected them to use their initiative. But he would review the paperwork. Ann came rushing in and, seeing the bloody lobby and glass everywhere, then Marcia and Cheryl with blood smeared across their clothes, nearly lost it. Ann asked how Steve was and Cheryl told her they were waiting for the doctor to call but he was probably still in surgery. Sharon and Claire were dead. The others would be okay. Ann shook and cried and moaned that she should have seen something like this coming. Cheryl

The Price of Success

hugged her and they comforted each other as they both calmed down. Ann said that she had to go to Grace's place and help with the kids. She'd be back later.

The cleanup crew arrived and promised to have it all cleaned up within a couple of hours. Cheryl would have to arrange for a new glass wall though. She asked Larry if she could borrow his assistant, Topaz, as she seemed to still have her head screwed on tight. Larry agreed and Cheryl told Topaz to work with Marcia. Cheryl then told Marcia to arrange for a new glass wall and ceiling ASAP. She continued: that's one of our companies so I expect it here immediately. Marcia set Topaz to work setting up the boardroom for the meeting, then called Grace. Grace had brought the kids home from school and rounded up Samara and Sergio. Grace and Ann were wondering if they should send the two older kids down to the office so they would feel part of the tragedy while they waited for the doctor to call. Cheryl said it was their call. And of course the phone continued ringing off the hook. The police downstairs called up and asked if someone was coming down to talk to the gathering press mob. Meanwhile, half the office was busy fielding calls from the Premier's office on down the line. Many others were paralyzed with grief and shock at Sharon's death. As Sharon had the day-to-day responsibility for all corporate operations, the company immediately fell into disarray. However most of the junior managers, rising to the occasion, slowly brought the company back to life. Their responsibility to the company had been constantly hammered into them, and now it paid off. Sharon may be dead, but Quinn Enterprises would survive and prosper.

By 2:05 all 36 presidents, senior managers, Peter Thayer, and Marcia to keep notes, were present in the boardroom. Everyone had blanched when they came through the elevator doors and saw the blood and broken glass everywhere. Sergio and Samara, who'd insisted they go to the office, also arrived and both kids barely kept their lunches down. Cheryl, still in her bloody clothes, opened the meeting by having everyone stand up and introduce themselves, including Sergio and Samara. Standing behind Cheryl was her partner Toni Fox, with the occasional big tear running down her cheek. Toni, in a panic that Cheryl may have been shot too, had rushed downtown as soon as she heard the news. Cheryl then continued the meeting by relating what had happened, then summarized, "Sharon is dead. Claire is dead. Lia and TT are in the hospital with gunshot wounds, but their wounds didn't look too serious when they were taken away."

"The only thing she knew was that when Steve was taken away, he was still alive." Except for the nervous shuffling of feet the room remained silent.

Cheryl went on, voice quivering, "You all know Steve and Sharon, some of you better than others. You all have discussed your job descriptions and corporate goals with them. You all know what your corporate duties are, and you also know what your growth goals are. You all know that your responsibilities include doing whatever is required to further the goals and protect your company and Quinn

Enterprises. Even if from time to time you have to bend the rules, corporate and otherwise. After all, that's why we employ Peter Thayer."

As a weak laughter rolled over the room, Cheryl paused, leaned forward, then continued, "And so it is with my position. As the only remaining healthy member of Quinn's senior management team, I must do, as Steve and Sharon would expect me to do, whatever is required to protect and keep Quinn operating."

She took a deep breath and continued, "With Sharon having passed and in Truckin' Ted's, Lia's and Steve's medical absence, I'm now the only functioning senior operating manager of Quinn Enterprises. I have a legal opinion that I can and should immediately assume Steve's position and authorities until we know when and if he can resume those duties." Head down she paused to let that sink in. Lifting her head, Cheryl continued in a quiet voice, "How does everyone feel about that? Will you accept me and my directives acting as the temporary President of Quinn Enterprises?"

Cheryl sat back as a wave of sound covered the room while Toni discretely squeezed her shoulders. As everyone discussed the question with his or her neighbour, on everyone's mind was the added unspoken question of whether they were willing to accept an openly gay woman as the Boss. Samara and Sergio, after a moment's discussion, stood up together. Samara said, "We know we have no standing in this meeting but we want everyone to know that dad thinks very highly of Cheryl. We think he'd be pleased and in complete agreement to have her sitting in his chair."

With that, one by one of those present agreed to accept Cheryl as acting president. Except for one. Brian Patterson continued to be an asshole and said, "I'm not sure you can legally promote yourself like this." The room went silent. Cheryl asked Peter to handle the situation.

Peter Thayer stood and introduced himself as the managing partner of Thayer LLC, and Quinn's outside counsel. He said, "Steve, when he wrote out the job descriptions for his managers, including your own job description Brian, deliberately left them vague and open in many areas. He felt very strongly that none of you would want headquarters and especially the chief jerk, meaning himself, to be second guessing you. You were hired for your ability to achieve the goals Steve set, not for your ability to follow the rules, even if it means that Lia and I are kept busy dealing with some of your shenanigans!" The crowd again laughed weakly. "And so it is here. Steve expects you all, including his most senior people, to do whatever is required, not just what the rules allow. That being the case then, there's no doubt in my mind that Cheryl assuming Steve's position is perfectly legal. And indeed, expected."

Cheryl looked at Brian, "Satisfied?"

The Price of Success

"Well, I'm still having trouble with it. How do we know that you're going to do what Steve wanted? Or that the banks won't object? Or - who knows - give yourself a big raise?"

Peter chimed in, "In fact if Cheryl wanted to, she is now the Boss and could quite legally give herself a raise."

Cheryl looked at him as the room again laughed weakly and said, "I never thought of that!"

She turned back to Brian, "Will you accept my direction in this position? Yes or no."

Brian replied with a sneer, "Why can't I be considered for the job?"

Peter answered, "Because you, nor anyone else in this room, have the training or experience for the position. Even Larry as a senior vice president can't do this job." With Larry nodding in agreement, he continued, "Cheryl is also two management layers above you. Now, please answer the question."

It was now obvious that Brian would not agree, but the reason was not clear. Speculation later came to the conclusion that it was because Cheryl was gay. Meanwhile the room was getting restive at his foolishness.

Cheryl, pressing forward, asked, "Your answer?"

Brian was silent.

Cheryl said, "One more time. If you do not give me a positive answer, I'm going to assume that you can't effectively do your job with me running the company; therefore I will take whatever action I have to manage the company." She paused. "I'm waiting."

Brian, even though he'd just been put on notice, looked up and shook his head. The room gave a collective gasp.

Cheryl leaned back in her chair and said, "Effective immediately, you are terminated. Larry, please have Brian's final cheque prepared immediately. Larry and Jake (the manager of the welding/fab company) will you please escort Brian down to his office and make sure he cleans out all his personal stuff in the next 15 minutes? Only his personal stuff. Make sure you recover his office and warehouse keys and company credit card. Larry, make sure that he does not touch his computer. Then escort him to the front door." She paused. "I'm sorry Brian that it's ended this way, but for the good of Quinn Enterprises, I have no choice."

A silent Brian, looking around, could see that he had no support. Shaking his head, he, Jake and Larry left the room.

Cheryl called for Topaz, "Go get Andrea for me please."

In a moment Andrea appeared. Cheryl addressed the room, "Andrea is my chief freight and courier analyst and has directed much of the reorganization of Patterson and Rayner. She also did all the preparatory investigative work prior to the two companies expanding into our neighbouring provinces." Turning to Andrea she said, "Sorry for putting you on the spot without warning, but you're now the acting president of City Express. Please take a seat."

As the room weakly applauded, Andrea turned pink and took Brian's chair. Just then Topaz stuck her head in the door and said, "The hospital is on line one."

Cheryl picked up the phone, put it on speaker mode and with a suddenly shaky voice introduced herself. Doctor Allenby, the ER head, told her that Steve was alive, but in critical condition. He'd come through the surgery, but there was still a question of whether his heart had been nicked by a bullet. He'd also suffered a huge blood loss and because his blood was so rare, they were down to their last liter of his blood type. If anyone they knew had AB Rh negative blood with a K factor, the hospital immediately needed them. Cheryl looked at Samara, but she shook her head. Allenby continued that more was being flown in from Winnipeg, and they were all praying it got here in time or that he didn't suffer another major blood loss. The next 48 hours were critical, and he'd keep her informed. He went on that Truckin' Ted, - and was that his real name? - had his arm set and would be released tomorrow. Lia too was out of surgery and doing well. She'd need some rehab later but would be released in four or five days. Cheryl gave him her private phone number and thanked him profusely. She hung up and, with tears in her eyes, turned to the room.

Talking directly to Samara and Sergio she suggested that they call Grace so that she could talk to the boys. She asked Marcia to create an intra company bulletin and get the news out to everyone. With everyone cheering, she asked if there was anything else that they needed to talk about. Topaz, still in the room, nervously raised her hand.

Cheryl asked, "Yes?"

"I'm thinking that since Sharon, Steve, Lia, and TT are so well known, perhaps we better issue a general news release. The phone calls are coming in from the media as well as his friends. If you like, I can draft up something and show you. And someone should go downstairs and talk to the media."

"Write the bulletin, and quickly. And everyone, I'm going to ask you not to talk about this to the media. I'll go talk to them right now. It's enough of a tragedy without some asshole news outlet chewing on it."

With nothing else to discuss, the meeting broke up, just as the new glass wall was being delivered. By quitting time the lobby was clean, the new wall and ceiling was up, and Cheryl was trying to decide if a new lobby carpet was in order. She decided it was and asked Topaz to call the architect's designer and get a new one ASAP. Cheryl then edited the news release and had Marcia forward it to all the media outlets. She then took the release downstairs and still wearing her bloody clothes, read it to the media. She did not answer any questions except to say that Steve was still alive. Exhausted, she and Toni then called Topaz, Marcia, Peter and Larry in for an end-of-week drink. This was a tradition Steve had started after any particularly harrowing week, and Cheryl decided that this week certainly fitted that category. After all it was fitting that they raise a glass to Sharon, first.

Chapter Twenty One - More Reorganization

Ann stayed in the city for the weekend and slept in Steve's apartment. She tidied up, although with Steve being as organized as he was, it didn't require much. On Saturday his housekeeper came in and, weeping most of the time she was there, gave it an extra dose of cleaning. Samara, who'd been looking for a better place to live, asked Ann if she thought Steve would mind if she moved in until he returned. Ann called Cheryl and they agreed that having Samara there was a good idea as long as she respected Steve's stuff. Besides, they thought that Lia would also move in when she was released from the hospital, just as she'd done after the bike accident. Samara could help look after her while she was in rehab. Also on that Saturday, Ann tried to find Sharon's estranged kids. She knew the eldest was an engineer and worked somewhere in Ontario and the daughter was a hairdresser. But the last time Sharon had said anything was to say that her daughter was in New Zealand. Ann had no idea where her ex-husband was. It was a fruitless search. Ann decided to talk to Cheryl about it on Monday. Otherwise she decided to turn the issue of Sharon's estate over to Peter and let him deal with it.

Sunday many of Steve's friends and employees gathered at Anne's country house in remembrance of Sharon. In spite of Sharon's temper and direct method of solving most problems, she was very well liked and respected. And not only by the company employees, but many in government and industry as well. She was recognized as having played a large part in Quinn's success and having climbed the ladder from a poor beginning to a woman of power and influence. But the biggest question was what affect her death would have on Steve? If Steve survived.

Monday came all too quickly for everyone. Truckin' Ted returned to work in spite of the doctor's orders and his wife's entreaties. Cheryl knew that Friday had not been a bad dream when Truckin' Ted greeted her with, "Mornin' Boss." By noon Cheryl was exhausted and buried under the workload. Truckin' Ted stopped by her office and told her she was coming to lunch with him. He looked at her and said, "And here is your first lesson as Boss with a capital B." He turned to Marcia, "Marcia, we're out for lunch, look after the place, please."

Marcia replied without even looking up, "Got it."

As they waited for the elevator they heard Marcia calling for Topaz to come and help her. Truckin' Ted said, "And that's how it's done, Boss."

They went downstairs and as soon as Luigi saw them he hustled them into Steve's corner booth and said that lunch was on him. He asked how Steve was and was told he was alive and they should know better later today. Then he congratulated Cheryl on her promotion and said that now she was the Boss, her lunches were on him. Over lunch Cheryl started to relax while listening to TT's early day stories about Steve. She suddenly realized that being "The Boss" was different from being "a boss". She really was going to have to learn to delegate and handle only policy and senior personnel questions. She'd often seen Steve with his feet up on the corner of the desk while he studied some document. Now she knew why. Steve often said his job was to supply enough money and muscle to his managers to allow them to accomplish his goals. The "Boss" job was a thinking man's job, not one of much action. She reached over and taking TT's rough hands in her own, thanked him.

Back in her office she asked him who he thought they should get to run the multi company division. He said that it was a very difficult problem because they needed a mini Steve, and he didn't think they had one. After all, they were talking about 30 or so different companies in many different fields with sales in the multi millions. TT wondered about a banker. Their banker was skilled at watching over many companies at once, but primarily from a financial point of view. Cheryl knew their banker had been interested in Quinn and its growth for years and maybe was ready to try his hand at real management. Cheryl decided to give him a call and ask him to come and see her. She then told Marcia to hold her calls and started back into the morning's problems with a view to delegation. She realized with a shock that she was also going to have to replace herself!

By Thursday, Steve was still in critical condition but was now stable and the odds of survival had swung in his favour. Lia was out of the hospital and living at Steve's with Samara, with Ann occasionally staying overnight. With Larry, Lia and Truckin' Ted's agreement, Cheryl promoted the manager of the computer services company to her old position. She'd also approved all the subsequent personnel moves caused by the promotions, and this included Topaz. While Larry objected, he recognized that Topaz had earned the chance, so he gave her up to be Cheryl's acting assistant. And for practical purposes, to have taken Lia's position. If Topaz worked out, Cheryl would bring her along by moving her into other management positions. Cheryl too had taken to spending some nights sleeping at Steve's place simply because her days were so long she was too tired to go home to her partner. The apartment was full, but everyone was too tired to worry about it, and everyone

The Price of Success

thanked God that Luigi had appointed himself the official supper supplier to the apartment. He even looked after the wine.

For the first time Samara saw at first hand the enormity and complexity of the company her dad had built and its management requirements. She listened fascinated as business matters were discussed over supper with Lia and Cheryl. Lia wasn't back to work yet but was trying to stay involved and contribute as best as she could. Slowly Samara realized that this was for her. Being an accountant with a car sales company paled beside the excitement of the fast-moving world of trucking, couriers and the other 30 or so businesses Quinn owned. When she rather hesitatingly brought up the subject of a job at Quinn, Cheryl had her doubts. Not about Samara's abilities, because obviously she was quick and well educated, but about her temperament and the fact that she was Steve's daughter. Larry reluctantly agreed to take her as a replacement for Topaz, and Cheryl laid down the law about her temper. One fuck up and she was gone.

Samara realized that everyone knew who she was, so she'd just have to prove that she belonged at Quinn. For the first few weeks she felt very lost in the tremendously complex world of Quinn, but slowly it started to make sense. She put in long hours and was never late with an assignment. Samara's only real problem was an analyst who didn't like her or who she was. The analyst began moving papers on her, hiding her coffee cup, diverting her mail, and failing to forward phone calls. Others, including Larry, saw it happening and wondered just how Samara was going to deal with it. Samara, who after all had her dad's temperament and knew how Sharon had sometimes solved vexing problems, caught the analyst in the washroom and, putting her considerable size and strength into it, punched the analyst right on her left boob. She then grabbed the stunned woman by the throat and, going nose to nose, told her that if she had any more problems she would take the woman and shove her face into a shit filled toilet and hold her under. Did she fucking understand? The other two women in the restroom watched, fascinated, as the analyst nodded her head in surrender. And that ended that. When Cheryl heard about it from Larry, he said, while laughingly relating the tale, there was now no doubt Samara was Steve's daughter. While Cheryl didn't agree with the violence, she also knew from Sharon's training that it sometimes was the only solution.

Two weeks after being shot, Lia returned to work. She and Cheryl had had several long conversations about Quinn's management and Lia suggested that Cheryl continue as president, while she resume her VP's role. Topaz would continue as Cheryl's assistant but would be available to Lia as required. After all, the company required someone to make final decisions and it would look much better if Cheryl continued doing that. Cheryl however, after some weeks of being the Boss, was not happy with the responsibility. She suggested that Lia and she share the president's job. They decided to ask Peter Thayer what he would suggest. His opinion was that Lia was right. The company needed a Boss and Cheryl was increasingly being seen as an effective Boss. Maybe even better than Steve because she didn't have Steve's menacing appearance or manner. Peter suggested that if she wanted, they could on a practical basis share the job, or even each take on tasks they were comfortable with. No one outside the management circle need know just how everything worked, just that it worked. Cheryl was very surprised at the praise. And the praise boosted her confidence, just as Peter had intended.

The Price of Success

Chapter Twenty Two - Another Change in Direction

Two months later, with Quinn settling down to function under the new management arrangement, a surprise phone call. West Freightways wanted to have a meeting in the week following. West was a division of Jake and Jones Freightways, one of the largest freight companies in Canada. The western manager of West and the VP of Finance for J&J, as it was usually called, had a proposition for them. He wanted to talk to them about an acquisition. Cheryl agreed to the meeting and immediately called in TT and asked what he knew about West. TT said he wasn't surprised by the call; West had been trying to expand in Saskatchewan. They probably wanted to buy Rayner and possibly City Express too. Or possibly they wanted a cooperative setup as Rayner had an excellent system of cross docks, while West had only one hub and one old dock. Whenever West and Rayner had gone after a client, Rayner usually prevailed. TT laughed and said that the reason was Merit's analysts. He said that Merit even suggested when they should lose a customer as it was either not profitable enough or it would fuck up West's routing and delivery routine. TT still laughing, told Cheryl that he'd never seen anything like it, deliberately not taking a client. They'd been doing it for about six months and it was driving West, and others, crazy. Cheryl then called Larry and Lia. She wanted to know what Rayner and City Express were worth. She asked Lia to think about the sale of the two companies and just what it would mean to Quinn. Lia suggested that Topaz and Samara be given the assignment of what the sale would mean to Quinn. It would be an excellent test of the two girls' ability to work together and test their out-of-the-box thinking ability.

Truckin' Ted stayed behind and asked Cheryl if he could bring up a delicate subject. Cheryl was very surprised as TT wasn't known for tact, and said okay. TT closed the office door and, humming and hawing for a moment, said, "It's about the way you dress. If you're going to be the company president, Cheryl, you have to look like one. Especially if we're going to meet with J&J."

The Price of Success

"What the hell's wrong with the way I dress? Steve always dressed very casually, and no one objected."

"Yeah well, guys are different. And Steve could carry it off. In this business, a woman can't, no matter who she is."

Jumping up, Cheryl said, "That's sexist! Jesus Christ it's because I'm gay, isn't it? God damn it TT, tell me the truth."

TT was in deep water now and he knew it. "Only partly. Women simply don't exist in the trucking world, never mind gay women, or gay men for that matter." As Cheryl was getting ready to really explode, TT continued, "Look, why don't you ask Lia to help you with a business wardrobe. I'll bet she'd be happy to do that." And before Cheryl could say anything more, he opened the door and sent Marcia to find her. With Lia in the room and the door closed again, TT asked Lia if she would help Cheryl select some presidential clothes. Quinn owned the only high-end women's clothing store in Regina, and it was well attended. Lia was delighted and said, "And how did this subject come up? TT, did you bring it up? Good for you! Because, Cheryl, I was going to suggest we talk about it."

Cheryl, who had in fact been increasingly concerned with how she looked but hadn't known what to do about it, all of a sudden was relieved. The next morning they went shopping, then later made a long visit to a hair salon. As Quinn also owned the high-end salon, the service was excellent. Cheryl didn't know she could look so feminine and attractive. Her life partner, Toni, was wildly enthusiastic with the makeover, and that sealed the deal. From then on Cheryl took the time to appear "presidential" and also noticed that she was treated with a great deal more respect by everyone. She and Lia now looked like the power duo they were. They went out for lunch more often and were asked by the mayor to attend select meetings at City Hall and the Chamber of Commerce. The two of them were becoming well known.

The day before the meeting with West, Larry and Lia came in with a replacement value of approximately $85 million cash for the two companies, plus good will. Lia was of the opinion that if the price were right, they should sell. But she cautioned they should leave the final decision to Steve. They called in TT and asked what his reaction would be to such a sale. His answer was immediate; I'll retire. I'm getting old, the kids are gone and the wife wants to travel. I don't need to work and that would be the excuse I need to quit.

Samara and Topaz's report, while rushed, was remarkably complete and suggested that a major problem would be reassigning those trucking staff that didn't wish to leave Quinn's employ. Another issue would be realigning the company's growth direction. But the biggest problem they saw was the access West would have to Rayner's computer systems and programs. Rayner's scheduling and routing programs were in advance of anything anyone else in the industry had, and Samara and Topaz didn't think they should be sold cheaply, if at all. The two weren't even sure that West knew of the program's existence! TT suggested they also talk to

Andrea. They knew she was doing a hell of a job, in spite of women being few and far between in the light trucking industry. She just may want to come back to work at the corporate level for Quinn. Or they had another possibility for her. A company president had died from cancer and they needed a replacement.

The meeting was scheduled for 10:00 a.m. in Peter Thayer's boardroom. Lia had suggested that having J&J meet with Cheryl in their office could spark speculation, something no one needed. Peter offered to make himself available, if required. As they all gathered in his boardroom, Eric Slaughter, Manager of West Freightways, without waiting for Cheryl to offer a coffee, opened and took control of the meeting. He passed on his and Andy Weslake's personal condolences over the tragedy and hoped that Quinn Enterprises was recovering from what must have been a shattering blow. Cheryl, Lia and TT, somewhat pissed off, acknowledged the sentiment and Cheryl replied that Sharon and Steve had built a management team deep enough in talent to carry on.

But there was an immediate problem. Eric kept wanting to address Truckin' Ted, not Cheryl. The idea of doing business with a woman clearly was not to his liking, and it was irritating Cheryl. She bluntly asked him if he had a problem with her. Andy Weslake jumped in and smoothly covered up Eric's gaffe. He went on that they had thought they would be talking to the company president. At which point Lia interjected and said, "You are, asshole. Now if that is the limit of your manners and homework, this meeting is over."

Caught unaware by this tiny female wop fearlessly attacking them, the visitors were immediately silenced. Andy regained his composure first and said, "No, wait, wait! We understood Steve was back at work and had resumed his management position. We meant no disrespect to you, Cheryl, or you Lia. Please forgive our misinformation. Can we start again?"

Cheryl and Lia couldn't believe that these two idiots were real. Lia glanced at Cheryl and as they were just about to ask them to leave, TT tried to rescue the situation.

"All right. Let me explain. Cheryl Letti is President of Quinn Enterprises. That is, she's the Boss. Lia Barchetti is the VP of Operations for Quinn, which means she oversees all day to day company operations. I'm Truckin' Ted, President of Rayner Freight Lines. The President of City Express, our courier company, is away on business. We both answer to Lia. Steve Quinn, while the sole owner of Quinn Enterprises, currently has no operational management position within the company and is absent on medical leave. Everyone clear on the situation? Any questions? Now what would you like to talk about?"

Andy Weslake, now looking directly at Cheryl said, "We want to make an offer for either all of Quinn Enterprises or just Rayner and City Express." He paused. "Cheryl, you seem surprised."

The Price of Success

"Well, we expected a possible interest in Rayner and City Express, but not for the whole company."

She continued, "Just to get this straight, you're interested in all of Quinn? Including all the other divisions, the real estate, buildings and equipment? Or possibly just Rayner and City Express, because they go as a package. And either deal is a share deal? For cash?"

Andy nodded and continued that he wasn't sure though about a cash deal though, then added, "We would offer $72 million for Rayner and City Express combined or, based on an examination of your books, a minimum of $140 million for Quinn Enterprises."

Cheryl, Lia and TT sat there, simply amazed. "Well," Cheryl said, "That's interesting."

Lia, ever the lawyer said, "Do you have that in writing?"

Andy pulled a sheaf of papers from his briefcase. "These are the tentative offers, good for 30 days. We understand that there will be many items to discuss, so that's the reason for the long open length of the offer. Here are our sale conditions." As he handed them over, he asked, "Are we in the ballpark?"

As Lia looked over the papers, Cheryl said, "You're low for the freight operations, and as we were not expecting an offer for the whole company, I'm not ready to discuss that amount. My gut feeling is though that for the whole company, you are significantly too low."

TT said, "Tell me why you want to buy our operations. You have a solid presence here in the west and, as far as I know, aren't hurting for work."

"We want to expand and, after looking over the market and the competition and the cost to grow, we decided that it would be easier and cheaper to buy our way in rather than go head to head with the competition."

"So that must mean that you feel the volume of business in the west is set to increase?"

"We think, as you do, that a natural resources boom in the west is coming, and we want to be part of it. We see coal, grain, potash, uranium, and all the support goods needed by those markets, booming. We even see oil and gas prices significantly improving."

"But why do you want the rest of Quinn? You've no history or experience with multiple businesses in a bunch of diverse markets."

"For the same reason you have them. Cash flow. Our finance people think this setup is brilliant. A bunch of diverse top end businesses throwing off cash to support the growth of the freight businesses. They wish they'd thought of it."

Lia quietly sat back to listen. She knew that J&J were wrong, and she wasn't about to correct them. If J&J needed a separate source of cash to support freight operations growth, then their freight operations were not as profitably run as was Rayner. Nor, it seemed, did they have the approval and level of support of their financial institutions that Quinn enjoyed. At that, Lia figuratively patted herself on the back for following TT's suggestion and talking Cheryl into hiring a senior account manager from their bank as the VP of the multi company division. She had no doubt it occurred through the backdoor, and had no objections to the bank being kept abreast of Quinn's ongoing success. Quinn's freight operations, Rayner Freight Lines, was able to be a standalone operation and highly profitable, thanks to hard work, tight organization and Merit Consulting's continuous oversight and analysis. Lia felt the familiar stirring of an audacious idea. She smiled as the meeting droned on around her. The meeting began to break up with an agreement to meet again next week. Quinn would see about a counter offer regarding Rayner and City Express, and J&J would revisit the valuation of Quinn. But Cheryl refused to release any of Quinn's financial data other than to say that last year's annual corporate sales were in excess of $275 million. This year the budget was for sales to exceed $310 million, and to date they were on track to significantly exceed that amount. It was Andy's turn to be surprised; they had no idea it was that high.

As a parting remark Lia said, "You know, I thought you might be here to discover if we were interested in your Western Canada courier operations and creating a relationship to locally deliver your incoming shipments."

Andy stopped and looked at her and said, "That would be expensive."

Lia replied, slowly, "A cash deal of course."

Andy, realizing that he'd been smartly stepped on, wisely didn't reply. Andy then promised to take that idea back to Toronto for discussion.

After the visitors left, Lia, TT and Cheryl sat in silence. Then TT laughed drily and said, "You know, you two, you're a piece of work. Did you see the look on Eric's face when you offered to buy their courier operations? For cash? I thought he'd have a crap right then and there. That was a brilliant move. It shows them we aren't intimidated by their size, and it also tells them we're loaded. That makes us very, very dangerous competitors. When they come back I betcha they bring a lot more horsepower and will be a lot more careful. God, I love it!"

Cheryl said, "Well TT, I'll send over a couple of analysts so that you and Andrea can determine just how big their freight and local delivery operation is. We better be ready for them if they agree to move in that direction."

On the way home, each one realized that they'd been presented with not only a company-changing situation but were at a personal life changing juncture as well. Lia suggested they enlarge the special committee to follow up this issue, and as they all were busy with routine matters, they bring Larry, Samara, Andrea and Topaz into the committee. But no one else.

Lia and Cheryl went to see Peter to ask him to review the J&J paperwork and to suggest a selling price for Quinn. Then they decided they had to bring Steve on board. It had been several months since he'd been shot and it had been a difficult time for him. He'd struggled with recurring infections until the surgeons realized

The Price of Success

that he must have parts of the bullets still in him. Even though his weight had dropped to 165 pounds, the surgeons decided that they had no choice. Three weeks ago they'd opened him up again and found a piece of bullet wadding in front of a rear rib, the reason the x-rays couldn't see it. With its removal, he'd started to recover. He was now back to 170 pounds and for a few minutes each day was riding a stationary bike. He was regaining his appetite and had had no signs of infection or fever since the latest operation. But he still had very little endurance and looked like hell. When anyone went to see him, the visits had to be short and uncomplicated. Cheryl went alone to see him.

She outlined the meeting and asked Steve if he was interested in selling. Steve looked at her in silence for a long few minutes, then said, "How do you like managing the company?"

Surprised, Cheryl said, "I like it but I'm finding it hard work. I was happier in my old job. Fortunately Lia is a great help. I couldn't do this without her, or for that matter, without the others."

"How much are you paying yourself?"

Cheryl, again surprised, replied, "$75,000 annually."

Steve looked at her and said, "Double it, and give Lia a raise to $125,000. Give me a piece of paper. Because I'm only the owner now, I don't know if this is required, but get Larry to put it in your employee file." He then scribbled a note to Larry to give Cheryl and Lia the raises. Then he added, "Make sure you're paying your senior people enough too, don't be chintzy."

He continued, "How's Samara doing?"

"She's doing well. She's controlling her temper, at least for the most part, and we've put her on the team to investigate the sale."

"Good. Samara is smarter than she knows and tougher than Wang leather. The way to keep her out of trouble is to keep her busy and overloaded with work."

He continued, "What will you do if the company sells?"

"I don't know, I've not had time to think about it."

"The answer to your first question is in what you do afterward, and what will become of the team we've built. Ask Lia the same thing. Otherwise, it's your call. Let me know what you decide."

Cheryl left the hospital in a daze. How the hell was she supposed to make that kind of decision? They were probably talking about hundreds of millions of dollars! And what became of the team was the answer to the sale question. Fuck, she thought. That goddamn man was going to drive her crazy!

She called Peter and set up a meeting for the next day. She needed more input.

The Price of Success

Chapter Twenty Three - Decision Time

    Needing to think, Lia went for a bike ride. She rode some 20 miles north of the city until she came to her favorite contemplation site, an abandoned pioneer cemetery about a mile off the main highway. There was a bench under a large ancient poplar tree on a high spot looking out over grain fields. The cemetery was old, quiet, and very peaceful. As usual the cemetery was empty of people, and Lia let her mind relax and wander.
    Cheryl had really caught her off guard by asking what she'd do if the company were sold. It was obvious that J&J wouldn't give her the type of job she now had. It was also clear that J&J didn't even know the secret to Quinn's success. Silly assholes! They just figured that Rayner and City Express operated the way everyone else did in this industry. Their minds were probably closed to even thinking there was another way to operate. If Andy's performance in the meeting was any indication, they certainly wouldn't give a woman a chance at anything! Especially a tiny, abrasive, noisy, perfect little wop lawyer.
    Lia's mind wandered back to when she'd first started working full time at Quinn. After three months Steve had called her in and asked her how she liked it. He then, in that quiet deadly voice he used when he was pissed off, asked her when she was going to get her ass in gear. Lia had been so shocked that she was speechless. Steve had continued that if he'd wanted a good looking female lawyer for the company, he could've chosen any one of a dozen. But he'd hired her for her brains, ability to think outside the box, and aggressiveness. So when was she going to start working for her paycheque? As she sat there trying not to cry, he told her that their high-end hair and makeup salon had something wrong with it. He didn't know what, but she was to go fix it. She would never forget when he leaned forward and told her she was to fucking fix it, not just come back with a story about what was wrong. "And," he said in dismissing her, "Change that goddamn name. It's ridiculous!"
    After reviewing the company files until late that night, she couldn't see anything wrong other than the sales had actually decreased somewhat over the past three

years. Lia knew that the salon was the only high-end salon in Regina and, in this economy, should be booming. Maybe Steve was right, the name "Super Face" certainly wasn't a winner.

She remembered walking into the place, nervous as hell, and introducing herself to the manager. As the manager, Marian, showed her around introducing her to everyone, Lia realized she was also nervous and wasn't showing her everything. Lia excused herself and wandered around looking at a surprisingly small inventory with few operating supplies. As she poked around in the storeroom, one of the technicians stood behind her and suggested in a low voice that Lia come to the back door at 8:00 tonight. The technician then picked up her supplies and moved on. Just then a delivery truck, and not one of City Express's, came to the back door with a shipment of hair salon supplies. Marian, trying to shield her actions, paid the driver in cash, cash that she took from her pocket. Lia asked about the cash transaction and Marian told her that she got a better deal for cash. Lia nodded, and said she'd be back in the morning.

Lia went back to the office and stopped at the second floor. Questioning the City Express manager, she discovered that they had never been asked to make deliveries to or from Super Face. This was in spite of a standing order that no company other than Quinn-owned companies were to be used for company business. Lia then went upstairs to see Cheryl. She wanted to talk to the analyst that last looked at Super Face, but Cheryl said they hadn't looked at Super Face for several years. Growth had been so intense that analytical efforts had been slanted to new companies like the Barchetti deal and not toward existing operations. She said that the division didn't have enough analysts to cover everything.

Lia, looking out over the grain fields, remembered going back to her office to think – and having a funny feeling in her stomach, one that made her twitchy and excited.

That night, dressed all in black, Lia casually walked around to the back door of Super Face. From several doors away she saw a car stop at the door and a woman ring the bell. Lia watched as Marian brought out several boxes and took some cash from the woman. Over the next hour, Lia watched as a number of visitors came to the door and all traded Marian cash for supplies. Finally, Lia waved one down and asked her about getting supplies from Marian. The car driver told her that all she had to call Marian during the day and order what she wanted. Then pick it up at night.

Lia still remembered how excited she was when she'd put it all together. Marian was buying the supplies, probably stolen, and selling them on the side. Lia also bet that any cash from the regular hairdressing work disappeared into Marian's pocket, hence the lack of sales. But what was she going to do about it? Well, she thought, Steve told her to fix it.

The Price of Success

The next morning Lia, carrying a small cardboard box, went into Super Face, called Marian into her office and fired her. She gave her the box, told her to clear out her desk and leave her office keys and company credit card. And to stay away from the computer. Marian was shocked and refused to believe it. Lia picked up the phone and called Larry and asked him to have Marian's last paycheck in the mail today. Marian then called Cheryl and was told that whatever Lia wanted, Lia got. Hanging up the phone, Marian, in a complete daze, let Lia walk her to the door and out onto the street. Lia then called in the tech who'd given her the tip and asked for her history. Lia discovered that she'd been a salon store manager in Winnipeg until her husband had been transferred to Regina. Lia asked her if she wanted the manager's job on a temporary basis. She jumped at it and Lia told her that an analyst would be down in a day or so to show her how to operate the reporting system. And if she stiffed Lia in any way, Lia would hound her to the grave.

Lia, sitting in the sun under the tree, smiled at the memories. Sitting in her office later that day long ago, Lia realized that the overall problem was rooted in the analyst division. That was what was causing her jittery stomach! So she went to Cheryl and told her that Cheryl should assign analysts to all the businesses to help them, not just the new ones. Cheryl was pissed off at being told how to run her division by a newcomer, even if she was probably her superior, and said so. Lia, realizing that she'd overstepped apologized. Cheryl, appeased, asked Lia what she had in mind. Lia outlined her idea to Cheryl, and Cheryl told her that she too had been thinking they were missing a huge area of concern. Lia told her that she could perhaps divide her staff into two parts. One side would look after new clients and the other would be assigned to take a constant look at existing businesses. Analysts should be rotated through the businesses on a regular basis and have the power to look at anything that interested them, including the competition, and the market.

Cheryl said that she'd need at least three new analysts to do that, and maybe more. Lia took a deep breath and told her to hire them. Steve had told her to solve the problem, and she was solving the problem. Cheryl laughed and laughed. Steve is going to have a heart attack when he hears what you've done, and he has no one to blame but himself! In fact, when Steve heard about it, he smiled his small smile and didn't say a word.

Lia realized, as she sat there under the tree, that had been the real beginning of the modern Merit Consulting, and Merit was the real core of Quinn's success. She smiled and wondered if Steve had figured this all out long before he leaned on her. And said to herself, "Of course he did!" You tricky son-of-bitch, she thought. How can you be so fuckin' smart? Could she walk away from this? Could she walk away from Steve? They didn't have a relationship, but from time to time they enjoyed a weekend together. But, thank god, no more tornadoes. She admitted that he could turn her crank, and she blushed at some of the things he'd shown her how to do. She knew she didn't have a great sex drive, but when Steve turned her on, she was really turned on!

She just didn't have another plan. Her time at Quinn had followed that first pattern, and she knew that was why she was now second in charge at Quinn, or was half of the presidency, take your pick. The pay was very good and with bonuses would be well over $250,000 this year. Where was she going to find an equal situation? And the team! They had a great, productive cutting-edge team. They should let the team continue running and go as far as possible. She'd been wrong. They should not sell, rather continue to grow. Besides, they could always sell in the future.

She climbed back on her bike and returned to the city.

Larry sat in his office and nervously rapped a pencil on his desk. His desk was covered in papers and reports and he was waiting for Samara and Topaz to come in. He was upset with the notion the business could be sold. He was a happy camper, in fact had never been happier than working at Quinn. Virtually no one told him what to do, he was well paid, and he was able to explore all manner of new financial management procedures in a constantly changing business mix. He didn't know what he would do, or could do, if Quinn were sold. He was too young to retire and didn't have enough money to retire the way he wanted to anyway. He shrugged. No sale was his preference. Plus, he looked after Steve's personal financing. Who would do that and continue the program that he'd designed for Steve? Steve was now a multi-millionaire and his private income exceeded his Quinn income. However, and the most important, he knew that regardless of what happened, Steve would look after and protect him.

Topaz and Samara each felt the same way. They loved the work and the pay. They recognized that if the company were sold they were out of a job. No sale, in harsh terms, was their vote. Topaz was surprised when she told Samara that she was lucky, it didn't matter because her dad owned the company, and Samara replied that it would make no difference. Her dad had made it on his own, and he strongly felt that the kids should too.

TT had come to the opposite conclusion about the sale. He loved his job, but he could afford to retire. It was clear now that J&J didn't understand how or why Rayner was so successful. And he didn't want to work for J&J under any circumstances. Besides, he needed a reason to pack it in before his wife really got ugly about it.

Cheryl, though, was having a very unpleasant time trying to decide what to do. She did realize that she'd be out of a job but probably would receive a sizeable severance package. She was so troubled that she closed Steve's office door and went back into his apartment. She poured herself a glass of his excellent Italian Chianti and plopped herself into his man chair, then got up and turned on the music system to play Lalo Shiffrin, then some Pink Floyd. She'd gone to see Peter and had come

The Price of Success

away disappointed. Peter had looked over the offer papers and told her that they were okay but needed detail work. But, he said, that's not why you're here. No, Cheryl said, and outlined the conversation she'd had with Steve about making a decision to sell.

"Why did he do it? I can't make a decision about $200 or $300 million or more of his money."

"Because Steve is telling you this is about far more than money. If this were about only money, Steve would sell tomorrow. But it's not about money. It's about a team of people working together to create an extraordinary organization. It's about the very clever method Quinn uses to be successful. And whether you want to continue as president. Steve, now that he is regaining his health, knows that this is only the first move in what's coming. Quinn is getting big enough to be drawing national attention, and soon international attention. He needs to know if you can, or are even willing, to continue to grow into such a management situation."

"Peter, I don't know if I can do that. If we don't sell I know that means we'll probably begin another breakneck expansion. We already have a backlog of consulting work in Saskatoon, and TT has been talking about Manitoba and Alberta. I just don't feel I can do that. I want to run Merit Consulting and be at the heart of everything. I want to present all the facts and recommendations and have someone else make the big decisions. That's my style."

Peter sat back, a troubled look on his face. "Are you sure you can run Merit? It too is going to grow and get involved in some huge, difficult situations, and Core Computing is also moving into new markets."

Cheryl answered, "Peter, I'm not an aggressive decision maker. I'm an analyst of facts, trends, possibilities, and a seeker of the truth. I do that very well and I like it. I probably should have been a fucking librarian or even a Jesuit priest. I don't care how big Merit or Core get or where we end up looking into things, I can do it. Larry and I are very similar that way. We were designed to be support people, very good support people, but always and nothing more than support people."

She paused, "Lia is who Steve wants. Really, he needs and wants Sharon, both as president and in person, but Sharon is dead. If Steve ever completely recovers, then he should resume the presidency, but I don't know if he'll ever completely recover. Ann is very worried that the long period of recurring infections he has suffered has damaged him in some way, and I know that he hasn't recovered from Sharon's death. He loved that woman and she loved him. She was a perfect consigliere for him and I know he's taking her loss very, very hard."

Cheryl stood. "Thank you, Peter, you've just helped me make up my mind. I'm going back to the office and create a new management structure with Lia as Acting President of Quinn, and me as President of Merit. Then I'll go see Steve and tell him that someone else can make the sell decision."

Peter had a troubled look on his face as Cheryl left. He knew that Cheryl had been doing an outstanding job as president, but also knew that she wasn't as comfortable as she could be. In the paraphrased words of Harry Truman, her ass hadn't quite grown to fit the president's chair. Lia on the other hand was a fireball, smart, tenacious, quick and able to work outside normal channels. She wasn't Sharon, but in some ways was better than Sharon; in other ways, not so much. She'd lived through the bike ride and the tornado and was as quick as Sharon - maybe even quicker - to respond to what she saw as an opportunity. Not being as big as Sharon, she'd developed less direct, but just as effective, ways to sort people out. She was also meaner and more vicious than Sharon ever was. And, although Steve didn't know it yet, Lia tried to protect him even more than Sharon ever had. He wondered about her love life. He'd never seen or heard of her having a partner; on the other hand, she'd lived with Steve for a week on the road. He threw his hands up in the air and sighed. This was one of those times when doing nothing seemed to be the way to go. He called in his own consigliere to talk it over again. Just before he did that, though, he wondered about something Cheryl had said. She claimed she wasn't a president; she was a support person. Was that true for him as well? He knew he could never do Steve's job; he wasn't aggressive enough, nor did he have the far-reaching imagination. The biggest difference though, was he just didn't have Steve's aggressive, in- your-face, get-the-hell-out-of-my-way, drive. But Peter was wrong. What he really lacked was Steve's sheer, immense brain power, something Peter and everyone else, except Ann, knew nothing about.

The Price of Success

CJ Vermeulen

Chapter Twenty Four - Steve Returns

On Monday of the following week, in a surprise move, Steve got himself discharged from the hospital and moved back into the apartment. Ann moved in with him, and Samara stayed, after talking to her dad and Ann. The other women had moved back to their own places. That first night Luigi sent up a special rib dinner and several very special bottles of wine from his own personal hoard. After supper Steve put a Willie Nelson CD on the music system, much to Samara's disgust, and settled back into his big man chair. He was asleep in moments so Ann covered him up and left him there. Sometime during the night Steve got up for a pee and crawled into bed with her.

For the next few days Steve, moving slowly, had Cheryl, Lia and all the division managers and presidents come and see him to bring him up to date. It was a slow process, and as a result the meeting with J&J had to be postponed. Ann was furious with Steve for not resting more but the activity seemed to recharge him. He made it clear to Cheryl that she was the Boss, all he needed was to be brought up to date. Since the company, as a matter of course, was managed across lines of responsibility, Cheryl had no trouble with it at all. One night Steve went back into the kitchen and for the first time in months whipped up a pasta, shrimp and scallop dinner with garlic. Lots of garlic. Combined with a smooth B.C. Pinot Grigio, it was the best meal Ann and Samara had had in a long time.

On Thursday Cheryl booked an hour of Steve's time and, dressing down to jeans and a pullover cashmere sweater, went to see him. Cheryl told Steve that she'd created a new management structure and would he please review it. The plan basically made Lia the Acting President of Quinn and Cheryl the President of Merit Consulting. An option was Lia VP of Operations and Steve as president. If Lia were president, then the position of VP of Operations was still open. Topaz would remain for the time being as the president's assistant. Larry, Cheryl, and the other division VPs plus the presidents of Rayner and City Express all reported to the VP of

The Price of Success

Operations. Cheryl said that she'd finally come to the conclusion that she was not a president person. Like Larry, she was a support person. She thought Lia was a president, and maybe Samara and Topaz would be someday too. But in her opinion no one else in the company was made of the right stuff. She sat back, calm and relieved that she'd finally come to grips with her place in the company and in life.

Steve asked her if she'd talked to anyone about this, and Cheryl answered her partner Toni and Peter. Steve finished reading her report and placed it carefully on the coffee table. He slowly got up and asked, "Would you like some coffee?"

Steve made some and, while waiting for it to finish perking, started slowly pacing back and forth across the living room. "Well," he said, "I won't argue with you. I don't like it, you've been doing a hell of a job, but you're the Boss." He went to pour the coffee. To give himself time to think, he said, "Were you able to do a senior payroll study? Yes? So everyone is now being paid appropriately?"

"I also asked all the VPs and presidents to do the same and submit a payroll plan for their own staff. Samara and Topaz are the resource for that task too. It's not done yet, but the study has shown that pay equalization was badly needed. And before you ask, gender or sexual orientation was not to be taken into consideration. I personally had a meeting with them all and made it clear that if I saw any indication of it, somebody would be fired. Scared the crap out of them, I did!"

Steve chuckled and said, "I bet that's the first time you've done that."

Cheryl nodded.

Steve stopped pacing, sighed and said, "Okay, make your part of the plan work. Leave Lia's and the VP Admin position to me and send Lia in. But before you do, though, you haven't answered the question about J&J. What do you recommend?"

Cheryl, all of a sudden very serious and starting to sweat, stirred up her courage and said, "No, I won't recommend anything."

Steve looked at her and chuckled again. Carefully pulling her up, Steve gave her a big gentle hug and said, "Good for you. You've stuck to your guns. From here on in you are absolutely forbidden to leave Merit!"

Cheryl, crying, with tears flowing copiously, hung onto Steve and could only nod.

After lunch Lia came into Steve's living room for the most important meeting of her life. Steve asked her what she thought about the suggested sale of Rayner and City Express. Lia looked at him, aware that until this very second she hadn't absolutely made up her mind. While in the beginning she'd favoured selling, after thinking of her own future and that of the team, wasn't so sure anymore that was the right answer.

She finally asked, belligerently, "What's your future? If the company sells, you'll be a 42-year-old multi-millionaire, single, able to do anything you want. Since it's your company and you built the team and you created the corporate culture, I don't think it's fair to ask me that question."

She was quiet for a moment, "Besides, the real question is: What are we going to do if we don't sell?"

Steve looked at her with his small smile and asked her for her answer to that question as well.

Lia, taking a deep breath, told him that they should turn the offer around and offer to buy the Western Canada local delivery and courier operations of J&J. She explained that to do so would give them two things; one, an easy way to approach and sell all their superior freight services to J&J's western customers and two, it'd give them fully operating bases in Edmonton, Calgary, and Winnipeg, something they didn't have now. With that foothold, Lia said, she didn't have any doubt they could gain market share and grow to dominate those markets as they did in Saskatchewan.

But she warned there was a downside. It was going to take money, and lots of it. It would require a careful plan to absorb the new company and attack these new markets in an orderly manner that wouldn't get Quinn's current management overstretched. And people, they'd need people. Steve asked her how much money, and Lia suggested it probably would cost $10 to $15 million to buy the local delivery business, convert West to City Express standards, and upgrade the delivery equipment and computer systems. Perhaps some of those funds could be found in Merit and Core Computing as they too could expand into those markets. Steve sat there tapping the desk with a pen. He then picked up the phone and called his bank contact. Yes, he was back, thank you, and off and running and could he please have $15 million to make a possible purchase and he needed an answer by Monday. His contact laughed and laughed and agreed that yup, he was back!

Steve looked at her in silence, slowly started to smile, and then laughed wholeheartedly. "You're a great little broad, aren't you? During our bike ride you sure showed me just how tough you are, but until now I wasn't sure just how adventurous you could be."

He stood up, slapped the desk and said, "Okay, you're the new VP of Operations. Would you like a drink to celebrate your promotion? Okay? Wine or Bourbon, or I believe I have a bottle of 25-year-old Scotch here somewhere."

Lia, who'd been sitting opposite Steve with her mouth hanging open, said, "Wait! Wait just a minute! What about Cheryl?"

"Cheryl requested she be reappointed President of Merit Consulting and be relieved of her position as President of Quinn. I've honored her request. She found another slot for the existing head of Merit. Now what do you want to drink?"

Lia jumped up, leaned over the coffee table and said, "No! Yes! Scotch. Goddammit, just a minute! I'm just a 42-year-old girl wop lawyer from the Italian district of Regina, what the fuck do I know about running a $300 million dollar a year company? I don't have the right education or even an MBA!"

The Price of Success

"I dunno, I guess we'll find out. But so far you're doing just fine. You're the only one that sees the J&J offer as an opportunity to do something different. Besides, I don't have a business education or an MBA either. I'm just a lowly economist, for Christ's sake! Here's your drink. Cheers."

Steve stood there looking down at her. "You know," he said, "As you've heard me say a few times, my old man was a lawyer and to this day I hate the ground he walked on. He did, however, teach me several useful lessons. The first was that the most important consideration was to hire the right people, have them agree on the end goals, give them the tools they required and then leave them alone to achieve those goals. You," he said, pointing at her and stealing a phrase, "Are made of the right stuff."

Lia took her drink, sat down, gave him a level look and said, "You can be a real son of a bitch. How do you know I won't turn it down?"

Steve with his small smile said, "You won't. You'd never forgive yourself if you did. You want to see if you can do it and show your brothers and Frank just how good you really are, and live up to Sharon's assessment of you. And stuff it to some asshole men."

Lia jumped up and let out a shriek. "You fucking bastard! That's not fair! If this Scotch wasn't so good I'd throw it at you!"

Steve laughed quietly. "I'd make you the acting president today, but we also need a VP of Operations, so finding a replacement for yourself will have to be your first job. Besides, Peter tells me that I should resume the presidency for the sake of company continuity and to show everyone that I'm fully recovered and in charge again. And that the company is off and running once more. Especially as word of the possible buy gets turned into a full-blown rumour. In fact, we need a press release sent out announcing the management changes and discounting the buy rumour. Do we still own that raggedy assed publicity company? The one no one wanted to buy? Let's get them in here and get this out today."

Lia called Topaz and asked her to get someone from the publicity company in immediately.

Steve then asked Lia to set up the J&J meeting for Wednesday of next week. Her next task was to rough out an acquisition plan with the special committee. As Lia stood up to leave she said, "You know I haven't taken the job yet."

Steve, awkwardly getting down on one knee said, "Lia Barchetti, will you please consent to be my new vice president?"

Lia laughed, but with tears in her eyes, nodded and muttered, "Asshole!"

After the Lia meeting, Steve was tired. He was still at least 25 pounds underweight and his endurance was still much diminished. His slow recovery rammed home just how close he'd come to not surviving, and for the first time in his life Steve realized he was actually mortal. The truth was he needed Lia to run the company; he just couldn't do it yet. He wasn't even interested in working on his old Jeep. Steve decided he needed a break, so he changed his clothes and asked Ann if she wanted to go for a ride. He phoned down to TT to have someone take the cover off his Mercedes 500SL convertible and make sure it would start. Truckin' Ted told him he'd started it every weekend and even had it washed a few days earlier. He told Steve that he thought he'd want it soon. When Steve and Ann got down to the second floor, all the employees and drivers stood, applauded and cheered.

Steve yelled, "TT, dock 'em all five minutes pay for wasting company time!" The staff all hooted and hollered, obviously glad to have him back.

Steve dropped the car's top, pulled out onto the street and asked Ann where she wanted to go. Ann didn't care, it was warm and sunny, a great day to be alive. Steve drove down Albert Street to the Legislature grounds and parked by the lake. They got out and went to sit on a park bench and sitting side by side in the sun, holding hands, they had nothing to say. It was enough they were alive and were able to look forward to tomorrow. Ann, seeing that he was getting tired after a few minutes in the sun and fresh air, suggested they return home. Steve didn't argue.

The next day, Ann arranged to see Steve's doctor by herself. During a long discussion, Ann told the doctor that Steve was not yet back to normal, not only physically but, more importantly, mentally. Whereas before he was full of pee and vinegar, now he was quiet and at times seemed to be elsewhere. Ann thought that after Sharon's death he'd realized just how much she meant to him and now he was remorseful and full of self-pity for what he'd lost. The doctor deferred to her expertise but advised that Steve was still in physical trouble. He was healing, but in the doctor's opinion, far too slowly. While the doctor could find no concrete reason for Steve's condition, he was very concerned. Ann asked him to give Steve the green light to begin a serious exercise regime and in particular to begin training again for his "age-class" bike racing that she knew he loved. She hoped that his normally very competitive nature would resurface and he would get back on track. The doctor, warning her that Steve wasn't really ready for this step, and would have to be carefully monitored, nonetheless would bow to her intimate knowledge of his psyche. He agreed to give Steve his approval to begin serious exercise.

Then Ann went to see Cheryl and asked her if Quinn owned a training gym of any kind. When she discovered they did, she went to Lia and asked her to have them install a mini gym in Steve's apartment. Lia jumped at the idea and over the next two days, despite Steve's doubts, one of the bedrooms was converted into a mini gym. Over the next week, Steve began a very limited exercise routine and discovered that Samara also loved having a home gym. Slowly Samara began to push her dad, teasing him whenever she outdid his efforts, which was most of the time. Ann watched carefully as he began to spend more and more time getting into shape. As she hoped, she saw the old snarl on his face when he was bested by Samara.

The Price of Success

CJ Vermeulen

Chapter Twenty Five - Lia Finally Rebels

Lia arranged that Peter, Larry, and Steve review the girls' report on the company sale. Samara and Topaz, working with the other team members, had come to the conclusion that Quinn should ask for $375 million, although Peter wanted a higher number. He thought $425 million would be better as it should include a significant premium for the Merit Consulting programming and analysis secrets. Lia then called a meeting of the special management group, plus Topaz and Samara, to discuss the report and to decide what to do.

The consensus was that if the entire company were sold, they should demand $400 million. Steve, keeping quiet, let Lia run the show. Lia, taking a deep breath, dropped her bombshell. She suggested that the company not be sold and that Quinn should instead make an offer for J&J's local delivery and courier operations in Manitoba, Saskatchewan and Alberta. For cash. Then Samara, very nervous at being in the first business meeting ever with her father, suggested there was another path, one that had not been discussed but was a legitimate option. That is, Quinn would turn down West's offer and do nothing. Quinn would continue on its own path, growing in its traditional way. She wasn't supporting such a move, but she felt, since they were talking about the company's future, all options should be looked at. Steve, smiling his small smile, agreed with her. Steve continued, saying the bank had confirmed that Quinn could have access to $15 million for the purpose of buying a company. Steve asked Larry to call the bank and give them whatever info they required to complete the loan. Larry, looking concerned, reminded everyone that they were now talking about some serious money.

As the discussion wore on and started to slow down, Peter suggested that Lia hold a vote. First, whether the company should be sold, then whether Quinn not buy part of J&J, then whether Quinn Enterprises should tackle buying part of J&J. Lia, following Peter's suggestion, called for a vote, from which Steve excused himself. The result was a unanimous "no sale." The next vote, to purchase West, was also

The Price of Success

unanimous. The third vote therefore was not required. Peter then suggested they talk about how they'd integrate West into City Express, since that was going to be the real problem. He knew that if they could decide on an integration approach, then the group would forget about spending so much of Steve's money!

Lia, now on familiar ground, asked for integration suggestions. Cheryl suggested that Truckin' Ted and Andrea be brought in so that TT could give the committee the benefit of his West research. Lia sent Topaz to find TT and Andrea. When the two arrived, Cheryl went on to say that it seemed to her that they should tackle the problem of integration in separate steps. They should start where Rayner's competition with West was weakest in order to be able to learn, as quickly as possible, the particular idiosyncrasies of doing business with West. This would include determining if any of the West staff was worth retaining. Steve, speaking up on this topic for the first time, was concerned about showing Rayner's computer systems to any West staff. He pointed out they'd never acquired just part of a company before and the possibility of critical information leaks was rather high. He added that West could easily add a ringer to whatever they bought with the express purpose of stealing Rayner's methodologies and systems. After all, sooner or later West was going to figure out just how Rayner operated and why it was so successful.

Truckin' Ted said, "As far as I'm concerned West is just another run-of-the-mill freight company. They don't have exceptional staff, nor do they have good management systems. Their western problem is that, in spite of having a Western Canada Manager, they're still basically managed from Toronto, and you all know what that means. Management problems increase exponentially with the increase in distance from head office."

Lia said, "Exponentially? I didn't know you knew that word!"

TT, blushing slightly, snapped, "You didn't know I have a Master's in Business Admin either, did you?"

Steve, stepping in, said in an admiring tone, "I don't think anyone knew that, Ted. But you know, TT, I've always wondered about you. In spite of your boots!" Everyone laughed, and everyone also knew that Lia had just been subtly chastised. To her credit, she apologized to TT.

Truckin' Ted continued, "I think Steve's idea is the right way to go. Since we're strongest here in Saskatchewan, this is where we should start. That would also allow us time to set up in Manitoba second, checking out West's staff and getting Merit involved in setting up the Winnipeg office."

Steve asked a clearly nervous Andrea, "What's your opinion, Andrea? This is your company and, after all, most of this expansion work will fall on your shoulders."

"I agree with Ted's approach, but you realize that I'm still new in this job and I'm not sure I know how to do this."

"Well Andrea, you've done a good job so far, and on these big deals we all work with each other. You won't be alone. You'll have Merit helping full time and I'm sure that Core Computing and Lia will also get in your way. I might even stick my nose in from time to time. However, think it over and come see me sometime in the next few days and we'll talk about any of your concerns."

Lia, changing the subject, said to TT and Andrea, "Why wouldn't you just take over J&J's offices?"

"Because then we'd also be working with J&J's freight operations right next door and that's not good for security. It's also easier for us to start something new rather than try to convert another operation and culture to Rayner's style."

Andrea spoke up, "Which reminds me, as part of the offer we should guarantee to retain existing staff for a maximum period of only three months in Saskatchewan, six months in Manitoba and nine months in Alberta, no longer. That'll give me time to evaluate them and to decide who to retain."

Steve sat back and smiled. He knew Andrea's ass would grow into the job! He'd just have to make sure that TT allowed her room on the team. He made a note to talk to Lia and TT about it.

Lia, feeling that a consensus had been reached, asked for a vote. There were no dissenting votes.

Peter asked Steve, "How're you going to negotiate with J&J? Or were you going to delegate it? Because I think this is your job, no one else's."

Steve replied, "No, the negotiations are mine, and I'll use TT and Andrea as resources. Lia, you and Peter are to keep yourselves informed. However, I personally don't want to get into the actual investigation of West. That's TT's and Andrea's task, with Cheryl and anyone else they need for assistance. Andrea, you have a free hand asking for any assistance you think you need. Just keep me informed."

After the meeting, Peter took Steve aside and suggested that it was time a proper corporate board of directors be created. Steve called Lia in and had Peter repeat the suggestion. As for the board, the only suggestion she had was that Ann Bazvsky and Jamie Price be considered for board seats.

Lia looked at Steve and said bluntly, "Ann, because I think she's the only one around here that has a clue about how you think, and Jamie because he's busted his ass for us and seems to really know his corporate law. With all due respect to you, Peter." As Lia finished, she saw for the first time in many months a brief flare of anger in Steve's eyes.

Peter said, "I'd rather not be on the board anyway but would rather attend all the formal meetings as Corporate Counsel. From what I hear, Price knows his stuff."

Steve looked at them both and said, "Done."

So it went down. Steve led the next meeting with J&J and negotiated a deal for their western courier and light truck operations. The deal included all the real estate,

The Price of Success

rolling stock and all other assets used in the operation. The final price was to be established after a thorough examination of the West assets by Quinn. During the negotiations it became clear to Steve that the J&J negotiators were under secret orders to sell. Cash had done the trick again.

Over the next two months, as Steve slowly continued to regain his health and strength, the team of Andrea, Truckin' Ted, and analysts from Merit and Core descended on the various offices of J&J. They were not happy with the discoveries they were making. Clearly West was not a well-run operation. Management was weak and sloppy, equipment was old, staff was demoralized and the cross docks were in need of modernization. The computers were simply junk. The more Quinn staff looked at the company, the lower the price became. The Quinn committee, which had been having progress meetings with Steve every week, even raised the possibility of withdrawing from the purchase. However, Steve refused to do that. He knew that in the long run the original plan was valid. He would just have to buy the company at the right price.

Steve, after some stiff negotiations ending in a personal trip to Toronto with Truckin' Ted, Andrea, Lia and Peter, bought the western Canada courier and local delivery operations (West Courier) from J&J. For cash. For less than $7 million. This price included an agreement that City Express would have exclusive rights to deliver all of J&J's freight in the Prairie Provinces. J&J didn't even include a clause that they were to be Rayner's exclusive shipper for freight going east! Or more importantly, that Rayner stay away from J&J's freight customers. Steve had arranged that a senior VP from his bank's Toronto head office also attend the meetings. When Steve met the owners of J&J, he knew the smell of cash was the final argument. Particularly when he, with the bank's VP watching, offered to write a cheque for the full purchase amount right then and there. Steve also came away with the knowledge that competing with J&J was going to be a piece of cake; the second-generation family owners just didn't have the balls anymore to be worthy competitors. On the way home in a chartered jet, he told Lia that she better get ready to buy the rest of the western operations of J&J, and down the road to think about buying the entire company. Lia and everyone else nearly choked on their celebratory drinks.

"And just when do you think we're going to be able to do that?" Lia asked.

"I betcha if I turned this plane around, we could walk back in there and buy the whole damn thing today!"

They all just looked at him, dumbfounded. Finally Lia got up and paced up and down the plane's aisle. She stopped in front of him and, hands on her waist, said, "No, no, no! You are not going to buy anything else until we've swallowed what we bought today!"

Peter, ever the peacemaker, started to intervene when Steve started laughing and said, "I always wondered when you'd finally say no to one of my ideas!"

Lia was so upset she was just about jumping out of her skin. Finally she threw her hands up in the air and shouted, "Asshole!" and went storming down the aisle to sit by herself.

And with that exchange Steve called for another drink and everyone withdrew into their own private thoughts. Steve knew, though, that they were already thinking about that next purchase!

By now Steve had regained another 10 pounds and was riding his bike on the cross-country trails behind Ann's farm. He wasn't yet ready for "age-class" racing but was happy to take the boys, Penny, Grace and her son Billy to Sergio's weekend races in his motorhome. On one of these trips, Sergio suggested he needed a larger, newer motorhome. This one was too small. He suggested Steve consider getting a diesel pusher; they were far superior to a front engine gas powered unit. Steve tucked that suggestion away for future consideration. He was also interested to see Sergio becoming more assertive and grown up. Grace reminded him that that's what a good woman would do!

With everyone available in the company now dragooned into integrating West with City Express, and Rayner approaching all the new City Express customers for their heavy freight business, Andrea and Truckin' Ted weren't seen around the office very much. Everyone else was busy building new computer systems, developing the new Winnipeg, Edmonton and Calgary offices, warehouses and cross docks and upgrading all the mobile equipment; no one had much use for Steve except to find the money to pay the bills and hire more senior people. Everyone was just too damn busy. Particularly when the bank branches in the new cities started asking for consulting assistance for faltering businesses. Soon the growth pattern of Quinn in Regina was being repeated in Winnipeg, Calgary and Edmonton. Steve knew that improving the staffing situation was critical, and he attacked it with gusto. Since existing employees were to be given first crack at the new positions, Steve's interviews also gave him an opportunity to re-examine the internal functioning of his company. He discovered that all the senior people were doing an excellent job, staff was happy and very involved. He also knew that Quinn was growing almost too rapidly, and for a change he reluctantly had to throttle back somewhat on everyone's expansion plans. Particularly the requests from the banks in the new locations. He also knew he was walking a tightrope between keeping the growth on track and staying within his company's resource pool of people and money.

The Price of Success

Chapter Twenty Six - Another Family Addition

Some weeks later Steve arranged a late afternoon meeting with Cheryl, Lia and Peter. Rather than meeting in his office, he invited them into his apartment. After getting them settled, he offered them both a glass of his excellent old Scotch. Clearly he was looking for a receptive audience. He outlined what he thought were the manpower and organization problems facing the company and asked for their opinions and possible solutions. Lia agreed with his assessment and even suggested that it was worse than he realized. Except for the money. Already revenues were up significantly and, while profit margins had slipped slightly, Lia had no doubt that they'd soon recover. She could see that Larry was going to have a fun problem on his hands! Meanwhile, everyone was overworked and, while no one was complaining yet, call-in sick days were up slightly. She had no solution except to try and work through it, but she was afraid that it might not be enough. Peter, who'd recently spent time in Calgary and Edmonton sorting out a City Express real estate ownership problem, agreed. And no, he didn't have a solution either.

Steve was quiet and slowly got up to pace the length of his living room. Stopping in front of them, he suggested they hire an outside management consulting company to review their organization and to suggest solutions. Looking at Cheryl, he said to her that this wasn't any criticism of Merit, he simply thought that at this point in their growth some outside opinions were now required. Cheryl told him she didn't have the time or manpower to tackle a problem like this anyway. While they digested that, he also suggested he'd like to bring Betty back as the VP of Administration with her emphasis being on admin but excluding personnel. Lia reminded him that they did have an admin department, but she hadn't yet found an adequate replacement for Betty; the person currently holding down the job just couldn't cut it. They didn't have a dedicated personnel department either. Peter agreed that they were now big enough to require a dedicated Personnel VP. Lia, after some thought and a number of questions, agreed. Peter offered to call a friend

The Price of Success

of his, the prairie managing partner of a very large national management consulting company. He wouldn't mention names but would inquire as to the availability of a top organizational consultant. If one were available, then Peter would get Steve to call the company and proceed.

That evening Steve called Betty in Calgary and asked how she was doing. Betty, very surprised at Steve's call, said that her father had died and her mother was now in a home suffering from terminal Lewy Body Dementia. Steve was upset that he didn't know about her father, but Betty said its okay, I didn't tell anyone at Quinn. To his question about returning to Quinn she hesitated, then told him she was ready to return to work, but that she had to put her young son first.

Steve surprised, said, "You're married?"

"No," she said, "No partner, just my son and me."

"Well, I can well understand why you hesitated when I asked."

"My mother doesn't know us anymore, so I guess it doesn't matter if I leave the city. It's time I had a new challenge in front of me anyway. What kind of job do you have in mind?"

"Things have changed around here as you prolly figured. We've bought another big freight company and are expanding right across the west. We need a VP of Administration, but without the personnel function that you had before. I don't have a job description written yet, but you have this knack of organizing us and all those background things that we badly need around here; parking, holidays, parties, office decoration, building maintenance, hell, even the coffee supply! We're soon going to have to expand onto one of the other floors and we need someone who can oversee that. Why don't you come down for a look-see and we can talk about it?"

There was a silence on the line. Then Betty sighed and said, "Steve, I'm interested but first I have to tell you something you may not like but that you should know." There was a lengthy pause. "My son, Steve, is your son."

As Steve absorbed this stunning admission, the line was silent.

Then, "What? What? Wait a minute, what are you saying?"

Betty rushed on, "I didn't set out to do it that afternoon but when I found out I was pregnant, I was very happy. I think he looks like you; he has the same blond hair and your blue eyes and is already tall. But he has my temperament and is a happy, healthy, outgoing youngster. And no, I don't want anything. I don't even want support. Thanks to my father's estate and insurance we have more than enough money."

"I'm speechless; I don't know what to say."

"Before I come down you should think about it, especially with regard to Ann and your other kids. Oh, that sounds so strange! Your other kids!"

There was another round of silence as Steve continued to digest this news, then he said, "Do you have a problem if people figure it out?"

Betty thought for a moment, "No, I guess not. I'm not going to run around and brag about it, but I'm proud and happy to have had your son. It's your name on his birth certificate, after all."

"Christ, I never thought about that!" Then after a pause, "Would you have a problem talking about it? After all, there are some here that will eventually put two and two together."

"No, not really. I don't want to advertise the fact but if we told Lia, Larry and Cheryl for starters, I wouldn't have a problem." She paused, "Are you still seeing Ann?"

"Yes. I'm not sure that we're a couple, but we do see each other rather frequently. I'd hope that this doesn't upset what we have, because I value her company and help. But I was also thinking of my kids. I don't think my kids will have a problem, it being a blended family anyway. But yes, I'm not sure how Ann will take it."

"Ann and I got along well in the past, maybe I'd better phone and tell her."

Steve paused to think about it and shrugging, said, "Okay, when do you want to come down?"

"Anytime. Better give me a few days to get organized."

"Okay, when you're ready, give us a call and we'll arrange all your travel."

"Okay! I'm already getting excited!"

Steve asked Lia to get their travel agent to arrange for Betty and her son to fly down for a visit, at Betty's convenience. And arrange hotels and a car for her, all at Quinn's expense. Then he sat at his desk, realizing that he had just been blind-sided in a manner that he had never expected. He sat at his desk for a long time, thinking.

Peter called and gave Steve a name and phone number. He also advised that this company did have a first-class organizational structural consultant that would be the only one he'd recommend for this job. He wasn't going to be available for a week or so though. Steve gave them a call.

The consulting company manager, Gregory, was pleased to receive Steve's call and suggested that they might want to get together somewhere private for a preliminary discussion. Steve suggested that Ann's B&B would work, and could they arrange the meeting for Monday next? Steve then checked to see that Ann's was available and that Peter could attend.

With nothing now to do except get in everyone's way, Steve decided that maybe he'd take Sergio's suggestion and go look at motorhomes. His preliminary research had found that Triple E, based in Winkler, Manitoba, was a manufacturer of top-of-the-line Class A rigs built to handle the Canadian climate. He called Triple E and arranged for a factory tour and a visit to their sales office. Packing an overnight bag, he told Lia that he'd be gone for a few days. She didn't even see him go, she was so busy. Down on the second floor he put the top down on his 500SL, turned on the illegal radar detector, exited the parking lot and rolled east to Hwy #1 with the stereo blaring "On the Road Again" by Willie Nelson. As soon as he was out of the city he

The Price of Success

let the Mercedes run, and whooped with glee when the engine burble rose to a shriek as the speedo whipped by 140 mph. He wished the car wasn't computer limited to 155 mph, but then thought that maybe it was a good thing. Steve, with a great grin on his face, let the Merc come back to a smooth 75 mph and simply enjoyed the ride, the engine's impatient V12 growl, and the sun beating down on his shoulders.

Two days later as he rolled the 400 miles west back toward home, he thought about his purchase. He was going to have to take his current unit down to the Regina Triple E dealer and then transfer all his stuff to the new rig. But his new rig wouldn't be ready for a few weeks yet, so he might as well strip out all the unneeded crap from his current rig and get rid of it. He also hoped he hadn't forgotten anything he wanted to be customized by the factory. The new rig was expressly set up for two people to live in for long periods of time away from the RV parks. It had very large fresh water and sewer tanks along with a 100-gallon fuel tank. A 10 Kva self-starting diesel generator and roof solar panels took care of the power needs. The cherry wood trim gave it a real dose of class. And he'd opted for the biggest engine available, a 500 HP diesel. The only disagreement had been when he didn't want any of the usual "Nevada whorehouse" interior trim, mirrors and lights. He laughed to himself. The way you've just spent about $380,000 on the rig and its modifications, you'd think you had money! Oh well, it was only money and the aluminum wheels, while an extravagance, certainly were pretty! That triggered the thought that maybe he should also do something about his present vehicle situation. With the jeep now finished, except for the new plastic top he was waiting for, he didn't need two toads. He'd given Sergio an older pickup truck, so Sergio didn't need the small Merc toad anymore; maybe he should sell it. Or maybe he could give it to Ann. Shaun had received a used Subaru sedan that he wanted, so he was okay. Steve usually drove the 500SL but not in the winter. Then he drove the big Mercedes sedan, but other than keeping the SL out of the salt and snow, he really didn't need it either. He should talk to Larry to see if he could spend some more money. While reading the Globe and Mail that morning, he'd seen an interesting high performance 4x4 Range Rover for sale.

When he got home he discovered that Betty had arrived and that Lia and Cheryl were happily looking after her. She was better looking than ever and, with a few extra pounds, now carried herself with a mature confidence. Li'l Steve (not Stevie!) as he was quickly named, was a good looking, quiet but very aware young man. After a brief shyness toward Big Steve, (naturally Steve's new name!) he made up his mind to like him and took to following him around, watching everything. In that, he was like most small children when they first met Steve. For some reason, he just captivated them! Betty later told him that he'd never been exposed to a man about the place so she had expected he was going to be nervous around Steve. Ann had been slower to accept the situation but, realizing that it was what it was, decided that she too could deal with it. The "other kids" thought having another brother was cool and quickly absorbed him into the family. Grace and Billy thought it was okay as well, and Grace offered to look after him while Betty was in town.

Steve asked Lia, Betty and Li'l Steve for supper and asked Li'l Steve what he liked to eat. Betty told him anything, as long as there was ice cream for dessert. When Li'l Steve heard "ice cream" his face lit up and he clapped his pudgy little hands. Steve said to Betty, "A chip off the old block!"

When supper was over and Li'l Steve had had his ice cream and been put to sleep in Steve's bed, the conversation turned serious. The upshot was that in a few days Betty would return to Calgary, arrange to sell everything she didn't need in Regina, and move down by month end. Thanks to a booming housing market in Calgary, she didn't think selling the house would be a problem. Tuesday she'd go and look at Regina houses with a representative from the real estate firm that Quinn owned. Lia also suggested that maybe she and Betty should talk about getting a house together. Betty would resume her old position as VP of Administration, less the personnel function and, like Lia, Cheryl and Larry, would be in the employ of the holding company, Quinn Enterprises.

Next Monday came with the Gregory and Peter meeting at Ann's B&B. It took only a few moments for Gregory (as he insisted he be called) to comprehend that Steve was even bigger, quicker, uglier and more aggressive than Peter had warned. He was all business, with no screwing around allowed. Steve served everyone coffee and outlined the company's current structure, its planned growth path and shortage of capable executives. Steve needed experienced operating and management execs that were ready to grow with the company, as there was much more growth coming. He also needed a management structure to accommodate the growth. Steve wasn't sure if managing province-by-province was better than industry-by-industry. With every province having a different business and cultural environment, he was favouring the former approach.

Gregory suggested they provide Steve with their top management analyst team, to begin immediate work first on the management structure. A preliminary report to be presented in two weeks. If Steve liked the suggestions, then the analysts would prepare a final report on how to achieve the goals. Meanwhile Gregory would have their Calgary headhunting division manager visit, and Steve and Lia could outline their needs. Since the acquisition of new employees was going to take longer than producing a management structure, both efforts could proceed simultaneously.

Gregory then asked Steve if he minded that some of the analysts were female. Peter, wincing, told him before Steve opened his mouth that most of the Quinn senior execs were tough smart females and that his analysts had better be aware of that fact. Gregory nodded, but privately thought, oh boy, this is going to be different. The meeting ended with Steve setting up a future meeting with Lia and Cheryl and him to meet the structural analyst team.

The Price of Success

Two weeks later when the preliminary structure report came in, it recommended that each province have its own managers for heavy truck, light truck and courier, administration, and finance including payroll. The courier and heavy freight managers would report to the respective Regina based presidents of their companies. The other managers would report to the Regina based VP of Administration or Finance. The Regina VPs would in turn report to the Executive Vice President of Operations. But each province would not have its own overall VP. Merit Consulting would operate out of Regina with its pool of operational, management and financial analysts used across the company and provinces. Core Computing, with its equipment located in Regina, should also continue to operate in a centralized mode. Both should be headed by presidents with Merit alone reporting to the President of Quinn Enterprises.

The big problem was with the multitude of other companies that Quinn owned. Privately it was called "The Dog's Breakfast Division" and the report suggested that each province have its own "Dog's Breakfast" manager reporting to a "Dog's Breakfast" VP in Regina. However, the report noted that one person in each province completely responsible for a large number of diverse businesses was going to have his hands full. To solve this problem it was suggested that the provincial manager would be responsible only for the companies in his province achieving the yearly growth and profitability goals. But not how the goals were achieved. Therefore his/her responsibility would be primarily to supply the companies with the muscle, money, and other resources as required to achieve those goals. Merit, on the other hand, would be responsible for the operational excellence of the companies. Merit too would be available to audit and/or to assist the companies as requested. In practical terms therefore, the company managers, rather than the provincial division manager carried the can for each company's success. The report also noted that with a potential 75 or more subsidiary companies in the corporate-wide "Dog's Breakfast Division", resource and management demands on the corporation would require careful allocation.

The final recommendation of the report was that the concept of the "Dog's Breakfast" and all the other divisions being monitored and assisted by an independent Merit Consulting, without interference from the troubled company's management, was one that should be reinforced and strengthened. Merit Consulting should become the premier company within Quinn and should report directly to the company president. This move was critical as Merit's investigations and opinions formed the basis for most of Quinn's major business decisions. Just as important, Merit was responsible for maintaining Quinn's unique culture across the company.

Steve was impressed. He asked Lia and Cheryl for their opinion. Cheryl said in a fake English accent, "My dear boy, unless you are wearing the president's hat, I cannot speak to you!"

Steve and Lia both laughed. Then Cheryl and Lia both said that it was perfect but that they'd talked it over and didn't want Cheryl's job to be more highly rated than Lia's. Perhaps Cheryl could have a split reporting responsibility. Reporting responsibility for routine analysis or even requested analysis of existing companies would remain with Lia, but new companies and business expansion would be the president's baby. Thus, from only a Quinn Enterprises overall point of view, in crude terms, Lia would run it and Steve would grow it. With that broad agreement, which did not create boundaries or limits to anyone's actions, the three of them signed off on the report.

Meanwhile, the staff acquisition team had met with Steve and Lia and had immediately run into a problem. The team leader was a man who clearly didn't understand the nuances of dealing with female executives, particularly tiny perfect volatile wop lawyers. Within minutes Lia had torn a strip off of him, and Steve had called Gregory and demanded a replacement. Steve let Gregory know that he wasn't happy with this development. Gregory had been expressly told who he was dealing with and now he'd seriously blown it. One more fuckup and he and his company were gone. Then he told the team leader that he was lucky he wasn't dealing with Sharon, she'd prolly have killed him. Lia explained who Sharon had been.

Gregory apologized and didn't understand how that particular team leader had ended up at Quinn. He promised to fix it and find out what happened and, as compensation, give Steve a free week of the team's services. Steve relaxed and decided to let Lia proceed with the preliminaries; he'd get involved when a list of candidates for the senior positions was presented. Gregory called back a few minutes later and apologized again. Apparently his secretary had given the assignment to the wrong team leader, and the secretary was now on a week's administrative leave without pay. The team leader was also on leave and had been assigned to a sensitivity class, also without pay. The correct team leader was being flown in from Calgary and would be there tomorrow. To assuage Gregory's feelings somewhat, Steve complimented his team on the structural report. After all, he did have to work with the man for some weeks yet.

However, on one point Steve was adamant. Potential senior management candidates must be considered from within the company, first. The corporate culture must be maintained and strengthened by advancing, wherever possible, existing staff. Managers of the companies within the "Dog's Breakfast" were to be considered the primary pool from which senior Quinn managers would be drawn. Only after all internal possibilities had been exhausted was the consultant to look at the Transportation Division and then outside the company.

The Price of Success

Chapter Twenty Seven - A Revelation

With the minute by minute control of the business having disappeared, and the day to day operational management now slipping away from him, Steve over the past weeks had been feeling less and less motivated about the business. He began to realize that with only cycling as his other immediate interest, without a business involvement, he had little to occupy his hyper intellect. He decided that some thinking time about this situation was required during a long top-down ride in his jeep. He went down to the second floor and had the standby courier driver take him over to the warehouse bay where his shop and the jeep were now stored. After taking off the jeep's top he checked tire pressures and fluid levels and fired it up. After gassing up he headed north toward the Qu'Appelle Valley, confidant that he would be able to find a peaceful spot to park and think. Finding a short stretch of empty city street, he suddenly slammed the jeep into four-wheel drive, shifted down into second gear and floored it. With his left foot momentarily on the brake he waited for the turbo to spool up, then when the waste gate started popping, slid his foot sideways off the brake pedal. Even in second gear all four tires instantly lit up and enveloped the jeep in a huge cloud of white smoke. With the turbo howling, the engine shrieking and the tires squawking, Steve disappeared down the road in a cloud of smoke and burnt rubber.

With Ann's help over the last weeks he had come to realize that the combination of losing Sharon and being nearly fatally shot had changed him. The accumulation of stress from the daily struggle he endured from years of living in a kindergarten world had also worked their insidious poisons into his soul. He hadn't lost or even suffered a diminishing of his senses or brilliance, but now how he regarded his gifts was changing. The biggest issue was his anger; he was angrier than ever at the world and the assholes that inhabited it. That anger now often spilled over to his own feelings about himself. Ann had talked to him about this situation developing into a vicious circle and Steve was worried that it was happening. As he drove, with the

The Price of Success

turbo charger quietly whistling in the background and mufflers barely suppressing the V6 rumble, he had an epiphany. The real reason for all the corporate changes was to allow him to withdraw from the rat race of day to day corporate management! His unconscious was telling him that the daily rat race was not fun anymore and was indeed driving, in the form of stress, his personal demons. He didn't laugh as much, and he was drinking more. The number of meals he prepared had also diminished, a point that Samara had commented on the other day. His poor vehicles were taking more abuse than they should and if he didn't slow down his driving, he was going to kill himself. And his downhill racing! Sergio had told him that he was getting crazier and crazier with the chances he was taking. When Steve had suggested a trip to Moab, Utah, for the annual downhill racing meeting, Sergio had flatly refused to hear of it. Steve had been so surprised at the vehemence of Sergio's objections he hadn't raised the subject since.

Steve glanced at the speedometer and lifted his foot to slow down to within at least sight of the speed limit. That was prolly why he'd bought a new RV and rebuilt the jeep. His unconscious was smarter than he was. It was a sobering thought to realize that his unconscious knew he was in serious trouble before he was consciously aware of that fact.

Steve found a quiet lay-by with a view out over the valley, stopped, got out and leaned on the fence to think. He had long ago come to terms with his gifts, slowly realizing that there was a terrible price to pay for having them. He now knew that his inability to admit to loving Sharon was part of that price. He had so insulated his feelings to protect himself that openly loving anyone was now prolly impossible. He'd never really loved Claire; she'd trapped him into marriage and had built a family of natural and adopted kids to hold him in the marriage web. Fortunately, he and the kids, and that included Billy and Li'l Steve, now got along very well. Like many aggressive, driven men, he had a special affinity toward children, and they knew it. Being unable to work with most men was also part of the price. He was just too goddamn smart and aggressive to be another man's friend; he knew that most men were very wary around him.

Women on the other hand all seemed to want to be around him and look after him, and that he didn't understand. He never went out of his way to be nice, he just treated them all as equals, so maybe that was it. He shrugged; women, he thought, were the least of his problems. He and Ann were tight and he'd had a long discussion with Betty. The upshot was that Betty didn't want to interfere with Ann's relationship and they would remain friends, particularly with regard to Li'l Steve. Betty, realizing that Big Steve and Li'l Steve were forming a tight bond, didn't want that upset. Strangely it never occurred to Steve that Ann would feel threatened by Betty and particularly by his relationship with Li'l Steve. Steve, like any parent as their kids grew up and established their own lives, was feeling somewhat abandoned by his original family and had welcomed having Li'l Steve around. Both Betty and

Ann didn't know whether to laugh or cry when Steve brought a happy Li'l Steve home, after Li'l Steve had "helped" fix a vehicle, both of them covered in dirt and grease.

Maybe getting away for a while, or even further limiting his exposure to his empire's management issues, was required. But he did owe his team big time. He just couldn't walk away from them; that wasn't fair or reasonable. After all, he'd built the team, and when it needed it he had nurtured it, pushed it around, trained it, and rewarded it very well for its performance. And the team had made him a very wealthy man. While the overall outstanding success of Quinn Enterprises was his to claim, the amazing growth, profitability and successful daily operations were the team's claim to glory.

Perhaps the solution was to get away in the new RV. He and Ann could take a short trip to Winnipeg and have a general meeting with all staff, sort of like the one they just had in Regina. As far as he could tell, the supper meeting in Regina had gone well with all the new West staff integrating quite well with the Quinn staff. When Steve had outlined the new management system being explored, and that all existing staff would have first crack at the new positions, he'd received a standing ovation.

As Steve leaned against the fence lost in thought, an RCMP cruiser pulled in behind him. The officer, walking over to him, startled him by calling his name. Steve turned around and the officer asked him if he was okay, and if he had some identification. Steve pulled out his wallet and assured the officer that he was fine, he was just out for a drive to find some private thinking time. The officer suggested that Steve call his office as they had asked the police to find him.

The officer handed back Steve's ID, hesitated, then, taking off his hat, said, "I'm Dale Spacek. I was the one that stopped you and your friend on the highway outside of Moose Jaw and told you to get to shelter. I was stationed in Moose Jaw and after the storm when I saw the wrecked motel, I still don't understand how you survived."

Steve replied, "Yeah well, climbing out of that safe room and riding to Regina is something we try to forget about. I think we both still have nightmares about it."

"I also saw the pictures and video of you at the hospital. How in the world did you and - Lia is it? - actually manage to ride to Regina? Did anyone ever find the truck that hit you?"

"No, no one ever came forward and admitted to hitting me. I'm still not too sure how we did that ride either. One thing the news left out was the brutal ride we had done the day before. They didn't mention that we hadn't gotten enough sleep or even enough food that morning to ride the road again. So in the hospital not only did we have to heal from the crash, but we had to recover and rebuild our abused bodies."

Dale just shook his head. He then looked Steve's jeep over very carefully and with a frown asked if it was really street legal. Steve assured him that it was, see, it

The Price of Success

even had windshield wipers! He asked to see under the hood and surprised Steve by correctly identifying the Buick V6 Grand National engine. He also noticed that the turbo was not the stock unit but was a larger aftermarket unit complete with a larger aftermarket intercooler. He said they had a report of a very loud yellow jeep street racing in the city, so he expected Steve to behave on his way home. He further suggested that Steve wait until he'd moved on before he started it up! Steve shook his hand and said he'd head back shortly; he hadn't realized that it was so late. On the way back Steve found a small gas station and called the office. Lia said that when she heard that he'd taken out the jeep, she became concerned. She knew that when he drove the jeep he was not in a good frame of mind and she worried about him. She hoped he didn't mind that she'd called the RCMP to find him. Actually, she said when the police heard his name they were happy to help. Was there something she didn't know about his relationship with the cops? Steve ignored the question and reassured her that he was fine and would be back in a couple of hours. Lia then told him to behave on the way home. She continued that a City courier driver had seen the whole burnout thing and everyone at City was talking and laughing about the Boss's antics!

The next day Steve called and asked Ann if she wanted a homemade supper. Since Ann had been expecting this call, she quickly agreed. She wasn't sure if Steve wanted to talk about Betty and Li'l Steve or something else. She was worried that Betty was unfinished business and that with Li'l Steve around, things were getting complicated. She'd been watching Big Steve for years through the building of his business, the deterioration of his marriage, the recovery from the bike crash, the beating from the tornado, the stress of being shot and finally the loss of Sharon, his general womanizing, and she was concerned it was all coming to a head. And the West foolishness! Why the fuck did that have to happen when Steve wasn't really ready for it? Although he was now back to his usual weight of 205 pounds and was doing his usual gruelling training rides and working out, Ann knew there was something still not right. She recognized the anger pulsing just below his usual agreeable manner. She'd also heard about the jeep rides! His spending nearly $400K on a motorhome and another well over $100K on the hot rod Range Rover was just not his usual behavior. He usually was so tight with his money that before he spent a nickel, he squeezed it so hard that you could see the beaver shit. (Canadian nickels have a beaver reverse) But strangely not if he was spending money on others. He was always very generous to his employees, family and charities. Christ, he'd even given her the small Mercedes! So much so that Larry had recently taken away the right of charities to ask him directly for money. She smiled, wondering if Steve knew yet that skinflint Larry had made that move. That reminded her that she was going to have to take Steve shopping for clothes. They were getting a little ragged and, while he didn't seem to notice or care, Ann wouldn't let him look like a poor relation. She'd received a notice that the Hong Kong tailor was coming to town and

Steve did need a couple of suits and a new sports jacket or two and some slacks. He normally wore casual clothing from "Lands' End" and it was time for more of them, but she thought it was also time he had something more formal in his closet.

Steve raided his fridge and pulled out a package of homemade spaghetti sauce and some homemade goat meatballs with garlic. He knew that Ann had the additional fresh spices he needed, and he'd stop and get some white and red Italian wine, bread and some Asiago cheese for later. Loading it all into a cooler, or chilly bin (as he had learned it was called Down Under from an Australian friend), he set out for the market, then on to Ann's. When Ann saw the Italian meal, she became doubly worried because, to Steve, Italian was comfort food even though he didn't have a drop of Italian blood in him.

After supper Ann cleared the table, cut the Asiago into slices and brought out a bottle of Taylor Fladgate Port that she'd been saving. Steve had been slowly pacing back and forth and finally stopped to take a crystal glass of port and a slice of cheese. As he turned to pace some more, Ann screwed up her courage and said in a quiet voice, "Why don't you just tell me what's wrong?"

Steve stopped with his back to her and said, "I don't know where to start."

Ann, now convinced this was about Betty and Li'l Steve, and with the ugly snake of fear crawling through her stomach, said, "Look at me and just say it."

Steve gave a big sigh, turned and, looking her right in the eyes, said, "I've just put myself out of a job and I'm happy I did it."

Ann's knees instantly turned to rubber and she stammered as she collapsed on a chair, "What? What do you mean?"

"The new management structure for Quinn moves all day to day operational responsibilities to the executive vice president's office, which is Lia. All growth plans, long range strategic decisions, and senior personnel decisions remain with the president or, in other words, me. In time that will be Lia's job and I'll be just the Chairman of the Board. I'll bring the finalized structure and the personnel plan to the Board sometime in the next few weeks."

Ann just sat there with a dumfounded look on her face. Mistaking the look, Steve said, "Yes, I know I should have brought it to the Board first, but it seemed like it was the obvious way to proceed, so I went ahead."

"But, but, I don't understand. What are you saying? Why did you do that? What are you going to do?"

"Well, I figure that a couple of hours a week at the office should be enough to discharge my required involvement. Well, prolly more than that, but it means all of a sudden I'll have a lot of time on my hands. Cheryl will prolly want to put me to work, which I won't refuse, but my direct official responsibilities will diminish significantly." He thought some more, "Actually I'll prolly start spending more time with the kids. I've found that I rather like them all."

The Price of Success

Ann, still thunderstruck, just sat there, mouth open. Frowning, Steve said, "I've never seen you without something to say."

Ann, trying to buy time to think, stood up, smoothed her slacks, and went over to give Steve a hug. As she clung to him, she told him that she had to think about this first, it was an absolute game changer. "Come," she said, "Let's go for a walk."

Carrying their glasses of wine, they slowly started down the path to the barn, while Steve continued, "I guess I've finally realized what you've been trying to hammer into my thick skull. I really am subject to the vicissitudes of the world. I just can't continue to ignore what the world does to me and survive by powering through it. I can't count on my intellect to get me through anything that happens. Sharon's death finally taught me that lesson. And you and everyone else knew that and I didn't. As I lay in that hospital bed recovering I guess I had an epiphany. I finally realized just how much you look after me, and how much Sharon, Betty, Cheryl and Lia and others worked so hard to insulate me from the real world. Even Grace and Cynthia have worked at arranging my life and smoothing out the bumps."

He stopped to look at her and continued, "That epiphany included the fact that all those people were doing it without my organizing it. I really, really don't understand that. I also don't understand our relationship. Why do you put up with me? Why do you try so hard to keep me sane?"

After a few minutes, he said in a very low voice, "Nor do I understand why I've never met anyone like me. Am I so strange and bent out of shape that there are no others like me? Am I so strange; would the world even miss me?"

He started walking again, "My world is coming apart, Ann, and I can't cope anymore."

Ann was completely stunned. She mentally kicked herself and thought, oh my god, oh my god, oh my god, what do I do now? She suddenly realized that she really, really didn't know this man and had been fooling herself all these years. As Sharon had repeatedly warned her, he was truly unknowable. Her professional mentor had warned her that this might happen. After all he'd said, this man is off the smart's chart, so why do you think you have a hope of really understanding and helping him? Ann clutched Steve's arm as they slowly and silently followed the path around the barn and back to the house.

That night in bed, she asked him to just make one promise to her, he wouldn't do anything unfortunate until they'd discussed it again. Steve lay there for a long time and finally promised. Both of them did not sleep well; Steve because he should have taken a Zopiclone and Ann because she was terrified about where he was going. During her sleepless night she decided that come hell or high water she was going to try, again, to help Steve not only cope, but now how to even survive. She didn't think he would end it, but then she admitted she couldn't say that with certainty. And it didn't matter what it took, she was going to try.

The next day Ann called Peter. She asked him, "Do you remember us talking about Steve ever being interested in something other than his business? I don't know what you had in mind but Steve is about to bring to the Board a new organization plan that in effect severely limits his direct involvement in the company's management. I know you know about this so I'm not talking out of turn, but I thought you should know that Steve now has the problem of keeping busy. If you've got something for him, better get to it."

Peter said, "Well, I've been meaning to talk to you about something. I've been approached to see if Steve would be interested in public service or even running for a public office. It seems that the story of him and Lia surviving the tornado and then riding to Regina has become part of Saskatchewan folklore. Sort of like the movie "The Man That Shot Liberty Valance" or whatever it's called. Plus the fact that he's a home grown, self-made multi-millionaire makes him pretty attractive to the voters.

"Well, I don't know Peter. I don't think Steve has the patience for elected office. He might be interested in sitting on the board of a Crown Corporation (a government owned business) but then he'd probably end up running the damn thing!"

Peter laughed and said, "I wonder if the world of Crown Corps is ready for someone like Steve! Let me think about it, it may be that he'd be better on a private industry board. Or perhaps better yet, the board of a foundation, or even a public facility board like an art gallery or museum."

"However, Peter, first I'm going to get him to take an extended holiday. I don't think he was ever happier than when he made that bike tour from Vancouver. He has talked a lot about the elemental nature of that ride, just him against the road. He's said over and over that it was life at its basic simplicity, and I think he needs to experience something like that again. He needs something to distract him, to get his mind off Sharon once and for all. Somehow we have to get him to move forward into a new life. Several times now he's mentioned driving the Dempster Highway up to Inuvik in the North West Territories and showing me the Arctic before it all melts. From what I've seen of the literature about driving the Alcan and Dempster Highways, it could be just the challenge he needs."

"Okay. I'll think about it and have another look."

The Price of Success

Chapter Twenty Eight - The Final Moves

Two days later Steve asked Lia if she had a moment, he wanted to know how the people search was going. Lia was clearly enthused with the outside consulting staff. They'd created preliminary job descriptions and had started interviewing the Saskatchewan staff. Betty had been sitting in on the interviews and seemed pleased that the interviewers had correctly interpreted Quinn's cultural needs. The goal was to fill the top positions first, then fill the resultant lower level vacancies. This approach would also work in conjunction with the suggested growth path in the consultant's management report. Lia asked if he was aware that this was going to be a long-term process; the management plan called for the positions to be filled in a particular order, as the business growth demanded. That way, the management of the Quinn companies would suffer only a minimum of disruption and confusion. Finally, Lia said, we'll shortly be ready to have you interview the final three candidates for the first of the new positions.

Lia stood up, picked up a laser pointer and walked over to the new large org chart taped to her glass wall, then continued, "First we're going to strengthen management here in Saskatchewan. We need new energies, new ideas, and a new people mix. Once that's done this will allow the freight and courier, Merit and Core Computing company presidents and managers to allocate sufficient time to Manitoba first, then Alberta. So the first new jobs are the finance positions, specifically in Regina, then for Manitoba. Then a new VP Personnel, then the courier operations, administration and Merit people. Depending on growth, then freight, and dog's breakfast. Then we do the same for Alberta, BUT, and this is a big but, it will depend on how the various divisions grow and are able to penetrate their particular markets."

"Have you and Larry interviewed the finance finalists?"

"We have one more to do, but we think we've selected who we want."

The Price of Success

In a rare display of anger, Steve said, "Okay get me involved ASAP, and DON'T tell me who you want! We gotta get moving dammit, West is just sitting out there directionless."

"Yes Sir. Right away Sir. How about in two hours Sir? Now please can I get the hell out of here so I can get back to work? Sir!"

After the interviews, with the Saskatchewan and Manitoba Finance Managers having been selected, Steve set up interviews the next day for the senior Regina Admin and Merit positions. They did need more Admin help, they were running short of office space and Betty was going to have to get them more. That meant either clearing out some offices on the third or fourth floor or finding a new building. Merit needed to find the staff to send down to West to help with its integration, and more staff to send to Manitoba to get that area's dog breakfast operation under control.

Now that he was divorced from the day to day operations and could concentrate on policy, growth, and senior personnel, Steve was finally pulling out of his doldrums. Unfortunately his anger was still barely under control, and everyone knew it. Lia, as the only one who dared confront Steve, now had the added task of riding herd on her boss. Steve thought they were lucky to have found so much of the potential staff in house, or at least three out of four. He was looking forward to the following day's interviews for the courier and heavy truck managers' positions. Before that could happen though, Lia took him out for a Luigi supper and wine and laid down the law. He was not to continue to piss of the staff! Yes, the long term employees were putting up with it but they already had a newbie question the thrill of working for someone who teetered on the edge. Her final words on the subject were to either slow down or stay home. Starting tomorrow. Steve, stunned at this very direct lecture and instruction, decided that maybe he should listen to his perfect little wop. If she had the cojones to confront him, it better be heeded.

Several weeks later Steve had finished interviewing and selecting the next round of managers, and now he had a break as everyone proceeded to integrate the new staff into the mysteries of their new jobs. He'd decided that he and Ann should go get the new motorhome, bring it home and load it. Then take it back to Winnipeg on a shakedown cruise and hold a staff meeting with the new Manitoba staff. If there was a problem with the rig, he'd be close to the factory for repair work. And that would get him out of the office. Prolly, he thought, much to Lia's liking.

And that is what they did. The West staff generally responded well to Steve, especially when he told them that those who wanted to work would be welcome at Quinn. No one would immediately lose their jobs and those who wanted to, or would be asked to leave the company after six months, would receive one month's salary, plus a week's salary for every year or part of a year they'd been employed by West. After the meeting, three employees quit. The reason given by all three was that they would not work for the new female Winnipeg manager.

On the return trip with the new motorhome running like a watch, and the jeep being towed without a problem, Ann raised the specter of them taking it on a major holiday. She suggested that it was the only time of the year that a trip up the Dempster would be possible. Or go the other way across Quebec to Labrador, then on to Newfoundland and the east coast. Steve thought about it and stopped to call Peter for his opinion. Peter didn't have, nor did he foresee, anything coming that would require Steve's direct input that couldn't be handled by phone. He wasn't happy with Steve being away during the frantic growth and reorganization, but agreed that as long as he was available by phone, his being away shouldn't present a problem.

When they returned to Regina, Ann closed down her B&B, and her daughter Janet came out to look after the animals. After a discussion with Lia, in a surprise twist, he'd decided that future interviews could be conducted on the road. Betty could bring them to Whitehorse, or Dawson Creek or wherever they happened to be for the interview. Peter and Lia weren't impressed with the idea and continued their objections with Steve being away during this frantic growth period. The kids, especially Li'l Steve, weren't impressed with his coming absence either. Steve showed them all his new cell phone and told them if they wanted him, just give him a call. Steve assured them all that they'd be back in four to six weeks. Secretly, he arranged that Grace and Betty, for a surprise holiday with the kids, would fly them all up and meet them in Inuvik.

With all arrangements completed and the new rig loaded, and Willie Nelson wailing, they went RVing.

To the north, as far as the road would go.

Thank You!

Thank you for reading my second book. I promise that the next Steve Quinn adventure will be even more exciting. There are two more being readied for distribution. If you enjoyed this book, won't you please take a moment to leave a review at your favorite retailer? Or if you have a suggestion about the content, please tell me! "The Broken Road" was greatly improved by readers' comments and suggestions.
Thank you,

CJ

Other Titles by CJ

The Road North
The Broken Road

About CJ Vermeulen

CJ, as he likes to be called is a retired Economist and sometime scribbler. He has been a long time contributor to RVing magazines and other publications. He's also a hard-core cyclist, gardener, and recently along with his wife, Kathy Rayner, completed the fifteen year-long restoration of their 125 year old stone house. He is vociferously Canadian and with Kathy, an inveterate RV traveler. These novels are based on CJ's personal experiences and travels and include many characters drawn from those experiences. He and Kathy have visited and explored many of the places described in these novels.

Connect with CJ Vermeulen at: janvlen@mts.net

Made in the USA
Monee, IL
21 February 2020